Praise for Trisha Sakhlecha

'A deliciously dark and original debut about love, loss and lies, with an ending that is impossible to predict'
Alice Feeney, author of *Sometimes I Lie*

'Original and evocative, I was completely hooked by the longing, love and envy simmering sometimes unseen, yet ever-present. With an ending I couldn't predict, this debut is one to savour'
Karen Hamilton, author of *The Perfect Girlfriend*

'Well written, with plenty of twists and an excellent sense of place'
Guardian

'I couldn't move until I'd finished . . . An original voice, and an intricate, unpredictable plot. It was really refreshing to read a psychological thriller set within a different culture. I loved it'
Emma Curtis, author of *One Little Mistake*

'Tense, twisting and infused with an intoxicating sense of dread. This is a seriously gripping thriller'
B. P. Walter, author of *A Version of the Truth*

'A book that you'll want to read again as soon as you've finished it to look for clues, wondering how you'd missed them the first time around. I thought I had it all figured out, so was "Wait . . . what?" when the reveal came. The sucker punch came from nowhere and lifted me off my feet – the sign of a great book'

Sandie Jones, author of *The Other Woman*

'This is a well-structured, twisty novel which has at its heart a very honest portrayal of a marriage and, no, I didn't see the twist coming'

Richard Skinner, author of *The Mirror*

Can You See Me Now?

Trisha Sakhlecha grew up in New Delhi and now lives in London. She works in fashion and is a graduate of the Faber Academy writing course. In the past, Trisha has worked as a designer, trend forecaster and lecturer, and is the acclaimed author of *Your Truth or Mine?* and *Can You See Me Now?*

TRISHA SAKHLECHA

Can You See Me Now?

PAN BOOKS

First published 2021 by Pan Books
an imprint of Pan Macmillan
The Smithson, 6 Briset Street, London EC1M 5NR
Associated companies throughout the world
www.panmacmillan.com

ISBN 978-1-5098-8634-0

1 3 5 7 9 8 6 4 2

A CIP catalogue record for this book is available from the British Library.

Typeset in Dante MT by Palimpsest Book Production Limited,
Falkirk, Stirlingshire
Printed and bound by CPI Group (UK) Ltd, Croydon, CR0 4YY

Visit **www.panmacmillan.com** to read more about all our books
and to buy them. You will also find features, author interviews and
news of any author events, and you can sign up for e-newsletters
so that you're always first to hear about our new releases.

For my parents

PROLOGUE

Look closely.

Can you see them? They're like fireflies. Shimmering, dazzling, buzzing with promise and confidence, plaid skirts hiked impossibly high, ties askew, shirtsleeves rolled up to show off matching friendship bracelets on slender wrists.

Take it in.

Watch how the other girls trail after them, hoping some of their magic will rub off. Watch how the boys pretend not to notice them. Watch how they indulge their audience for a minute before returning to their private little world.

Oh yes, they know you're watching.

Keep looking. Watch how the one at the centre throws her head back when she laughs, how she adjusts her hijab, the silk sliding off curls that want to run wild. Notice how the one on her right rolls her eyes then takes her friend's arm, their bodies naturally in sync, matching each other step for step. Look, finally, at the third girl – the timid one; look how she picks up pace, moves closer, tries to flick her hair and move her hips the way they do.

Look closely. The beauty. The intimacy. The possibilities. Together they're dynamite.

Remember this moment.

Remember what it was like before.

Because by the end of the year, this trio, this friendship, will no longer exist. They'll burn out, quick and bright, the way fireflies do, and leave darkness in their wake.

One girl dead, one lost and one on the run.

Bound together by a secret that will haunt them forever, and a crime they will never escape.

ALIA

I stand in the shadows and watch the last few members of the audience settle in. The lights have been dimmed but the mid-morning sun filtering through the windows is enough to illuminate the auditorium. It's packed, nearly every seat occupied by graduates and their professors.

I shiver. Even though it's nearly November, the air con is turned on and the thin *chanderi sari* I'm wearing provides little warmth. I realize I'm standing directly underneath a vent and take a few steps to the right until I'm practically engulfed by the thick velvet curtains.

I can hear my staff in the background, talking in low murmurs. They know not to speak to me before a speech.

I run through the talking points in my head one final time, then I go into the news app on my phone and hit refresh. I reread the message my husband sent me this morning before his flight to New York. I scroll through my emails. Twitter. Instagram. WhatsApp.

Everyone has a different response to nerves. Some people take deep breaths, go still, and tap into an inner space of calm and reflection.

Me, I've never been that person. I'm the eccentric method actor before a premiere. My breathing becomes shallow. My heart rate speeds up. My mind races. I fidget. I'm used to this so I know that it's not until I'm out there, mic in hand, my skin warm under the spotlight, that the anxiety will melt away and a false confidence will take its place.

I'll step into character.

But I can sense an edge to my usual dread today, an irrational foreboding that has crawled under my skin and wrapped itself around my chest.

I look around even though I know my team has already swept the auditorium. I see my personal protection officer standing a few feet to my right, hand resting casually on his hip, cradling his holster. I can't see him, but I know the second PPO will be standing in an almost identical position in the wings across the stage. The two additional PPOs that my chief of staff, Omar, insisted I bring along are standing at the back of the hall keeping an eye on the audience. With three months to go until the general election, every precaution is warranted, every bizarre security measure necessary.

I flex my fingers and turn to look at Omar on my left. I follow his eyes to the stage where a young woman is introducing me.

'. . . here she is. Women and Child Development Minister, senior member of the INP, *India Today* Youth Icon of the Year and the woman who is changing the face of Indian politics, Alia Sharma.'

I hand Omar my phone and take a deep breath. I remind myself why I do this. I put on my well-practised smile, warm, welcoming but not too wide. It's important to get my face just right.

I give it a few seconds before I step out of the wings.

The applause as I walk onto the stage is deafening and amidst that roar, my heart stills. I feel the muscles in my spine unclench. My shoulders relax.

They love me.

They *will* love me.

The secret to capturing an audience? Striking the right balance. You have to come across as confident but humble, charming but honest, persuasive but relaxed. It's a tightrope act, and not an easy one, but on the few occasions that you do get it right, the result is spectacular. I can tell halfway through the speech that today, I've got it right. The audience is buzzing with energy, and I'm bouncing off them, the dynamic so alive, so charged that it feels almost hypnotic.

'I want all the women here today to know that you can have a future in the Indian National Party. I want you to know –'

I am so focused, so engrossed that I almost don't notice when Omar appears next to me and places a handwritten note on the podium.

Almost.

I glance at it. Four words, barely a sentence.

I swear my heart stops, just for a second, and I'm convinced I can't go on. All I can hear is the blood swishing in my ears. I take one shaky breath, then another. I look at the note again, hoping desperately that I read it wrong.

I didn't.

I flip the note over. I push down the lump that has lodged itself in my throat. I blink away the tears that are threatening to spill over. I do what I always do, what I must do in order to survive. I compartmentalize and I carry on. There will be time for myself later. Right now, I have a job to do.

I have a responsibility.

'I want you to know,' I continue shakily, 'that if you decide to seek party membership, you will be welcomed and supported. And, for those of you who are elected, we will make sure the parliament offices and assemblies you work in are the modern, equal, safe workplaces that we all have every right to expect.'

I dismount the mic from its holder. It seems impossible that my legs have the strength to carry me, yet here I am, walking to the centre of the stage.

There is a beat or two of complete silence as I try to remember what to say next. I can practically feel the audience quivering with anticipation.

'But if there's one thing I want you all to take away from this talk, it's this: I am not someone who expected to have the life, the career, the choices that I have now. I didn't have a political legacy or a trust fund to rely on. My story is one of struggle, of hard work, of tenacity.'

I pause, letting my words echo through the auditorium.

'I am here because I sat in an extremely uncomfortable chair, in an office lined with leather-covered books, listening to a man tell me there was only so much I could do, only so far I could go, not because I wasn't good enough or smart enough or determined enough. No. I wouldn't make it, he said, because I was a woman. A woman.'

I look around the auditorium, I take a few steps forward and then I begin wrapping up my speech, the panic rising through me too sharp to ignore anymore.

I *need* to get off this stage.

Here is what I say:

'I am here because I sat in that chair and I decided that I was going to prove that man, and every other man who has ever said those words to any woman, wrong. I am here because I decided, right then, that I was going to spend every single day fighting for the millions of women who have been told they are second-class citizens. I am here because I worked for it. I am here because I earned it.

'So remember this: I am a wife and a daughter-in-law. I am a patriot. I am a feminist. At thirty-one, I am the youngest cabinet minister in our government. And yes, I am a woman. I am a woman and I have the life I was told I couldn't have. So can you. So. Can. You.'

Here is what I don't say:

I am not who you think I am.

I am a liar.

ALIA

We are on the move in less than five minutes. Omar fills me in as we slice through the chronic Delhi traffic – heart attack; there will be a state funeral later in the week but the body has been flown to the ancestral residence to allow politicians and party workers to pay tribute. I draw in a deep breath and turn to stare out of the window while Omar continues talking. There are whispers about an emergency election for party president, but no news yet if Faraz is in the running for the position.

'I saw him just last night,' I murmur and Omar pauses.

'I'm sorry, I –' He hesitates, takes a breath. 'He didn't suffer.'

I nod, the conversation from last night still fresh in my mind. I'd dropped in unannounced after a particularly gruelling day at the constituency and even though it was close to midnight, Javed Uncle had welcomed me in with a wide smile. With the general election fast approaching, he knew I was stressed about my nomination. He had reassured me with a quick squeeze of my shoulder and a reminder that with the full weight of the alliance behind me, I had nothing to worry about. We'd scheduled Sunday lunch at the hole-in-the-wall Chinese restaurant that he loved.

'The media will be expecting a comment,' Omar says, startling me out of my thoughts.

I lean back into the cushioned leather seat. I open the window and close my eyes.

'Write something up,' I say.

Javed Qureshi, my mentor, my ally, my *friend*, is gone.

The drive to the Qureshi estate takes just over an hour. I roll up the window and take my sunglasses off as we exit the highway. I have avoided this region for the last fifteen years and I am surprised to see how much it has changed. Gone is the bumpy gravel road that had sent us into fits of giggles as girls. The dense forest that used to flank the road has been cut down to reveal acres of fields, shimmering golden in the late afternoon sun. In the distance, I can see the derelict water tank that had held particular fascination back then.

The driver slows down as we approach the final turn leading to the house. I am prepared for a smattering of party *karyakartas* and media but the crowds take my breath away. The road is a blur of white as hundreds of supporters in white *kurta pyjamas* and skullcaps spill over from the pavement onto the road. In the makeshift parking area to our left, I can count at least a dozen TV vans. There's armed police all around and cordons have been set up to keep the crowds under control.

It's all very different from the last time I rushed here, a

lifetime ago, when the only mourners allowed in were a handful of schoolgirls.

We honk our way through and I hand the driver my ID as we approach the first cordon.

'WCD Ministry. Madam's in the car,' he says, holding up my ID.

The policeman peeps in and nods to me in the back seat. '*Namaste*, madam.'

He jots down the registration number and waves us through. The lane is packed with cars, and we inch along towards the wrought-iron gates where a second cordon has been set up. The forest I remember so clearly from that winter lines the curved driveway, the trees tall and gnarled, the underbrush a tangle of leaves and ivy, threatening to take over the narrow road.

I catch glimpses of the house as it reveals itself in snatches through the trees and suddenly I am fifteen again, squashed up next to Noor and Sabah in the back seat of an Ambassador. Just the thought of their names, always uttered together in a single breath, brings them back to me. Noor's kohl-rimmed eyes, Sabah's throaty laugh, the identical bracelets they wore, and the heady intoxicating smell of the perfume they both claimed to have stolen from the other – Obsession.

Noor.

Sabah.

And lurking somewhere in the shadows, me.

We stop at the wrought-iron gates and I climb out of the car, stretching myself as discreetly as I can manage. I step through the metal detectors while Omar signs us in. At first glance, the house looks exactly as it did fifteen years ago – overwhelming in its scale and opulence – but as my eyes linger over the building, I realize it is shrouded in neglect. The family has spent hardly any time here since that winter and it occurs to me that it must have been even more painful for them to return here after everything. All I was hiding from was a year's worth of memories; they had a lifetime's worth to contend with.

I circle the fountain, dry and covered in moss, and climb up the short flight of steps. Inside, I hesitate for a moment, bracing myself, before I turn left and go straight into the living room.

That's when it hits me. The room, which is big enough to hold a few hundred people, has been cleared of all furniture. A clear-glass coffin rests in the centre. A large picture of Javed Uncle from his last campaign has been propped up next to it. I lean on the door frame, my legs refusing to move further, my heart rejecting what my brain already knows. I wipe the tears away and take a breath to steady myself. I make my way over to the coffin, walking past groups of men, and bow down to pay my respects. I could not stomach looking at a dead body as a teenager and I can't do it now. I barely glance inside the glass box at the body that's been wrapped up in white muslin before I step back.

This is not how I want to remember him.

I spot Faraz and the family lined up a few feet from me and I head over to them instead. Faraz is standing there immobile, hands folded in front of him as people murmur their condolences and move on. It's only when I am standing opposite him that I notice the tears streaming down his face.

'Faraz,' I say. I'm not sure if he hears me or registers my presence.

'Faraz,' I repeat, placing my hands on his. It's a bold gesture, one that I know will send ripples through the political circuit, but Faraz and I go back a long way. Grief, I've realized, binds you to people in a way that joy never can.

My touch sparks something in him and as his eyes focus in on me, I can no longer hold back the sobs. He pulls me into a hug.

'Alia, he's gone,' he whispers, his words heavy, weighed down. 'He's really gone.'

It had hit Faraz the hardest. He had pulled me aside at the funeral to ask me about some detail, something so minor that I can't even remember it now. He had been obsessed with the specifics – he wanted to know everything from the colour of her dress to what time we snuck out – almost as if by piecing together the exact chain of events that night, he could change what had happened. I should never have left the city, I should have been there, I should have protected her, he had screamed.

I told him over and over again that it wasn't his fault.

That she had walked into that party on her own.

That he couldn't have done anything to stop what happened next.

There was so much that I didn't know back then. So much that I still don't know. But I have often wondered if my conviction that day came from knowing, deep down, that if I looked at the chain of responsibility, I'd find that it started with me.

ALIA

Fifteen years ago

Everyone always assumes that having lived in London my whole life, I would've found life in Delhi quite mellow, but the truth is, it was the opposite. Put a bunch of bored, overprivileged teenagers in a school with rules that are more repressive than a fascist regime and you'll get more scandal and gossip in an hour than in an entire season of reality TV.

The memories from that time shine so bright, with such vivid clarity and detail that they almost feel false. It was my first day at Wescott, and while first days are bad enough for most people, for me, being the new girl held a special horror.

The headmistress had sent me off with a timetable and vague directions to the classroom in a building that felt more like a multi-level concrete labyrinth than a high school.

I was terrified, so naturally, I acted blasé.

I went off, quite purposefully at first, certain that she had told me to turn right, go down the long corridor that connected all the buildings, which for some reason, they liked to call blocks, and then turn –

I looked around at the identical grey buildings. I was lost. I tried to search my brain for the rest of her instructions as groups of students walked past me in all directions, the clamour of their voices making it impossible for me to focus.

I saw the door to the girls' toilets on my left and ducked in.

I was washing my hands and trying to remember if the headmistress had said block F or H when a very tall, very skinny girl stepped out of one of the stalls. She came and stood next to me at the sink. I remember staring at her in the mirror. She was alarmingly pretty, with none of the spotty skin or facial hair that had haunted me since the day I turned twelve. She had a heart-shaped face and pouty lips, her deep black eyes framed by thick kohl. She was wearing a *hijab*, but the silky scarf was barely enough to contain what I could tell was a wild tangle of hair underneath. And though I would never have admitted it then, it was her easy beauty, that shock of the bright pink *hijab* against her creamy skin, that first made me want to be friends with her. At fifteen, I was convinced that if I hung out with the pretty, popular girls, I would somehow transform into one myself.

'Do you mind?'

I averted my eyes, embarrassed to have been caught staring, and she laughed. She leaned in and stuck her hands above mine under the stream of water.

'I don't like touching *anything* in here,' she said, wiping her hands on her skirt. There were no hand dryers or even paper towels in the toilets. Of all the things that shocked me about this supposedly elite school that I had been shipped off to, the complete lack of hygiene struck me the most.

'Are you new?' she asked. I saw her eyes scan my face in the mirror and watched them soften as she took in my expression.

I nodded, not trusting myself to speak as I blinked back the tears. I followed her lead, wiping my hands on my skirt instead of the filthy brown towel that was hung by the door. I handed her the timetable. 'Do you know where this is? XI-R?'

'That's my class! Banerjee's not great at orientations, is she?' she smirked.

It took me a second to realize that she had just referred to the headmistress by her last name alone.

'Relax, she can't hear us,' she smiled. 'I'm Noor, by the way.'

'Alia.'

'Okay, so, all year eleven classrooms are in block F, which is the tall one right next to the assembly ground. We're in section R, so that'll be top floor, by the water cooler.' She picked up her backpack and slung it over one shoulder. 'Come on, I'll show you,' she said, pushing the door open with her hip.

I followed her out of the toilets and down yet another long corridor. She pointed out activity rooms, science labs and faculty lounges as we passed them, her voice rising over the commotion that was hundreds of students back on their first day of term. I had visited Westminster as part of a school group the year before and I could recognize the same whiff of power and entitlement in the halls at Wescott. I felt just as out of place here as I had done in Westminster that day, being led by a person clearly accustomed to sashaying down the corridors.

But then, I suppose I felt out of place everywhere.

'Homeroom starts in six minutes,' she said, looking at her watch as we power-walked three flights up a concrete staircase. 'Four periods before the break, and four after. Most seniors use the cafeteria in block H, but you can go wherever you want. There's a—'

'There's more than one cafeteria?'

'Yeah, there's, like, four thousand students at Wescott.'

'Oh, right.'

One of the few things Mrs Banerjee had been at pains to explain was that students didn't go from class to class in Wescott; instead, the teachers came to us. I tried to picture four thousand students cramming into this maze of narrow corridors and stairwells after every period and suddenly it made sense.

I was about to thank Noor for the tour when I realized she was distracted. Her face broke into a grin as she waved at the girl waiting at the top of the stairs. 'That's Sabah,' she said before running up the final few steps. I watched the two of them drape around each other while talking a million miles a minute, several weeks' worth of chatter condensed into urgent whispers, interrupted only by giggles and shrieks.

Sabah was pretty. Extremely pretty, with sparkling hazel

eyes and dark brown hair pulled back into a sleek ponytail. Her nose and forehead were dotted with freckles and though she was slim, her face had a healthy fullness to it, giving her the kind of wholesome appearance that was every teenage girl's dream.

'Hey,' Sabah said, taking me in with one sharp glance after I'd slogged my way up the remaining stairs. I could feel myself blush as her eyes lingered over my starched uniform. She was dressed in the same uniform that I was wearing, but while mine felt stiff and restrictive, Sabah looked like she had just stepped out of *Teen Vogue*. Her plaid skirt finished halfway down her thighs, her shirtsleeves were rolled up to reveal a delicate charm bracelet and her tie hung loose, top button undone. She was wearing the same white socks with the red stripe running through, but hers were scrunched down to her ankles, revealing ridiculously long legs for such a petite girl.

I felt myself shrink under her scrutiny.

'Hi, I'm Alia,' I managed to say before she spun around.

'Come on, we're already late,' she said, linking her arm through Noor's and marching down the corridor to the classroom. She leaned in to whisper something into Noor's ear and Noor swatted her away.

All I could do was imagine what she might have said, what words she would have used to dismiss me.

'Here we are,' Noor said, turning to me and swinging the door open.

The room was crammed full of desks, arranged in pairs and lined up in four rows. Students were scattered in groups of twos and threes across the classroom, leaning on desks, the girls talking in shrill voices and the boys pretending to ignore them. Though the layout and scale was very different to my comprehensive in London, somehow it felt exactly the same.

'Pick any desk you want,' Noor called out as Sabah dragged her over to a group of girls clustered around the window, all of them slim, all of them gorgeous. I watched for a minute as the girls rearranged themselves to let Noor and Sabah claim their spots at the centre. Noor dumped her backpack on the floor and hoisted herself on top of a desk.

In less than a few seconds, the group closed around them and all I could see of Noor was a flash of her *hijab* and her distinctly non-regulation trainers resting on the chair.

I took a deep breath and made my way over to an empty seat at the back of the room. I reminded myself that I didn't need friends. I'd been fine on my own in London and I would be fine here.

I slipped into the chair and busied myself with studying the timetable that I already knew by heart.

ALIA

Fifteen years ago

I nearly jumped with relief when the bell rang, signalling the start of the forty-minute lunch break. I swept my notebook and pens into my backpack and zipped it shut. The homeroom teacher had left some sign-up sheets on her desk and a group of girls had clustered around it.

I waited till they had trickled away, their attention seized by a group of boys, and then stepped through the aisle. I flicked through the sheets, amazed at the sheer number of options. There were at least fifteen different clubs and a dozen activities coming up in the first term alone, everything from the traditional swim team to a model United Nations conference and a social outreach society.

I watched the girl I had spent the morning sitting next to walk out with not so much as a glance in my direction. I chided myself for the unwanted flutter of disappointment. I had already decided to spend the lunch break reading. I knew that over time these faces would become familiar but until then the thought of walking into a packed cafeteria on the first day of school and trying to work out where to sit filled me with dread.

I was scrawling my name on the sign-up sheet for the track team when Noor and Sabah sauntered over.

'Hey,' Noor said, as Sabah put her and Noor's names down on a couple of sheets in elaborate looping letters. Even her handwriting was prettier than mine.

'Hi.'

'Are you going for lunch?'

The only thing worse than facing hundreds of new faces at lunch was admitting to one of them that I wasn't brave enough to go.

'Yeah, in a minute. Are you?' I asked, trying to sound nonchalant.

'There, done,' Sabah said, straightening up to face Noor and me.

A look passed between them, and I could sense some sort of agreement being reached. I tried not to get my hopes up.

'Yep, do you want to walk with us?'

'Sure,' I shrugged, even as my heart spun cartwheels inside my chest.

The seniors' cafeteria was on the ground floor in the block across from us. Noor and Sabah led the way, arms linked, pleated skirts swaying in sync. I tried to keep up with them in the narrow corridor but every few steps I'd have to hang back to let someone pass.

One of the boys from my bus route waved at me from across the courtyard as we crossed it on our way to the cafeteria.

'You know him?' Sabah asked.

'Dhruv? He was at my bus stop this morning. Why?'

'He's a senior, and newly single.'

'Oh.'

'And super hot,' Noor grinned.

I could feel the colour rising in my cheeks.

'You don't have a boyfriend, do you?' Sabah asked.

'No,' I said, then noticing the satisfaction creeping up Sabah's face, I added, 'Not anymore, I mean. I broke up with Chris when we moved here. Long distance,' I said with a shudder. The lie was only small but it sent a ripple of excitement through me, especially when I saw that the girls were suitably impressed.

'What about you?' I asked as we climbed up the short flight of stairs at the entrance of the cafeteria.

'Noor doesn't really do boyfriends,' Sabah said.

'Oh, of course, I –' I stammered, mortified that I hadn't clocked the significance of her *hijab*.

'No, no, nothing like that. All of this' – Noor twirled – 'is for my parents. What she means is, I prefer not to be tied down at sixteen. Not like Sabah, who's been in love with the same boy since we were, like, eight.'

'What can I say, unlike *some* people, I have no interest in getting half the swim team's opinion on which bra matches —ouch,' Sabah squealed as Noor pinched her arm.

It didn't take a genius to figure out this banter was part of their act and the sudden stab of longing took me by surprise.

These girls were seriously cool.

We pushed the double doors open and stepped into a large hall lined with long wooden tables and benches. A huge skylight and massive windows overlooking the main courtyard lit up the room and turned what would otherwise have been a claustrophobic space into something open and welcoming. Or as open as it can be with the entire senior class crammed into it.

I felt the burn of hundreds of eyes on me as we weaved through the hordes of students to get to the snack station.

'Wow,' I muttered. I tugged at my skirt self-consciously.

Sabah laughed and took my arm, pulling me to the front of the queue. 'This is what happens when you're with Noor. You'll get used to it.'

'Boys, this is Alia. She's new, so be nice,' Noor said as we approached a table along the back wall.

'Vineet,' Noor said, pointing to the ridiculously good-looking boy who was still in his cricket jersey. 'Mohit.' The dark one with tightly curled black hair and rimmed glasses. 'Yash.' The one who barely looked up; he was taller than the others and clearly belonged in a computer lab.

After a chorus of uninterested hellos, the boys went back to dissing the Campion School cricket team, and we went back to ignoring them. The message was clear: I might be at their table today but I had to earn the right to be part of the group.

'So you moved *here*? From London?' Sabah asked, dumping her bag of Cheetos on the table as she slid in next to Vineet. With his deep olive skin and floppy Nick Carter-esque hair, I didn't need anyone to tell me he was the Ken to her Barbie.

'My parents got transferred to Turkey,' I said, sitting down across from her. 'I would've gone with them but they weren't having it. Too dangerous, apparently. I'm living with my grandparents now, which is cool because I can basically do anything I want.'

Noor sat down next to me. 'What do your parents do?'

We were sitting at a table next to the windows. Though the cafeteria was busy, bustling with students trying to find an empty seat, there were only six of us on a table large enough for ten. It was obvious, even to me, that this was the top table. I'd learn later that being from London gave me instant cool quotient, but for the moment, I couldn't quite believe that I was eating lunch with girls like Noor and Sabah. It felt crucial to build up a picture of myself that would fit in with them, even if that meant stretching the truth a little. This was supposed to be a fresh start, after all.

'They're diplomats,' I said, which was technically true.

'Nice,' Noor said. She reached across the table to help herself to a handful of Cheetos.

'What was your school like in London?' Sabah asked. Her poise unnerved me.

'Small. We had five hundred students there in total.'

'Wow.'

'Yeah, everyone knew everyone,' I said, breaking off a small piece of the *samosa* I had bought.

'Did you live close by?'

'Kind of. It was, like, a fifteen-minute walk.'

'It's so cute how you can walk everywhere in London.

My aunt lives there, near Notting Hill,' Sabah said, by way of explanation.

'That's not too far from where we are.' I paused to correct myself. 'Were. Kensington.' Even back then, I knew how to play to my audience. As Noor and Sabah quizzed me about my life in London, my state-funded comprehensive in Harrow quickly became a grammar school in Kensington, and our damp two-bedroom flat became a Victorian red-brick a quick stroll from the palace.

'What, you mean, Buckingham Palace?'

'No, don't be silly. *Kensington* Palace. Buckingham Palace is so touristy,' I said, adopting the slightly haughty tone that Sabah had used with me earlier but to my dismay, her attention was elsewhere.

I turned around to see what she was looking at.

Two girls wearing matching Nike trainers were approaching our table. There was something menacing in their gait, and I found myself shrinking back in my seat.

The tall one, who I would later come to know as Nivedita, or Niv, slid in next to Noor. Her friend hovered at the end of the table, looking as uncomfortable as I felt.

'Enjoy the holidays, Niv?' Noor asked.

'Don't think I don't know what you're up to.'

'All I did was tell my friends what I saw. There's no rule against that, is there?' Noor said, her face the picture of innocence.

'Oh yeah? You know, you aren't the only one who can tell people what you saw. You think you're so high and mighty, walking around like you own this place.' She brought her face closer to Noor's, looking her square in the eyes. 'I know where you really went for the holidays. I saw you. And if you don't—'

Sabah, who had been a silent observer until now, leaned across the table and put her hand on Niv's wrist, stopping her mid-sentence. She smiled sweetly, and for a second I was fooled. 'You do know you can get expelled for cheating on a final, don't you? I still have those chits I found,' she said. 'Not that I'll need them. Everyone knows how you get your perfect scores.'

Niv shook her wrist free, rubbing it with her other hand where Sabah's grip had left an angry red mark. 'No one is going to believe you.'

'Really? Shall we walk into Banerjee's office and see?'

I looked at Sabah, this dainty, innocent-looking girl who had until now seemed a bit uptight, but harmless overall. The ferocity underneath her girly exterior dazzled me.

'I didn't think so,' Sabah said after a minute, picking up a single cheesy puff from her never-ending bag of Cheetos. 'You can go now,' she said to Niv, before popping it in her mouth.

ALIA

Outside the house, people are milling about talking and sipping *chai* out of disposable plastic cups. A marquee has been set up in the back garden. Politicians, bureaucrats and industrialists elbow for space as TV presenters broadcast comments and interviews to thousands of homes live across the country. A couple of reporters approach me and I oblige them with a short, teary comment. Optics is everything.

I learned that the hard way.

The scandal, when it broke, stayed in the papers for months afterwards. It had to, considering the people involved: Noor, the daughter of a cabinet minister; Vineet, the son of the city's most prominent property developer; and me, the cast-off daughter of two civil servants. Sabah, in contrast, had had it easier to begin with, until someone let spill the details of what had really gone on at our parties and, overnight, she was the mastermind, the one who had led us down the path of total ruin. The coverage was brutal. In the absence of real facts, the media whipped up a storm, one ludicrous story at a time. Opinion pieces about the dangers of allowing girls too much freedom, articles condemning the school administration, books claiming to reveal the 'real' truth. Within days, stricter rules came into force in schools across the city, from the obvious to the utterly bizarre: longer skirts, mandatory counselling sessions, no after-school activities, no mobile phones, no outside food. Though the courts ensured we were never officially named, it was one thing banning the national media from printing our names, quite another trying to keep it from the mouths of gossipy teenagers. Our identities were, quite possibly, the worst kept secret of the time.

It had worried me, when I decided to run for office. I questioned myself incessantly. Did I really think I could escape that? Not only walk away scot-free but also build a life based on a mistake that had destroyed so many? Turns out, the world loves nothing more than a good redemption story and, in some ways, the media attention helped more than it harmed. I gave one single interview – an hour-long exclusive on CTV the week before I declared my candidacy. I spoke frankly about the school, about teenage mental health, about Noor and Sabah and what friendships like that could do to a naive teenager. It had been Arjun who suggested I do the interview. Take control of the narrative, he'd said. We hadn't been married then, but I trusted him. I took his advice. The country had loved it; it was better than any exposé or true crime documentary. They were hearing directly from one of the infamous Wescott Four. The non-profit I had set up as a young student saw a 200 per cent hike in donations that quarter and when I ran for office a few months later, I won by a landslide. Somehow, by admitting my guilt on national television, by talking about my anguish over trying and failing to help Noor, I had become a symbol for innocent girls who had been led astray. The country came together in their support for me and with one interview, the worst thing I had ever done became the foundation for the rest of my life.

Six months into my first term, Javed Uncle told me I was being vetted for a post as a junior minister. My relationship with Javed Qureshi, and the resultant vote base, gave me an edge within the party. As the leader of the Indian Muslim Congress, Javed Uncle controlled the majority of the Muslim votes and the alliance between our parties meant that I was the only Hindu MP with a 50 per cent Muslim electorate. It's a statistic that has served me well through both my terms as an MP. After three years as a junior minister, I was given a position on the cabinet. Javed Uncle had told me that after another term as WCD minister, I would be in line for the most influential portfolio on the cabinet – Home Minister.

It hits me again just how much I had relied on Javed Uncle's counsel – and influence – and I steel myself as a fresh wave of emotion threatens to overtake me.

I spot Faraz emerging from the house and make my way over to him.

'You okay?' I ask, touching his elbow lightly as he extricates himself from a group of *karyakartas*.

He nods, but doesn't say anything.

'If there's anything you need, anything at all—'

'I know,' he says. His gaze wanders over to the party workers huddled together across the lawn. 'Can you believe they're already talking about electing a new party president? It's been less than twenty-four hours,' he continues, his voice thick with outrage. 'Vultures.'

I let out a small sigh. I had hoped the rumours hadn't reached him yet.

'You'll need to act quickly,' I say, hating myself for even uttering the words. But I've seen enough parties split and alliances collapse with the death of the leader. 'Is Aziz advising you?' I ask, nodding towards Javed Uncle's chief of staff.

'He's putting in my bid this afternoon,' Faraz sighs. 'I hate to ask, but your support would go a long way—'

It's my turn to cut him off. 'And you have it. Like I said, anything you need.'

'Thank you,' he says.

I step back as a reporter approaches Faraz, her scathing questions wrapped up in layers of sympathy.

I swallow past the tightening in my throat and walk out of the marquee towards the forest we had so carelessly run into as girls. In my memory, it had become an extension of the garden itself, something small and easily contained. Now I see it for what it really is, a sparkling menace of foliage as alluring as it is forbidding, hiding inside it a darkness so profound not even the sharp afternoon sun manages to pierce through it.

I shiver. I wrap my *pallu* around myself as I walk right

up to the edge of the lawn, a barbed-wire fence the only thing standing between this stately estate and the wild unkempt forest surrounding it.

ALIA

Fifteen years ago

It didn't take long for me to secure my spot on Noor and Sabah's lunch table. It had become obvious that first day that my two ins were London and Dhruv and I played both cards with the precision of a regular at the Empire's poker table.

I was already at the bus stop when Dhruv sauntered over.

'So, one week in,' he said, eyebrow raised, lips lifted in a half-smile. 'Do we meet your standards?'

'Jury's still out,' I said, trying not to stare at him as the early morning sun bounced off his face. 'Though the bus is always late, the cafeteria snack selection is, frankly, disgusting and this has to be the most boring first week of term ever. So I guess not.'

Dhruv laughed. He brushed his hair out of his eyes, in a move straight out of the Leonardo Di Caprio playbook. 'Correct on all counts except one.'

'Really?' I said as the bus pulled up in front of us. Dhruv stepped back to let me go first and then climbed in himself, the metal floor shaking as we scrambled up the steps and down the narrow aisle. I turned to look at him over my shoulder. 'Which one?'

I slid into a window seat, trying desperately to slow my heart down and keep the heat from rising to my face. Dhruv leaned in and lowered his voice to a whisper.

'It's only boring if you don't know who to hang out with. Party at mine tomorrow night. You're coming. Bring your friends if you want.'

'I'll see if I can make it,' I replied, straight-faced.

I waited for him to walk past me to his usual seat at the back of the bus. It was only when I heard the thump of his backpack against the hard vinyl-covered seats, and the roar of laughter that meant he was busy with his friends, that I allowed myself a smile.

An invite to the hottest senior's house.

The hottest, newly single senior.

I was *so* in.

When I think about it now, I know it couldn't have been that simple. I couldn't possibly have reinvented myself into someone completely different overnight, but that is how I remember it. I had spent so long trying to fit in, to be liked and popular, that when I saw the glimmer of opportunity, I knew I had to take it. I learned how to make my lies roll off my tongue so naturally that they began to sound real even to me. I spent ages observing the other girls, the way they spoke, the way they dressed, the things they laughed at and the things they cared about. I had always liked music, but it took on a new meaning as we whispered secrets to each other in lyrics from the Spice Girls and Dido. More than anything else, I learned to loosen up. I had fun. *They* were fun. We did all the usual things teenage girls do – we talked about boys, we painted our nails, we giggled endlessly – but with Noor and Sabah, even the most mundane conversation took on the allure of something epic and life-changing.

But here's the thing: just acting like I belonged wasn't enough; I also had to *look* like I belonged.

Less than two weeks after I started school, I begged my grandma to take me shopping. I knew if I asked for the money outright, she'd say no, or worse, tell my mother, but if I could prove to her that I needed all these new things, if she could see for herself how much nicer the quality was, how much longer everything would last, I knew I could convince her.

Our first stop was Rio Grande. Here's something I learned early on: *always* start with the academic essentials. No adult can say no to a new notebook. Or five.

The ploy worked. I ended up with a bunch of the rainbow-coloured vest tops that were all the rage then, a pair of Levi's hipsters, a new dove-grey JanSport backpack to replace my tatty Sports Direct one, two new pairs of trainers, both Nike of course, black with a white swoosh for classes and white with a neon-pink swoosh for track club, and a dozen sparkly bracelets. I tried to pull Nani into Silofer to round off the kind of shopping spree that would make my mum livid with anger – I'd been hankering after a pair of sterling silver hoops that I'd seen all the girls wearing, but there my luck ran out.

'Maybe for your birthday,' Nani said, as I dug into my triple hot chocolate fudge sundae at Nirula's later. With extra fudge. 'How are you finding the new school?' she asked, her face, as usual, full of concern. A look that I had never witnessed on my mother's face.

'It's very different,' I shrugged. I thought about broaching the subject of the newly announced Oxbridge trip but after the amount of money she'd just spent on me, I decided I'd be better off waiting for another time. 'I have the track club try-outs soon.'

'Have you made friends?'

'A few. I was going to ask you if I could go to my friend Sabah's house after school tomorrow. I'm helping her organize a cleanliness—'

'Alia?'

The screech stopped me mid-sentence. I turned around in my chair.

It was Saloni, one of the girls from Noor and Sabah's group. From *my* group.

'Oh my God, how funny seeing you here,' she said, twirling one finger through her long, Pantene-commercial hair.

'I know,' I smiled. 'I've been shopping with my Nani.' I nodded to my grandma sitting across from me.

'Hi, Aunty,' she beamed, the coveted Silofer hoops sparkling on her ears as she moved. 'Wow.' She leaned over to look at my half-eaten sundae. 'I haven't had that since I was, like, twelve. My body just can't handle the calories, you know?' She rolled her eyes and patted the space where her stomach should have been.

I walked right into it.

'Don't be silly, you look great,' I said, taking in her waifish frame, even more pronounced in the cropped T-shirt and the Levi's 501s she had on, slung so low on her hips that I could see her hipbones protrude.

'Aw, thanks, Alia. You look . . . fine,' she said. 'Anyway, Mum's waiting at the salon. So . . . I'll see you at school?' she said before gliding out the door, laden with shopping bags and the one thing no one ever went to Nirula's for: a fruit cup.

'Is that what the girls at school are like?' Nani asked.

I shrugged, licking off the last bit of fudge from my spoon before pushing my half-eaten sundae away.

'Come on,' Nani said, 'let's get you those hoops. Your mother doesn't need to know everything.'

ALIA

I check my watch as I rush into the house, the front door unlocked as usual. There's little need for locks and bolts when you have fifteen armed guards scattered all over the grounds.

'We're going to be late,' Arjun says as I step into the living room and kick off my shoes. Between his trips to New York and my pre-campaign schedule, I've hardly seen him the past few weeks. I let my eyes linger over my husband's handsome, if tired face, taking in the slight stubble pricking his chin and the adorably mussed hair. I bend down to give him a quick kiss.

'It's only around the corner.' I perch on the arm of the sofa and wiggle my toes. Arjun's never understood that for me, even after so many years, being late is a move. It's a reminder: look how busy I am, but I made time for you.

'How's Faraz?'

'Good,' I say. 'The ceremony was odd, though. I was the only one there from the INP.'

'Are you worried about the alliance?' Arjun asks and I almost tell him the truth. I am terrified.

Less than a month after Javed Uncle's death, Faraz's swearing-in ceremony this morning had been a surprisingly cheerful affair. I was bewildered to see that while most of the senior leaders of the Muslim Congress were present, I was the only member of the INP in attendance. Javed Uncle had spent thirty years nurturing the alliance between the Muslim Congress and the INP. I found it disconcerting that Faraz hadn't used the opportunity to reassure the INP that the alliance between our parties was secure despite the change in leadership. When I mentioned it afterwards, Faraz assured me that it wasn't an oversight – he was planning to hold a separate, more intimate reception for the key members of the alliance in a few days. Yet something about his speech and the fervour with which he had promised to lead the party into a new 'era of inclusiveness' left me feeling rattled. With two months to go, even a small change in direction can cost me the election.

It can cost me everything.

I push the thoughts away. I am being paranoid. The alliance benefits Faraz as much as it does me, and he would never do anything to endanger it.

I run up the stairs to the private wing. I've lived in this house for nearly seven years now, but it still doesn't feel like home. Though, maybe it is a bit unfair to expect an eight-bedroom government-owned mansion to feel like home. Aside from the cavalry of staff – a cook, a maid, a cleaner and three drivers just for the residence – there is a sense of impermanence here. Too many others have been here before me and the walls hum with their secrets. One wrong move and I'll be the next one being ousted from here. I know Arjun feels it too, that niggle of uncertainty, but ultimately, this house represents little more than a place to sleep for him.

I try to focus my thoughts on the evening ahead as I step into the bedroom and close the door. I unpin my *sari* and peel it away, before stepping out of my petticoat and unhooking my blouse. With each layer that I strip away, I feel a little bit younger, more feminine, more me. I shake my hair out of its ponytail and twist it into a messy bun at the nape of my neck, letting a few loose strands frame my face. I slip into a red silk blouse and cropped trousers and dab on some perfume. The look I'm going for is off duty but powerful.

I find Arjun waiting in the hall when I go back downstairs. 'What have you done with my wife?' he says, wrapping his arms around my waist. 'You okay?' he whispers into my ear. My husband has always been attentive, but ever since the funeral last month, there seems to be a permanent trace of worry in his eyes.

'I'm fine, sweetheart,' I say, leaning back into him. I allow myself a moment before straightening up and forcing my feet into a pair of black Louboutins.

I take a deep breath and check my reflection in the hall mirror. Gone is the asexual politician touring her constituency; instead, I have transformed into a regular thirty-one-year-old who could almost be sexy.

Viewed from the right angle.

ALIA

Fifteen years ago

The transformation complete, in a few short weeks I became a permanent fixture by Noor and Sabah's side. I'd earned my spot on the lunch table and a week after the Nirula's incident, I had swapped seats in class so I was sitting right behind Noor instead of next to Tanvi, who I had learned by now was 'a bit slow'.

It happened quite casually.

I was standing with Noor and Sabah next to their desks when the homeroom bell rang, cutting Noor off mid-story.

I picked up my backpack from the floor and slung it onto one shoulder, ready to go back to my seat on the other side of the room when Noor touched my arm. She smiled at Saloni. 'You don't mind swapping seats with Alia, do you?'

'Oh, but I—' Saloni stuttered.

'I *really* need to talk to her. Thanks!' Noor continued.

I saw a smirk pass over Sabah's face as Saloni looked from Noor to Sabah, puzzled at this sudden dismissal, until finally her eyes came to rest on me.

I shrugged, an innocent smile playing on my lips.

Saloni may be skinny but *I* was wanted.

She muttered something under her breath, but then picked up her backpack and shuffled along, sullen faced, to the other end of the classroom. No one liked stepping out of Noor's orbit, but I knew by then that whatever Noor wanted, she got.

And as it turned out, when I was with her, so did I.

For a committee that prestigious, I was surprised to learn that the Student Council at Wescott wasn't elected. Any student in year eleven could apply at the beginning of the school year in April and as long they had at least two faculty endorsements and good grades they would earn a spot on the long list. Each applicant then had six weeks to submit a three-thousand-word essay outlining their plans for the school. You would think that was it, but the fight only got bloodier as term progressed. The school board then pored over the entries, and drew up a shortlist of students who would be interviewed by the board for the positions of Head Girl, Head Boy and half a dozen prefects. The whole saga took about nine months start to finish and ended in an elaborate investiture ceremony when the school reopened in January after the winter break, the next year's Student Council in situ, ready to step up after the year twelve students had graduated.

Both Noor and Sabah had put in their names, and while Noor was going for prefect, which everyone knew was the fun job, Sabah, of course, had her eye on Head Girl.

So a month into the school term, Saloni, Addi and I had been roped in to help with the multi-point plan that

Sabah assured us would result in her landing the position come January. Rumour had it that there had been over forty applications already, and with just two weeks left before the summer holidays, Sabah was getting antsier by the day.

While the other students were focusing on their essays, Sabah decided to up the ante. Not only was she going to give the school board an outline of what she was planning to do once she was appointed, she was also going to show them how committed she was to the school. Which was where we came in. From a community outreach programme to a cleanliness campaign, we filled our afternoons painting posters, handing out flyers and organizing assemblies while Sabah dreamed up scheme after scheme.

That afternoon Saloni, Addi, Sabah and I were working on posters for a blood donation drive when Noor walked in, late as usual.

She took one look at us, paintbrushes in hand, and flopped down on Sabah's bed. 'Seriously? You're a shoo-in for Head Girl. You can stop with the crazy now.'

Sabah didn't look up. She was painting an intricate border along the edge of the poster. 'I'm not taking any chances. Not all of us have Noor Qureshi's luck. Anyway, a blood drive for little boys and girls is hardly crazy,' she said.

'You know what I mean. It's Friday afternoon.' Noor sat up. 'Let's go see a film, have some fun.'

'We don't need to put these up until next week,' I ventured, not quite bold enough to put my brush down yet.

'The new Leo film is out,' Addi commented and I smiled.

I liked Addi. Her family had moved to India from Bristol and, unsurprisingly, it made us instant allies.

'Fine,' Sabah said after a minute, the word stretched out into a long sigh. She twirled her brush in the pot of red paint next to her.

'Amazing!' Noor leaped up. 'Let's go.'

'Just as soon as these posters are done,' Sabah said, grinning and handing Noor the brush.

ALIA

Fifteen years ago

I wasn't naïve enough to believe I knew everything that was going on. I'd walked in on enough whispered conversations to know that there were things I wasn't privy to, but I chose to ignore it. I chose to believe that while Noor and Sabah may have had secrets before, now that I was their friend, I knew everything they knew. I chose to look past the hushed giggles, ignored the times they blatantly hung out without me, moved past the anxiety that I was missing out and instead focused on the fact that for the first time in my life I had friends, real friends, the kind of friends who shared secrets and rang each other in the middle of the night.

I compartmentalized. I saw what I wanted to see, which was that we were just a bunch of teenage girls doing what normal teenage girls do: having fun.

I had always been one of the good girls in London – I turned my homework in on time, I paid attention in class, I was always polite, always helpful, and that, despite my mediocre grades, made me popular with the teachers and invisible to the cool kids. My group of friends had consisted of three other girls, as ordinary as me, who stuck together simply so we had someone to team up with for group projects. So it seemed fitting that I had somehow made it to fifteen without ever having cheated on a paper, cut class or tasted alcohol. I had once tried to skip Chemistry lab. I'd snuck out of school – not that anyone was keeping watch. I made it as far as the bus stop before turning around. I told the teacher I was late because I'd been sick. She waved me in and I slipped into my seat, test tubes glistening in front of me. I realized that afternoon that it's easier to be lonely in a crowded classroom than in an empty flat.

So when Noor asked me to meet her in the girls' toilets after PE one day, I didn't know exactly what she was planning but I felt a thrill run up my spine.

Addi, Saloni and I had already been waiting a few minutes when Noor walked in. Sabah wasn't coming. She was far too straight-laced to risk being late to class, and she would never endanger her shot at Head Girl.

'What are we doing?' I asked Noor, unable to bear the suspense any longer.

'You need to have some patience,' she said, slipping off her *hijab* to redo her hair. She shook her hair loose, wild curls tumbling around her face. She took her time teasing the ringlets apart with her fingers, scrunching up the ends, before twisting them into a tight bun and wrapping the silky scarf around her head.

She turned to face us when she was done. She smiled conspiratorially. 'And courage.'

She pulled out a handful of miniature bottles of vodka from her backpack and handed them out.

'Cheers,' she said and I watched all three of them knock the drink back without hesitation.

I was reminded of my parents, opening a bottle of champagne when their Turkey postings were approved, clinking their heavy whisky glasses after they booked my flight to Delhi, sipping on wine at their farewell dinner in London. A million tiny sips to celebrate one thing: they were finally getting rid of me.

I raised the little bottle to my lips and took a tentative sip, before following Noor's lead and knocking it back, feeling the cold liquid burn through my throat all the way down to my stomach. I pictured it entering my bloodstream, veins rippling as the vodka travelled through my body.

I felt the urge to cough, but I swallowed it down, hoping that the others hadn't noticed. I could feel them watching me, but no one said anything and the pretence that I was exactly like them continued.

We waited till another ten minutes had passed, and then halfway through the third period when Noor assured us the corridors would be empty, we slipped out of the toilets one by one and ran across the assembly ground.

Picturing it now, I am astounded at our idiocy. The assembly ground was spread out along the back of the school and anyone looking out of a window of D or E block could have spotted the four of us running across towards the brick wall outlining the school complex. We were aiming for the metal service gate. Students weren't allowed to use it and though it was locked, it wasn't manned like the main gates were.

Noor ushered us into a corner so we were concealed behind the trees clustered around the assembly ground.

'Now what?' Saloni whispered, even though there was no one around to hear us.

Noor pulled out a key from her pocket, that even today, I don't know how she got. 'Now,' she said, 'we break out of this place.'

Within moments, we were out, the door locked shut behind us.

'Look sexy, girls,' Noor said, sticking a thumb out as a few cars approached.

A Maruti 800 braked to a stop. A middle-aged man looked at us from behind the wheel.

'I'm *so* sorry to bother you,' Noor said, leaning down to talk to him through the window, her voice sweet as honey. 'We're on a school trip and we missed the bus. Could you please give us a lift to the Hyatt? We tried to get a rickshaw, but we don't have enough money.'

'You have a school trip to the Hyatt?' the man asked, not convinced by four girls standing fifty feet from school claiming they were on a trip to a five-star hotel.

'It's meant to be a treat for all the class toppers, you know. We were late because my friend,' she said, pointing to me, 'was sick and we went to get some water.'

Noor sounded so sincere even I almost believed her.

I tried to pull my best 'sick' face as the man peered at me, his eyes lingering where my skirt ended and thighs began.

'Please? It's only a ten-minute drive.'

'Okay, get in, but you should be more careful. Delhi's not safe, not for pretty girls like you.'

He went on talking at us throughout the drive, his words getting creepier by the minute. He took a diversion eschewing the main road for a deserted dirt track and I felt Addi's hand grip mine. In the front seat, Noor's excited babble slowed down. For a few minutes, I could've sworn we all forgot to breathe.

We burst into laughter as soon as he drove off, because of course, *of course*, we knew exactly what we were doing. He might have been sleazy, but we were clever.

We weren't scared. We were safe.

We were untouchable.

ALIA

I'm aware of the eyes following me as the hostess leads us through the packed restaurant and up the stairs. It's not that I'm famous exactly, but I have achieved a certain level of recognition over the past year, at least within the upper and middle classes in Delhi. I had been just another face in Delhi's political circuit until I came out in support of the decriminalization of gay sex two years ago. A controversial stance, but one that had won me a spot on nearly every televised debate and panel discussion in the lead-up to the Supreme Court judgement this summer.

Upstairs, the room has a distinct element of theatre, a peculiar mix of precision and chaos. The centre of the room is dominated by a handful of live robata grills around which groups of diners are seated bar style. Tables are scattered across the rest of the space, spilling out onto the terrace. Waiters glide around the packed room, trays piled high with fresh fish and sushi, and as I watch them thread their way through the room, I have a morbid sense of being trapped in a car that is about to crash.

We tail the hostess to the back of the space where I can see Saurav and Arushi already seated at a round table, along with Niv and a young couple who I assume are John and Maya.

This whole evening has been arranged so Saurav can introduce me to them, a political pimping out that's going to help him win the deal that will turn him from an heir to an entrepreneur and launch Europe's largest supermarket chain, which John owns, into the Indian market. It's usually the kind of thing I abhor, but Saurav is Arjun's cousin and the request came directly from my mother-in-law.

I know better than to give up my darling daughter-in-law status over one dinner. My marriage is another piece in the complex jigsaw that makes up my life. At first glance, most people would think it unnecessary, un-feminist, but take the piece away and the picture is left wanting.

Hugs and kisses are exchanged, introductions made, before we settle down around the polished wood table.

'Sake?' Saurav asks and I watch heads nod in agreement all around the table. 'Alia?'

'Of course, maybe a junmai?'

A few years ago I might have asked for champagne, not knowing that even a 2004 Dom Perignon can be deemed vulgar when paired with a platter of delicately sliced sashimi. I've had to work hard to learn the subtleties and tells of this world that Arjun so easily inhabits.

Saurav merely has to tip his head and a waiter appears by his side.

'We'll have the Shichida junmai, and' – he takes a moment

to look around the table – 'your signature tasting menu, please.'

'Very well, sir.' The waiter nods his appreciation, before bowing down and disappearing.

'Well done with the human trafficking bill last month, by the way,' Saurav says, once the sake has been poured and pleasantries exchanged. 'I know you were a bit worried.'

I've never once discussed the bill or the complexities surrounding it with Saurav or his wife, Arushi. Usually, our conversations centre around family weddings and the inordinate amount of gossip they generate.

'Alia's spearheaded a bill that completely changes how our justice system deals with the trafficking of women and children,' he adds, for John and Maya's benefit. 'Was it eight children and one woman being trafficked every hour, Alia?'

'That's right,' I nod. 'It's one of the world's biggest organized crimes.'

'Sure. But didn't you already have legislation in place dealing with that?' John asks, his inflection hinting at a posh north London upbringing.

'Yes, but the laws we've got in place only criminalize sexual trafficking, not trafficking for forced labour, slavery, begging or marriage.' I glance around the table, my words well rehearsed after presenting this bill to countless committees and MPs over the last few months. 'Effectively, we're trying to broaden the scope of the law and bring in stricter sentencing.'

'Isn't that part of the criticism, though? That the scope

is so wide, and the provisions so stringent, that it can freeze entire sections of the economy,' Niv says.

I try to hide my surprise. It's a double-edged sword, but one I have spent months wielding.

'Well, do we really want to protect the economy at the expense of teenage girls being shot with drugs so they are more sexually pliable? Or children having their limbs cut off so they have more clout as beggars?' Arjun chips in. I touch his arm lightly, affectionately.

I may be off duty, but this is still my gig.

'It's a simple matter of cost, Niv,' I say. I place my hands flat on the table and close my eyes, taking a moment to gather my thoughts. 'How much are we willing to pay to keep our women and children safe? For me, and I think for most of the country, the answer is whatever it takes. Don't you agree?'

No one speaks. Saurav gives me a quick nod and I lean back in my chair. After all these years, I still find it fascinating how even the whiff of power can sway people, alter decisions, change lives.

The waiter appears with our first course and we busy ourselves manoeuvring paper-thin sashimi and finely chopped salad onto our plates with chopsticks.

'Did you say you went to Cambridge?' Arjun asks Maya, expertly steering us back to lighter topics.

'Trinity, Class of 2009. From gilded corridors straight into the recession,' she says, smiling ruefully, as if someone like her would ever have had to worry about money. Her family practically owns the hospitality industry in India.

'Niv was at Trinity, class of 2007,' Arjun says. 'And Alia

and I were 2008, Corpus Christi. That's how we met actually.' He places his hand on mine and I find myself smiling at his touch.

Serendipitous. That's how Arjun always describes our meeting, and as I hear him recount the story for our new audience, I feel my chest fill with love, the warmth tempered only slightly by guilt as my eyes find Niv's across the table. I shift my focus back to my husband as he tells everyone how he felt his heart crack open the instant he saw me at Niv's birthday party nearly thirteen years ago, how he chased me for months before we started dating, how I turned him down twice before finally, *finally* agreeing to marry him. I let him carry the story until we get to the proposal. That part of the story is mine to tell and I see Arjun's eyes sparkle as I tell everyone about how he had proposed that third, and final, time, how we had snuck away for a secret ceremony in Bali before the elaborate wedding his parents had insisted on hosting, and how he had surprised me with a honeymoon tent in our back garden when the PM called an emergency parliamentary session, making the pre-booked honeymoon in the Maldives impossible. The story is timeworn and we both play our parts with practised ease, and yet it brings with it all the warmth and the excitement of the early days.

I lean in as Arjun throws an arm over my shoulder and pulls me close.

'I love you,' I whisper into his ear, allowing myself a moment before straightening up and turning back to the table.

I am as much his prize as he is mine.

'Did anyone read that piece in the *Sunday Times* about the Qureshis, by the way?' Arushi says, her chopsticks delicately balanced as she picks up a miniscule piece of tuna and dots it with wasabi. 'I'd forgotten you guys were at Wescott when all that happened.'

I resist the temptation to roll my eyes and focus instead on my sake glass. Arushi doesn't forget *anything*.

'Wescott is basically the Eton of India,' Maya explains, leaning towards John.

'You must hate that you're associated with that whole mess,' Saurav says, nodding at Niv and me. 'There was a *major* scandal there when we were growing up,' Saurav says, turning to John. 'Three teenage girls, one boy, all from prominent families . . .' He trails off provocatively.

I set my chopsticks down and take a slow sip of water. There are times when I love talking about where I went to school, when I jump at the opportunity to prove how far I've come, how much I've overcome, but tonight is not one of those nights. I feel Arjun's hand squeeze my knee under the table and I flash him a quick smile.

'It was ages ago—'

'And everyone's come a long way,' Niv says, cutting Saurav off, her read on me as sharp as my husband's.

'True. I mean, Sabah won a BAFTA, for god's sake,' Arushi says, rushing to swallow her sake. 'Does anyone know what her next project is, by the way?'

'Is she an actress?' Maya asks.

'She's a film-maker. She made the Netflix documentary about Harriet Clarke,' Niv says.

'Oh, I watched that,' Maya says. 'It was devastating. Can you imagine your little girl being snatched out of your own home?'

I find myself observing Niv as she leads the conversation into unsolved cases and true crime podcasts and away from the scandal that changed everything.

Niv and I had barely known each other when it happened. She was a year ahead of us and had always been at odds with Noor and Sabah. But when I reached Cambridge a year later, we had gravitated towards each other, the pull of our shared history too potent to ignore. It was a friendship borne of loneliness and strengthened over happy hour margaritas at the student bar. Niv had married straight out of university and moved to London. The divorce that followed was as messy as it was sudden and when she arrived in Delhi a few years later, I suggested Arjun hire her as his legal consultant. I went out of my way to pencil in regular girls' nights. But with political success comes a schedule that is almost entirely out of my control. I was pleasantly surprised when Arjun told me he'd invited Niv along tonight. I've cancelled on her twice in the last month and the guilt has been gnawing at me.

I look at the woman sitting in front of me. She's had a haircut since I last saw her, a sleek bob that highlights the high cheekbones and delicate bone structure I've envied for years. There is something oddly frenetic about her today, a strange energy I haven't seen in a long time, and I know instinctively that there is a man involved.

I watch as she throws her head back and laughs at

something John says, her skin shimmering golden under the pendant light, and as the collar of her blouse slips, I see it, the pebble-shaped love bite on the side of her neck.

It takes everything I have not to laugh out loud.

I've been trying to convince Niv to start dating for the best part of the last five years and as happy as I am for her, it irks me that she didn't tell me about this new romance.

I catch her eye, hoping she will be able to read the question in it, but she simply shakes her head and looks away.

I take a small bite of the *mochi* that's been placed in front of me, the sickly sweet dessert sticky in my mouth. I force it down with a sip of water and set my cutlery down, my gaze drifting back to Niv.

I suppose I shouldn't blame her for keeping secrets.

After all, I still have mine.

SABAH

Something happens to me when I find my way into a good story. A quickening of the pulse. A tingling on the back of my neck. A conviction deep in my bones that I am on to something. A secret. A missing link. A little-known detail that will turn the narrative on its head. The catalyst is always different, but the sensation is exactly the same. It's how I felt when I wrote the abstract for my dissertation. It's how I felt when I came across that crucial piece of testimony in the Harriet Clarke documentary. It's how I haven't felt in more than two years.

I edge my chair closer to the desk and read through the dozen or so documents open on my computer. Abandoned pitches, research notes, narrative arcs. At least twenty different ideas for my next documentary. Not one of them even remotely viable.

I feel Jenny's eyes on me and I give her a quick smile before I start typing into an open document, fingers flying over the keyboard, typing out sentences that make little sense. When I look up a few minutes later, she's no longer at her desk and I let out a quick breath. Though she's only twenty-four, Jenny is one of the sharpest production managers in the company and I've sensed her watching me over the past few weeks. I consider slamming my laptop shut and walking out. It's only midday, but I could quite easily say I have a lead I want to follow or that I'm meeting a source and no one in the office would think to question it. They all think I've been researching my next big project for the past two years. I've dropped hints along the way, used buzzwords that I know get the executive producers salivating – explosive, gut-wrenching, *award season* – yet allow me to keep the actual details shrouded in an air of secrecy. What none of them know is that the reason for the secrecy isn't that I'm working on sensitive material, it's that I have no material. There are no leads or sources, no explosive new ideas percolating in this film-maker's brain. I might have won every award under the sun two years ago, but I have no idea what to work on next. I am a one-hit wonder.

I've just about decided to leave for the day when I hear a knock on the glass panel behind me. The office is open plan with sheets of glass fencing off sections. The architect that the partners employed called it a dynamic, Instagram-friendly workspace that is segmented but not divided, with open walls and an ergonomic flow.

Whatever that means.

'Sabah.'

I wheel my chair around slowly. I tell myself the tightness between my shoulder blades has been there all morning. Andrew is leaning against the glass, his stocky figure an anomaly in the sleek office.

'Yes?'

'We need to talk.'

I slip into the chair opposite Andrew and set my notebook down on the conference table in front of me. The 'huddle' room is an airless cube on the mezzanine with black iron beams holding up panels of glass. The effect is oddly disconcerting, and sitting in the clear Perspex chair looking at Andrew across the glass table, I feel like I'm floating mid-air. I turn my gaze to the windows instead, letting the solidity of Tower Bridge and the murky waters of the Thames running beneath it ground me.

The hissing sound as Andrew twists open a bottle of sparkling water brings my attention back to him.

'I wanted to see how you're getting on,' he says, pausing to take a sip. 'We're all very intrigued to see this new proposal.'

I force my lips into a smile. Andrew is one of the executive producers at Arch Films and though I work as a freelance contractor, he is, for all intents and purposes, my boss.

'I'm nearly there,' I say. 'Just following up a few leads to make sure it all checks out.'

Andrew nods, the corners of his mouth twisting up into a smile. I wonder how much of it is a show. I find it impossible to believe that he can't see right through me, which is not to say that I am a bad liar, rather that we've been through this rigmarole so many times over the past year, I can't believe he is still willing to trust me when I say I'm nearly there.

'Great,' he says. 'That's great.' He flicks open his Filofax,

the old-fashioned planner remarkably out of place in a
room that could function as the set for a sci-fi film. I watch
as his fingers run through the week ahead. 'I've got you
pencilled in for ten thirty on Monday. Rachel will join in.'

Rachel is one of the partners and Andrew's boss. She
never attends pitch meetings. I try to work out if I can get
away with asking for another extension, but judging by the
expression on Andrew's face, I doubt he will allow it. I
swallow. Monday is five days away and I have nothing.

'I really am excited to see what you've been working on.'
Andrew hesitates. He loosens the bottle top again, the water
heckling with each bubble that escapes. 'But you are nearing
the end of your contract so just in case this pitch doesn't work
out either, we have put together an exit package for you.'

It takes me a second to process his words.

I don't know why I am surprised. I should've seen this
coming. Andrew had offered me a year-long development
contract after the success of the Harriet Clarke film. Pretty
much every major studio in London had made me an offer,
but Andrew had given me my first break and even though
his offer wasn't the highest, I signed with him out of a
sense of loyalty. In the two years since its release, the documentary has won more awards, but the money has long
since run out and despite two six-month extensions, the
groundbreaking follow-up I was expected to deliver hasn't
materialized. The exit package that he is talking about will
be no more than two weeks' pay, if the termination clause
on the contract I'd so happily signed is anything to go by.
I feel the tightness between my shoulder blades slither down

my back as I think about the stack of unpaid credit card bills on my coffee table, the overdrawn bank account, the texts from my mother asking when I'll be paying her back.

I know I should tell him the truth, beg him to give me a few more months to come up with something, but even though I seem to have lost my talent, I do still have some self-respect left. I'm thirty-one, broke, living alone in a flat I can't afford, but at least I still have my pride. I draw my lips into what I hope is a relaxed smile and say the words we are both anxious to hear. 'Don't worry, you're going to love what I have.'

I pop a ready meal into the oven and take my laptop and a large gin and tonic into the living room. Setting everything down on the coffee table, I sit cross-legged on the floor. I log in to the email account I'd set up exclusively for tips and scroll through the fifty or so unread emails, searching for something that might inspire a follow-through. Ever since the BAFTA award, I've been getting hundreds of tips every week. Pleas of help from victims' families, clippings of cold cases, unsolicited pictures and offers to give me exclusive access to dead-end stories. I hear the ping of a new match on Tinder and flip my phone over without a glance.

The reason the Harriet Clarke documentary had worked so well was because I'd put something of myself into it. I was in film school when Harriet disappeared and like the rest of the world, I'd watched, horrified, as piece after piece of the story was laid out by the media. A nine-year-old girl snatched out of her grandparents' house in the middle of the night. Where were the parents? Why did no one check on little Harriet till noon the next day? How had the kidnapper got into the house without so much as a broken window? And why were Harriet's pyjamas found in a rubbish bin halfway across the country? In the absence of any real evidence, the police had tried to pin the blame on the family but no arrests were ever made and though the case had been reported widely, not once in the ten years since Harriet's disappearance had the family spoken to a reporter.

When I first approached Harriet's parents, they refused to speak to me. After the way they had been treated by the media, it was no surprise. But I had been obsessing over the case for years. I wanted to tell a story that was not just about a missing girl, but also about grief and guilt and the pain of living with the unknown and I needed the parents on board to do that. I kept at it and after weeks of emails and phone calls, they agreed to an interview. It was the raw emotion lurking beneath the facts that made the film as heart-wrenching, and as widely distributed, as it was. Three months after the release, a woman in Greece came forward with a tip and a month later, Harriet's remains and her killer were found.

I force myself to take a deep breath and click on the next email.

I did it once. I can do it again.

I open up a new document, my fingers poised over the keyboard, yet the words fail to materialize. I think about all the abandoned ideas over the last year, all the false starts.

The winking cursor taunts me, mocking me for my inaptitude.

I spend a few minutes staring at the blank document before giving in. I open a webpage and type 'Javed Qureshi' into the search bar, just like I have done every night for the past three weeks. I scroll through page after page of pictures and news clippings from the funeral, typing in a handful of words in different permutations and combinations. It's futile and I know I should stop, but it's like the old wound you scratch away at, subconsciously, bit by bit by bit, until it peels off and fresh blood oozes out.

Oh, the morbid satisfaction of it.

It's all so different from Noor's funeral, which had been clouded with shame, the family closing in around itself.

I go back to my emails. I know what I have to do. In some ways, it is the only thing I can do.

I navigate into the deepest recesses of my hard drive and find the folder I'm looking for. In the background, I can hear the oven beeping but I stay rooted to the spot, my finger hovering over the trackpad.

Everything I've done in the past fifteen years has been leading up to this point. Consciously or not, it's why I went into investigative journalism, why I found myself drawn to Harriet Clarke and why I swore I'd do everything I can to help families find closure.

It's also why I left India, why I've spent fifteen years systematically cutting myself off from everything that reminds me of my past and why I swore I'd never look back.

And yet the folder on my laptop tells a different story.

It's heaving with pictures, clippings, notes and documents, bits and pieces I've collected over more than a decade, relics that prove how desperate I am for answers even though the questions terrify me.

With one final shake of my head, I click on it and watch as the past I've spent so long hiding from opens up in front of me.

ALIA

Fifteen years ago

'. . . and that's when she slit her wrists. Apparently, the day before, her mother had told her if she so much as spoke to him again, she would get her transferred to a Catholic girls' school.'

Sabah and I were sprawled out on the bed. I'd just painted her nails – baby pink with flecks of multi-coloured glitter. We were waiting for the topcoat to dry so she could do mine.

'She obviously did it to get him back,' Noor said. She was sitting on the window seat, playing *Snake* on Sabah's new phone. Her parents had bought it for her last week and since then, all three of us had been taking turns on it, trying to beat each other's scores. So far, Sabah was in the lead.

'Or she wanted sympathy,' I said, rolling over onto my stomach and running my hands over the bedspread. It was velvety soft and quilted with little love hearts.

'Same difference. She pulls these stunts so she can hold on to him. There are easier ways,' Noor grinned. 'And quicker, you know, considering she walks around in a swim-suit half the time.'

'Eeeww. Remember that trip in eighth grade?' Sabah giggled.

As if on cue, the phone emitted a series of beeps and Noor groaned in frustration, tossing the phone aside.

'Would you ever do it?' I asked, refusing to take the bait. Noor and Sabah had a long history and they never failed to remind me of it.

'What – slash my wrists? For a *boy*? Never!' Noor jumped up and climbed onto the bed, sitting cross-legged next to Sabah and me.

'I'm dry,' Sabah said, tapping her nails one by one. I sat up and handed her the pot of nail varnish. 'It's such a cop-out. If you're going to try to kill yourself, at least pick a more respectable way to do it.'

'I'd use a gun, go out with a bang,' I said, resting the tips of my fingers on Sabah's outstretched palm.

Back then, I was obsessed with the idea of dying young and I'd fantasized about it enough times to have a plan, a back-up plan and a back-up for my back-up plan. There was something incredibly romantic about it, about being so young, so beautiful and so, *so* messed up that ordinary life simply wasn't enough. There's a reason why no one ever wrote an opera about being content, why all the greatest stories are tragedies, and the greatest heroines broken beyond repair. Happiness was boring. I wanted love, drama, darkness and, yes, heartbreak. We all did.

Sabah rolled her eyes. 'Too basic. I'd jump off a cliff.' She paused to think. 'In Scotland.'

'Why Scotland?' I asked.

'Sounds cool,' she said, wistfully. 'Astonishingly beautiful girl jumps to tragic death, leaves heartbroken boyfriend behind.'

'You're both crazy,' Noor said. 'Have you paid the deposit for the Oxbridge trip?'

'Yes, Mum,' Sabah retorted.

'Whatever. There are only six spots and this trip is going to be *epic*,' she declared. 'Alia?'

'Yeah, done,' I said. I held my hand out and wiggled my fingers to inspect Sabah's handiwork. The glitter sparkled like the sequins on one of my mother's velvet cushions.

I'd pooled all my birthday and Diwali money and scraped together just about enough to cover the hefty 10 per cent deposit, but I had no idea where I was going to get the rest. My grandparents couldn't afford it, and my parents . . . they were clearly not an option. I was too far down on their list of priorities, if all the unanswered phone calls were anything to go by.

'Anyway, guess who else has paid up?' Sabah asked.

Noor raised an eyebrow. 'Who?'

'Ankit.'

'No way!' Noor said. 'What is the matter with him?'

Sabah fake-swooned. 'He's in *love*.'

My eyes darted from Noor to Sabah, but neither bothered to elaborate.

'Who's Ankit?' I asked, giving in.

Sabah grinned. 'Noor's stalker,' she said, conspiratorially.

Noor had her own guild of loyal admirers, but a stalker? At sixteen! I couldn't help but be impressed. 'Really?'

'She's exaggerating,' Noor said, acting annoyed, but obviously enjoying the attention. 'He's just—'

'I am not,' Sabah cut her off. 'Noor invited him to a birthday party, when we were – what, nine? – and he's followed her around ever since.' She turned back to Noor. 'Didn't he write you a love letter for Valentine's Day? And there was that whole phase last year when he would wait for you at the school gates and follow you to the bus.'

'Okay, yeah, maybe he's a *bit* obsessed,' Noor said, giggling.

'Only because you lead him on,' Sabah said. 'The poor thing. He actually thinks he has a shot.'

'Imagine that.' Noor shuddered. 'Anyway, what's happening with Vineet?'

School broke for the summer in less than ten days and nothing was without the element of urgency.

'We're going to go see a film tomorrow,' Sabah said, eyes twinkling.

'Let me guess, matinee?' Noor said.

'Yeah,' Sabah said, dragging the word out.

'You know what that means. Empty cinema, romantic film, your hand on his thigh . . .'

'You are so gross,' Sabah shrieked, shoving Noor so she landed flat on the bed, the mattress bouncing in retaliation.

'Does that mean you've never . . . ?' I asked Sabah after we'd stopped giggling.

'Of course not,' Sabah said, a touch indignant. 'He's not even my boyfriend. Yet.'

'Have you?' she asked me after a moment. 'With Chris?'

'Or someone else?' Noor grinned. 'We don't judge.' Then,

looking at Sabah's stricken expression, she added, '*I* don't judge.'

'I've fooled around,' I lied, 'but not, you know . . .'

'Sex?' Noor prompted.

'Yeah, no, not that.' I wondered if my face looked as red as it felt.

'You can say it, you know,' Noor said, smirking. 'You have to actually *have* sex to get pregnant.'

'Shut up!'

'Well, now that Sabah's all set, I can get to work on you,' Noor said, wiggling her eyebrows up and down. 'Not that you need it. You and Dhruv looked *very* cosy.'

To my relief, a knock at the door distracted Noor. A plain-looking girl, dressed almost exactly like Noor, stepped in.

In fact, I was pretty sure she was dressed in Noor's clothes.

'*Didi, khana,*' she mumbled, her words barely audible.

'Who's that?' I whispered to Sabah as we followed her down the stairs and into the hall.

'Who?'

'That girl,' I said, pointing to the girl just as she disappeared into the kitchen.

'One of the servants. Why?'

'She's wearing Noor's clothes.'

Sabah looked at me as if I had lost it. 'What do you do with your old clothes?'

I tried to imagine her reaction if I told her about the system my mother had established when I was eight. Every

spring, anything old or faded was given a new lease of life
by dyeing it in the bathtub or embroidering it with multi-
coloured thread, holes and tears darned over, and once
they'd lived through their resurrection, my clothes got one
final shot at life as nightwear. It was only when things were
falling apart at the seams that I was allowed to discard
them, and even then, they usually ended up being used as
rags around the house.

Yeah, I wasn't about to tell her that.

'Refugee camps, usually,' I said instead, injecting my
words with enough indignation for them to sound sincere.
'Or orphanages.'

Sabah nodded as we entered the dining room.

'*Aadab*, Uncle, Aunty,' Sabah said to Noor's parents before
sitting down at the table.

'This is my friend, Alia. She's just moved from London,'
Noor announced.

'Hi,' I said, sitting down next to the tall boy who I
assumed was Noor's brother. I had heard enough about
Faraz over the past few weeks to form a mental picture
and the reality felt somewhat jarring. The overbearing,
insufferable brother who Noor couldn't stop bitching about
seemed kind and, with his fair skin and the deep dimples
that appeared in both his cheeks when he smiled, insanely
good-looking.

'It's lovely to meet you, Alia,' Noor's father said.

Noor's mother smiled hello. '*Biryani* okay for you, *beta*?'

'It's perfect, Aunty,' I said as the maid started bringing
in the food. I looked at the family gathered around me.

Lively banter passed around the table as easily as the dishes heaped with *biryani, salan* and *raita*. I was amazed at how quickly and easily they had welcomed me in. I smiled as I unfurled my napkin and spooned some *raita* onto my plate. Everything about this evening, this family, was perfect.

ALIA

Fifteen years ago

What struck me that first time I met Javed Uncle was the way he spoke, not just to Noor and Faraz, but to all of us: his attention to the minutiae, his knack for making us feel like adults with important things to say. I remember how he zipped through dinner asking questions, knowing so much about me already. On the rare occasions that he could be bothered to tear himself away from the ambassador's family to sit down with his own, my father had barely taken the time to ask me how school was. Yet here was a cabinet minister, a man who moved amidst a swirl of staff, and he was actually *interested*.

As I sat there, talking about my parents, and the life I'd left behind in London, I felt an intense longing; grief for a relationship that I'd never even known could exist.

'Have you decided where you want to go to university?' Javed Uncle asked me, as he passed the bowl of salad to Faraz.

'I'm not sure yet,' I said.

'You still have plenty of time,' Fatima Aunty said.

'I'm going to Oxford,' Sabah said. Like that was something you could just decide.

I turned to Faraz. 'Are you at uni?' I asked him, even though I knew the answer already.

'We call it college here,' he smiled. 'I'm at St Stephen's, second year.'

'Faraz got into Oxford, Columbia and Yale, but he decided to stay here so he could get a head start on his career,' Javed Uncle explained, barely concealed pride punctuating his words. 'He's running for Student Union president next year.'

I could see then why Noor had it in for her brother. He was clearly the golden child in the Qureshi house, the one destined to carry the legacy.

'Wow. So you're going to go into politics?' I asked Faraz.

'What else?' he shrugged, strands of entitlement rippling beneath his modesty.

'Faraz was the Head Boy the year before last,' Sabah said from across the table.

'Which was actually quite dull but it made college applications a breeze,' he said. 'Are you still aiming for Head Girl?'

'Of course,' Sabah said, her lips pressed into a tight smile. 'Though I want to do things a little differently. It's not going to be dull.'

I smiled. Her excitement was contagious.

'Don't we know it,' Faraz laughed.

'We were all forced into attending your blood donation camp,' Javed Uncle said, holding up his arm to show off the plaster he still had on from that afternoon. 'What did it come to in the end?'

'Eighty litres, in total.'

He smiled, visibly impressed. 'Well, I can't imagine anyone better suited for Head Girl. Especially,' he said, looking at Noor, 'with Noor supporting you as a prefect.'

'Next year is going to be so much fun,' Sabah nodded, delighted.

'*Jaan*,' Javed Uncle said, looking at Noor, 'how are you getting on with your essay for the committee?'

'Fine,' Noor said. 'I'm almost done.'

'Do you need my help?' Sabah asked, putting her fork down and turning to Noor with a look on her face that I couldn't quite decipher.

'I'm pretty sure I can manage an essay on my own, Sabah,' Noor shot back.

'I'm sure Sabah didn't mean—' Javed Uncle started before Noor interrupted him.

'Of course she didn't. But it wouldn't be right to ask Sabah for help.' Noor paused, lifting her glass of water to her lips and taking a long sip. She set the glass down lightly, the sound of the clinking ice reverberating across the table. She waited till she had everyone's attention and then said, 'I'm running for Head Girl as well.'

'Really?' Faraz asked at the same time as Sabah said, 'What?'

'Yeah,' Noor smiled, tilting her plate so she could spoon the last of her *biryani*. 'It's going to be *so* much fun.'

ALIA

I flick through the folder Omar left on the dining table while I sip my morning coffee – drafts for proposals, letters to sign, documents to approve – homework from the night before that I neglected to do. I work through the papers methodically, pausing when I get to a copy of the press release Faraz's office issued after the ceremony. I flag it up to discuss with Omar later. If he's snuck this into my briefing folder, it means he's worried about the alliance as well.

I'm looking at the longlist for the sexual assault committee when Arjun comes in and switches on the news.

'*Chai*,' he calls out into the kitchen. 'Morning,' he smiles as I tilt my face up for a kiss.

I swing the folder shut and help myself to some more coffee from the cafetière. These twenty minutes are precious. Most days, this is the only time Arjun and I get with each other before my staff trickles in and the relentless rhythm of our jobs consumes us both.

'Last night was fun,' I say as Arjun sits down across from me.

'Saurav was pleased. He thinks John will sign with us within the week.'

Us? It finally hits me why Arjun invited Niv to the dinner and I chide myself for feeling wrong-footed. Arjun doesn't tell me about every deal he works on, just like I don't tell him about every campaign strategy or political move.

'This is horrific,' Arjun says, eyes glued to the TV. I shift my attention to the screen. We watch silently as the news reporter updates us on the Delhi University rape case that's been all over the news for the past week.

Last month, a seventeen-year-old girl was gang-raped in her hostel bedroom by her boyfriend and two of his friends. When she went to the warden to request permission to go to the police station – it was past the hostel's curfew – the warden dismissed her, accusing her of using rape as an excuse to go out after hours. The next morning she went to the police station. After questioning her for more than twelve hours, the police superintendent refused to lodge the complaint or even administer a rape kit. She had been at a birthday party on the night in question. *Her own birthday party.* She'd had a few drinks, which naturally made her a liar and a tease and a waste of police time. Next, she went to the university's internal complaints committee, who had much the same response. Two weeks later, she was found dead in her bathroom, naked with the word 'slut' written across her breasts. The police ruled it a suicide. Because of course she would undress and declare herself a slut before hanging herself. It came as no surprise when a few days ago, a leaked document disclosed that two of the accused came from influential families and the third was the son of a junior minister.

The news reporter cuts to a clip of the parents and I look away. The anguish in their eyes is all too familiar, the grief wrapped up in their words too raw. I reach for the remote and put the TV on mute.

'Those boys need to be arrested,' Arjun says, as the maid comes in and places a cup of tea and some digestive biscuits in front of him.

'*Didi, nashta?*' the maid asks and I nod my agreement.

'This is exactly why we need the independent sexual assault committee,' I mutter.

Arjun blows on his tea and takes a sip. 'The problem is bigger than that, though, isn't it?'

I don't trust myself to respond. I have learned to keep my *Guardian*-reading, leftist opinions under wraps – there is no room for naive idealism in politics – but Arjun's right. No matter how many victim support groups and committees I set up, nothing is going to change until the police realize they can't turn victims away irrespective of how wealthy or powerful the perpetrators are. And yet, it riles me that there's little I can do to effect that change.

I'm not usually one to get swayed by the news – maintaining a degree of objectivity is crucial in my line of work – but this case is under my skin. Everything about it – the refusal to believe that she was raped, the implication that she had it coming, the general sense that anyone with money and power is above the law – all of it makes me want to scream, but perhaps it is the sense of my own powerlessness that troubles me the most. I'd called the police commissioner when the news first broke, urging him to take action, but all that had achieved was an extremely uncomfortable, and ultimately pointless conversation. I went into politics to fight exactly this kind of thing, and yet the longer I am 'in power', the more I realize how meaningless that phrase is.

'How are things going with the Barclays deal?' I ask instead as our breakfast is laid out and Arjun and I help ourselves to our usual porridge, heaping fruits and seeds on top.

If he is surprised by the sudden change of topic, he doesn't show it. Arjun has had a front row seat to my struggles within the party for years.

'Good, so far. I'm reviewing the draft MoU this afternoon, but it's looking promising.'

Arjun had set up his own business when he was just twenty-five, fresh out of graduate school. As the heir to the country's largest consumer goods business, he could easily have cruised along – his father's business pretty much ran itself by now and there was enough money there to keep him – *us* – comfortable in our eight-hundred-thread-count Egyptian cotton and Siberian duck down cocoon – but Arjun had always been keen to strike out on his own. It would be childish to call him a self-made man when his name alone was enough to open doors that weren't even visible to most start-up entrepreneurs. But silver spoon notwithstanding, Arjun had worked tirelessly to set up the country's first large-scale sustainable energy business at a time when the concept of renewable energy was limited to the solar cookers that overambitious children hatched up for science fairs. The Barclays deal, if it came through, would be one of the largest energy replacement projects in Asia and the first step towards making Agro Tech a global business.

'Is Niv handling the paperwork?'

'She's been a godsend,' he says, barely looking up from his phone, a reminder that at ten minutes to eight, his workday has already started.

I glance at the TV. The reporter covering the rape is back on air, this time live from the university, where more than 300 students have gathered in a silent protest. I watch for a minute before turning it off, the specifics of the case spinning through my brain.

Maybe if even one of the people she'd begged for help had listened to her, stood by her instead of looking the other way, she would still be alive.

I push my coffee away, nausea churning through my stomach.

I scroll through the contacts on my phone, hovering over Omar's name before scrolling further.

Javed Uncle had always said that in politics, you can achieve a lot more behind the scenes than in public view. He said that the best way to get things done was through compromise.

But sometimes the only way to handle an issue is to take a stand. Shout about it.

I type out a message and press send before I can change my mind.

It's time I stepped out of the shadows.

It's time to speak up.

ALIA

Fifteen years ago

My granddad dropped me off at the school gates early on Saturday morning. I strolled in, trying to exude a confidence that despite my brand-new shorts and vest top, I did not feel. I adjusted the gym bag slung over my shoulder, making sure the Nike logo on the handles was visible. The school felt eerie without the din of a few thousand students whispering in the halls and I hurried to the sports block where I could see a few girls milling about.

Try-outs for the senior girls' track and field, cricket and diving teams were being held in the morning. Boys' try-outs would follow later in the afternoon. For what was considered to be a liberal co-ed school, Wescott went to great lengths to keep the boys and the girls separate outside of class.

I still had an hour to go before my slot so I sat down on the bleachers by the open-air swimming pool, enjoying the sun hitting my face. Even though I'd been in India for a few months now, and it was never anything but sunny, I still hadn't had enough. After years of living in a damp flat, perhaps I never would.

I topped up my sunscreen and leaned back on the hot concrete steps. I stretched my legs out in front of me, admiring the way the Nike swoosh sparkled every time I moved my feet.

The burst of activity in front of me made me sit up. Seven girls dressed in swimsuits were lined up in front of the open showers, ready to jump into the pool. The coach was looking at the girls, checking they had their caps on and goggles ready. I recognized Niv, and leaned forward. The flash of white on her wrists stood out, a stark contrast to her bright blue swimsuit, cut dangerously low at the back.

'Nivedita, what's with the bandages?' the coach asked when she got to her.

'Skating accident, ma'am.'

That was the same story I'd heard she'd given to the other teachers. I couldn't work out whether the teachers here were stupid enough to believe her, or if they knew she was lying but just didn't care, the effort of trying to work out why a seventeen-year-old would slash her wrists out of their contracted duties.

The coach stepped closer to her and said something that I couldn't quite make out. I watched what seemed like a heated exchange before Niv stormed off into the changing rooms.

I couldn't help it. I followed her in.

She was rummaging through her locker when I burst in.

'Hey,' I said. 'Are you okay?'

'The bitch won't let me into the pool with these bandages. I need to find some plasters.'

She pulled her bag out and turned it upside down on the bench, combing through the contents.

'Damn it,' she muttered.

I unzipped my bag and felt around for my kit.

'Here,' I said, holding out a four-pack of plasters. 'Will these do?'

Niv examined them. 'They aren't waterproof but better than nothing, I suppose. Thank you,' she said, already getting to work on loosening the bandage on her left wrist.

I turned to leave, the awkwardness of the situation too much for me to handle. Noor and Sabah didn't like Niv so I didn't like Niv, no matter how bad I felt for her.

'You don't have scissors, do you?' she called out after me.

'No, sorry.' I cursed myself as I turned around, walking back through the towers of lockers to sit down next to her. 'But I can try to help.'

'There are loads of knots on this,' I said after a minute as I loosened the first knot. There were at least a dozen more to go. The bandage was all wet and soggy from her shower, which was making it even harder to manoeuvre.

'I know.' Niv sighed. She looked at my outfit. 'Track and field?'

'Yeah. I got here too early.'

She nodded. 'Don't worry about your speed on the initial laps, focus on keeping your stamina up – Coach likes to do that to tire the girls out before the hundred-metre race.

That is all she's going to judge you on. And try and get a spot on the far left. The ground has a slight angle so that's the shortest side.'

'Thanks,' I said, surprised at this show of support.

She shrugged it off, bony shoulders rising and falling in a gesture of unexpected generosity.

'There,' I said as I got the last knot out and unfurled the bandage. 'All—'

'Thanks,' Niv interrupted, clamping her free hand down on her wrist but not before the gauzy fabric slipped off, giving me a glimpse of the skin underneath.

I gasped. 'Niv, I—'

'Thanks,' Niv repeated, the friendliness from earlier disappearing, 'I've got it from here.'

I went back outside and sat down on the bleachers.

I watched as Niv demonstrated one perfect dive after another, her sylphlike body slicing through the water without as much as a ripple on the surface.

All weekend, I couldn't get that image out of my head. The gauzy bandage. Niv's expression when she realized I had seen. It was heartbreaking. I wasn't sure what to do or how to help her so when I saw Sabah and Noor on Monday, I told them.

Sabah looked suitably shocked.

Noor, however, just smiled a sad smile. 'We should invite her to the party,' she said.

'Sure, just go ahead and help yourself,' Sabah muttered as Noor plucked a piece of the *samosa* Sabah had just bought.

'Stop being such a bitch,' Noor said.

We were sitting on the steps by the football ground: Noor, Sabah and me.

'Look who's talking,' Sabah bit back.

I looked at my apple like it held all the secrets to the universe.

They had been building up to an argument for days now and I had no intention of getting caught in the crossfire.

'You know what, Sabah,' Noor sighed, 'I've had enough of the snide comments. If you have something to say, just say it.'

'I don't know what you're talking about.'

'Oh, come on. We both know you're sulking because you're worried about the Head Girl thing. I get that you hate losing, but you really do need to stop acting like such a baby.'

'Excuse me?'

'Look, I'm not trying to take anything away from you, but—'

I had to look up at that.

'Because it's yours to take if you want it?'

The shock on Sabah's face said everything. I had only known them for a few weeks, but even I understood one thing: Sabah worked for everything she wanted and Noor just waltzed in and assumed things would go her way. It could be infuriating, when you weren't benefiting from it directly.

'I just meant . . . Look, just because we're friends doesn't mean I should have to sit things out. It's not my fault that you're so insecure.'

'And I'm sure it's not your fault that you're so arrogant.'

My eyes darted from Noor to Sabah. I had the strange feeling that I was eavesdropping, even though they could both see me sitting right there. I thought about getting up and leaving but that felt too dramatic. A few junior boys were playing football at the far end of the field. I fixed my eyes on them.

'Also, for the record, I'm not worried. I could win this thing without even trying,' Sabah continued. 'I'm upset that you have no issues screwing over your best friend just to prove a point. I thought things would be different this time.'

'What's that supposed to mean?'

'Do you really want me to spell it out? In front of *her*?'

'Sabah,' I started, too uncomfortable to keep quiet anymore, but the look she gave me would have been enough to silence a hundred wailing babies. I retreated, shrinking back into the concrete steps.

Noor stared at Sabah. I stared at the floor.

The silence was excruciating. I wondered, not for the first time, how well I really knew these girls.

'Yeah, I didn't think so,' I heard Sabah say.

Noor was standing at the foot of the stairs when I looked up. 'A real best friend would support me, not ask me to squash my ambitions,' she said, before stalking off.

'Good luck finding one,' Sabah called after her. She hurled her *samosa* on the ground. In less than a minute, a handful of pigeons swooped in to pick at its remains, delighted at their luck.

'Don't act so naive,' Sabah scowled at me just as the bell rang. She got up and brushed the crumbs off her skirt.

She looked down at me, still sitting there with my apple, brown and disgusting now.

'No one is born at the top,' she said before she walked off, ponytail swinging as she strode across the ground and disappeared amidst the crush of students.

I threw the apple away and made my way back to class. Sabah was sitting in her usual spot, but Noor had moved back one seat so she was next to me.

No one is born at the top.

I filled in the rest of Sabah's sentence myself as our Physics teacher drawled on about force and power.

No one is born at the top, but those who are willing to do whatever it takes can work their way there.

ALIA

'Thank you for agreeing to see me,' I say. 'I can't even begin to imagine how painful this must be for you. To lose your daughter like—'

'Divya,' the woman sitting next to me says, her words broken, punctured with grief. 'Her name was Divya.'

I look at the framed pictures propped up around the room. They all show the same girl at different ages. As a baby clutching her mother's hair, as a toddler grinning at the camera, as a teenager in her school uniform, as a fresher standing at the steps of her college. I feel the knot in my chest twist as I put my tea down.

I can feel Omar's gaze burn into me from across the room. He was very clear on the car ride over. No matter how bad I feel for the girl's parents, I cannot make any promises. With the accused's father, Saeed, not only a junior minister but also a member of the Muslim Congress, any comment would be construed as a move against the alliance. And with the election nominations due in a few weeks, I need to be on my best behaviour, putting my political interests above everything else.

I need to compromise.

I reach across the sofa and place a hand on her knee, which hasn't stopped shaking since she sat down. I murmur a few comforting words. My gaze keeps drifting back to the pictures, but the face that flashes before my eyes doesn't belong to Divya. The words slip out before I can stop myself. I take the mother's hand and look her firmly in the eye.

'Let me help.'

It's past midnight by the time I finish work for the day. I push myself to my feet, allowing myself a moment to stretch my back before stepping out of the office and through the corridor that leads into the house.

I roll my shoulders as I walk into the living room, wanting nothing more than a glass of wine and a hot bath. I go straight to the drinks cabinet and pour myself a large glass of wine in the moon-streaked dark, my mind still on the press conference scheduled for the morning. It's no secret that Saeed has been harbouring the three accused in his constituency for weeks now, just the mention of his name enough to keep them safe. Even though I've spent hours trying to find the perfect words, I know that no matter what I say, any statement I make will create a certain level of chaos. There is a reason no one has spoken publicly about this case. My heart clenches as I imagine the backlash and I force myself to breathe deeply. Faraz will not be happy – Saeed is one of the founding members of the Muslim Congress – and if Omar is right, this could be fatal for the alliance. It could be fatal for my career. But just the thought of letting this go makes me sick. Divya knocked on every door she could think of, and everyone she turned to let her down. I will not be one of them. Not again.

I glance at my phone, checking for a text from my husband, but there are no new messages. Arjun and Saurav had finally managed to lock John down into signing the contract and they were out celebrating. I was supposed to go along but I'd had to cancel last minute. Knowing him, though, he'll be upstairs in bed already. Arjun's never been a big drinker and the only time he stays out late socializing is when I'm with him. I pick up my glass and slip out of the living room.

I am at the foot of the stairs when I hear it, the sound of footsteps. I pause, standing completely still, my hearing amplified. I remind myself that it could be any of the staff, moving through the house. But it's nearly one a.m. No one is allowed in the house after the guards have done their nightly check at midnight. I have all but convinced myself I imagined the noise when I hear it again, this time accompanied by the sound that still turns my stomach: hushed whispers.

I tiptoe into the pitch-black darkness of the dining room and towards the kitchen. I want to turn, leave. Pretend that I can't see the small strip of light peeking out from under the door, that I can't hear the muted voices drifting from within. I force myself to swing the door open.

I can't decide if the feeling that rushes through me is relief or shock.

The first thing I see is the heels, kicked off and strewn across the floor, the red soles jarring against the polished white marble. Next my gaze lingers on the midnight-blue jacket, flung over a stool, the matching tie I'd help pick out in Harrods tossed on top of it. The Gucci handbag I know so well, snakeskin with gold trims, lies slumped on the floor.

I can feel my heart thumping as I lift my eyes away from the detritus on the floor and look at the people responsible for it. Niv is perched on the kitchen island, bare feet dangling. Arjun is standing next to her, elbow resting on the granite countertop, his back to me.

I am used to feeling like an intruder, but never in my own home.

I watch Niv nod along, her hand resting lightly on Arjun's arm as he talks, the words nothing but a symphony of murmurs that glide across the polished kitchen floor and crawl under my skin. It takes less than a few seconds for them to notice me, but a few seconds is all it takes for me to get drawn back, the memory of a different kitchen but the same man pushing at the edges of my brain.

'Alia,' Niv squeals, her fake cheer conveying more than a sharp remark ever can. It's a tone I've adopted hundreds of times myself.

Arjun steps away from her and I see the bottle of tequila sitting on the counter between them. 'Hungry?' Niv asks, holding out a Tupperware box towards me.

'We just got back,' Arjun says, his voice deep, his eyes restless. He's drunk, I realize. 'I didn't want to wake you.'

I don't say anything, letting the silence stretch and twist between us, the low hum of the fridge the only sound in the room.

Niv slides off the counter. 'Well, I should be off,' she says. She circles around me to slip on her shoes and pick up her bag.

'I'll see you out,' I say, on automatic, as I follow her through the dining room and into the hall.

Niv turns to me, arms outstretched, and in the milky moonlight leaking in through the porch window, she looks younger, far more like the schoolgirl I had known a lifetime ago than the woman I've come to think of as my best friend.

The schoolgirl whose secrets I had once betrayed.

She gives me a quick hug.

'Thank you for being such a good friend,' she murmurs.

Her words echo in my ear long after I have closed the door and climbed into bed, my husband snoring softly next to me.

ALIA

Fifteen years ago

The night felt important even as it was happening.

'Truth or Dare,' Noor yelled out to a chorus of rowdy hoots from across the room.

I plonked myself next to her, pulling my top down to hide the little strip of skin along the waistband of my jeans.

Noor's parties were legendary at Wescott and *everyone* was there. Everyone except Sabah, of course.

We were in the basement, sprawled out on beanbags and cushions munching on bread *pakoras* and chilli *paneer*. A few girls from our class were clustered in the corner talking in low whispers while a playlist of Justin Timberlake and Christina Aguilera songs played in the background. For a party that had been thrown together at the last minute when Noor found out her parents were away, it was all very well organized.

Dhruv grabbed a beer from the nearly empty bucket and sat down next to me as we all scrambled to arrange ourselves into a circle.

Dhruv and I had been flirting for weeks now. We'd gone out a few times, mainly with friends, but we always managed to break away from the group. It seemed to be going well, but even with my limited experience, I could tell something was holding him back.

I knew it had something to do with his ex but every time I tried to ask him about her, he clammed up. All I had managed to learn was that she was a senior like him, and they had had one of those on again, off again relationships. Other than that, I knew nothing. Not even her name or what she looked like. I could've asked Noor, but for some reason, that was the time I decided I had principles. And anyway, the one time I had mentioned to Noor that things seemed to be slowing down, she offered to invite Dhruv over after school, the subtext being that she wouldn't be there and I would. I laughed it off, both touched by her generosity and appalled at the suggestion. I was looking for a boyfriend not a quickie in my friend's bedroom.

'Are you ready for this?' Noor leaned in and whispered into my ear. She looked at my empty glass and poured a large shot of vodka before passing the bottle on.

She crawled forward and placed an empty bottle in the middle of the circle. I couldn't help but notice the way Mohit was looking at her, his eyes travelling across the deep hollow of her back and resting on her bottom. My skin crawled on her behalf.

'Does everyone know the rules?' Saloni asked after Noor was done positioning the bottle.

'It's Truth or Dare,' Dhruv smirked. 'How complicated can it be?'

'We do things a little differently,' Saloni replied. 'We'll spin the bottle, and whoever the bottle points to has to pick truth or dare. The person sitting opposite them chooses the challenge.'

'But,' Noor chipped in, 'we don't ask questions. If you pick truth, your challenger *reveals* a truth about you.'

I smiled. This was Noor's favourite game. She seemed to know everyone's secrets and she revelled in the power it afforded her.

'So . . . ready?' Noor asked, slinking back to the centre to spin the empty Smirnoff bottle.

The girl from Noor's art class went first. 'Dare,' she yelled out, looking straight at Yash sitting across from her, before picking up her glass and draining her vodka and Coke in one go.

'I dare you,' Yash said, 'to go upstairs and get another bottle of vodka from the kitchen.'

'What is this, kindergarten?' She straightened up, popped a couple of mints in her mouth and ran upstairs. She was back in less than five minutes carrying a bottle and a big bowl of popcorn. 'Lame,' she said to Yash before setting both on the floor and sitting down. She filled her glass up, adding a drop of Coke to take the edge off, and then leaned forward to spin the bottle at the centre.

I took a large gulp from my glass, the alcohol easier to stomach with every searing sip, and rearranged myself so I was a little bit closer to Dhruv. At some point during the game, his hand had come to rest on mine and I became acutely aware of the pattern his fingers were tracing, sending ripples of excitement through me with every agonizing graze.

The bottle slowed to a stop, pointing straight at Saloni, sitting across from Vineet.

'Dare,' Saloni said, a little too quickly.

'I dare you . . .' Vineet smiled, 'to pick truth.'

Saloni made a show of rolling her eyes. 'Fine. Truth.'

'Ninth grade. Finals. You cheated on the French exam,' Vineet started and Saloni shrugged, as if to say, so what, but Vineet just cocked his head. He leaned forward, resting his hands on the floor, and looked at Saloni for a long moment. 'You had the verbs written down on your thigh, snaking all the way up . . . Let's just say you're the reason Yash and I failed that paper.'

'You bastard,' Saloni shrieked. I found myself laughing with the rest of the group as she threw a fistful of popcorn at Vineet. The only person sitting quietly was Niv. I noticed her looking at me and shrugged. We were all friends here. I turned my attention back to Dhruv.

'Another drink?' he whispered, tightening his grip on my hand and leaning in so close I could feel the shape of his words in my ear. I nodded, not trusting myself to move.

Dhruv poured us both a drink and shuffled closer to me.

I became very aware of his hand snaking up and down my back and the sensation that generated between my legs. I felt Noor's eyes on me as I leaned forward, letting Dhruv's fingers slide lower as I reached out to help myself to some popcorn.

When I straightened up, Dhruv let his hand slip under my top, his fingertips cold against my skin.

It was electric.

I fought to keep a straight face, and focused on the bottle spinning in front of me as it slowed down and came to rest pointing towards . . . me.

I took a deep breath. I said a little prayer in my head.

'Dare,' I said, looking straight at Addi across from me, willing her to read my mind.

'I dare you . . .' Addi said, 'to kiss Dhruv.'

I just about managed to hide my smile.

A few of the boys cheered, as I turned to Dhruv, eyebrows raised. Though we'd been teasing each other for weeks, all we had done so far was hold hands. This would be our first kiss, and though he didn't know it, it would be my first kiss ever.

I waited for him to nod, and then leaned in, intending to give him a quick peck. But the curl of his hand on my neck changed everything. I felt my lips part as he kissed me softly, and in hindsight, a little sloppily.

I looked away when we parted, grateful that the dim lighting was enough to conceal the flush that I knew would be creeping up my neck.

I leaned forward and spun the bottle, quickly, carelessly. I laced my fingers through Dhruv's and looked around the room. Everyone looked happily drunk, and I found myself smiling until my eyes came to rest on Niv. She looked disgusted and made as if to get up but Noor stopped her.

'Hey,' Noor said, 'you know the rules. No one leaves until the game's over. It wouldn't be fair.'

'Fine, whatever,' Niv said just as the bottle came to rest, pointing directly at her, with Noor her challenger.

'Truth?' Noor asked, her words slurring a little. 'I'm not sure you can handle a dare from me, Niv.'

'Dare,' Niv replied without missing a beat.

'You asked for it,' Noor shrugged. She paused, as if she was trying to come up with something, and my heart clenched. I knew that look.

And I knew, instantly, that I'd made a huge mistake.

'I dare you to take those bandages off,' Noor said to Niv.

Niv looked like she had been struck. This was a step too far, even for Noor.

'What the hell, Noor,' I said.

'That's not funny,' Dhruv said at the same time and I looked at him, surprised. He was in the same year as Niv, but I didn't know they were friends.

'Lighten up, guys, it's just a game. And you, of all people, want to see this Dhruv,' Noor said.

'What . . . what does she mean?' I turned to Dhruv.

'I'm done here,' Niv said, getting up.

'I told you, you couldn't handle a dare,' Noor said to her. 'How about the truth then? There are no scars underneath those bandages, it's just another trick to lure your ex back.'

The whole room went quiet. Someone gasped.

'Is that true, Niv?' Dhruv asked and all of a sudden, it fell into place.

'You and your lies. I don't know why I bothered coming,' Niv spat before spinning around and running out of the room.

'Is she your—' I started, needing confirmation, but before I could finish Dhruv got up and ran after her.

'Prove me wrong. Show us,' Noor called out as the group fell into an uncomfortable silence.

'What?' Noor said, reaching out to spin the bottle again. 'It's true,' she added, looking at me. 'I've seen it.'

When I asked her later why she did it, why she humiliated Niv so cruelly in front of everyone, Noor looked genuinely confused. 'I thought you wanted her out of the way . . . so you could make things official with Dhruv. Isn't that why you told me about her?'

'I didn't even know she was his ex! All you and Sabah said was that he'd dated a senior. You never told me it was *her*.'

'Oh,' she said, giving me a wounded look. 'I was just trying to be a good friend.'

She looked so hurt and so puzzled that there was nothing for me to do but forgive her. I smiled and – this is the bit that haunts me to this day – I said, 'I know. I know you were. Thank you.'

ALIA

I wake in the milky pre-dawn light, the sheets a hot tangle around me, the memories from last night resurfacing even before I've had the chance to open my eyes.

I listen for the sound of Arjun breathing next to me, but the bed is empty and all I can hear is my own heartbeat. Rapid. Panicked.

There is a growing restlessness in my chest as I picture it, Arjun and Niv in the kitchen, drinking, laughing, *whispering*.

I flick on the bedside lamp.

It can't be real. My husband and my best friend. I try to separate the facts from my own insecurities.

All I had seen was the two of them talking. It's a scene I've observed hundreds of times before; the only difference is that usually I'm right there with them. It is practically tradition for Niv to come around for a midnight snack after we've all been on a night out.

'Morning,' Arjun says, snapping me out of my thoughts as he emerges from the bathroom. He leans down to kiss me, little droplets of water running from his face onto mine. He lingers by my side for a few moments before walking over to the wardrobe.

'You're up early,' I say, sitting up. My eyes follow him around the room as he picks out a suit and gets dressed quickly, efficiently.

I trust my husband. Implicitly. That niggle in the back of my mind says more about me than him.

I tell myself that it's just paranoia. I have never quite managed to shake the feeling of being an imposter, of having more than I deserve, but I cannot let my worst self ruin my marriage.

'I've got the flight to Mumbai,' he says, turning to face me as he buttons up his shirt. 'The Barclays meeting? I thought I told you.'

I search my brain for a memory of the conversation. He had said something about a trip last week but I'd been too tired to pay attention to the dates. I look at my phone and there it is, five days blocked out in my calendar.

'It must have slipped my mind,' I say, yawning. I watch as he loops a bright yellow tie around his neck.

'Did Niv get home okay last night? I was going to wait till we'd heard from her but I could barely keep my eyes open.'

I nod. Niv had sent me a text half an hour after I'd all but thrown her out, letting me know she'd arrived safely. Yet another one of our traditions. I feel a pang of regret and make a mental note to call Niv later to apologize. She must think that I behaved like a complete idiot.

I kiss Arjun goodbye, then haul myself out of bed and

go into the bathroom. I try to quell the unease that is swirling up inside me as I undress and step into the shower. Even though the day's barely started, I am exhausted. The DU rape case is getting to me and the stress is leaking into my life. I hadn't even remembered to congratulate Arjun for signing with John.

I take a deep breath as my insides twist and turn, the guilt and anxiety and anger melding together into one toxic combination, assaulting me from the inside, leaving me feeling raw and hollow. As usual in times of stress, my mind goes to Noor. I find myself wondering if she would still be here if I'd never met her. If I hadn't done the things I did.

The narrative I've built up over the years is one of redemption, of helplessness, of a girl who despite her best efforts was unable to save her best friend.

The truth is entirely different. It has the power to destroy lives.

I turn the shower off and step out. I push Noor away.

Some memories are best left alone. They are too dangerous to even think about, just the slightest tug capable of unravelling a whole life.

SABAH

'You said it yourself. This story's been covered to the death. There are already, three –' Andrew looks at me for confirmation and I nod. 'Three documentaries about the case. What makes this different?'

I know he's only playing devil's advocate but his words and the indifference with which they are delivered make me flinch.

I bend down to look at the laptop in front of me. I scroll through the images till I find the one I'm looking for, clicking on it so it fills my screen. I angle the laptop towards Andrew and Rachel, giving them a moment before I speak.

'It doesn't matter how many times it's been covered before. The family's never spoken to the press about it, nor have any of the key witnesses,' I say.

Across from me, Andrew looks unconvinced but his eyes are still fixed on the screen. Noor has the power to hold people captive, even in death.

'This is exactly like the Harriet Clarke documentary, except that I was there,' I continue. 'I have relationships with everyone involved. I know their stories, I can get under their skin.'

'The timing is certainly interesting,' Rachel says and I nod. It's no secret that broadcasters love anniversaries. 'The focus will be the scandal?' she asks, leaning forward.

I can tell I have her. She can see the potential in the story. It's topical, it's splashy, it's perfect for the post #MeToo world and, most importantly, considering the people involved, it's exactly the kind of thing the networks will lap up. There was a reason why Noor had captured the country's imagination back then, why thousands of people had come together in her defence. And that was before social media.

'The scandal. And everything that happened after.'

'You mean the—' Andrew starts and I cut him off with a quick nod. The scandal was just the catalyst. It was the thing that drove us all to the brink.

I twist the laptop towards me. My eyes flick back almost automatically to the screen. To the picture of Noor and me standing in front of the bright yellow Wescott bus, arms linked, big, beautiful grins lighting up our faces. I remember that day as vividly as if it was yesterday. We were on our way to Noor's for a sleepover. It was before the Head Girl drama, before the Oxbridge trip, before everything went so, so wrong. 'Best friends forever!' we had shouted into the camera just before the timer went off.

How had everything crumbled so swiftly after that? How did we go from being best friends to two girls who would do anything to destroy each other? Even before the thought completes itself, the answer comes to me. The guilt that follows feels as physical as a punch in the gut.

Noor was my best friend. I betrayed her and she ended up dead. I take a breath to steady myself. Rachel is looking at me, head cocked, eyebrows raised. Next to her, Andrew is bent low over his notepad, his pen moving furiously across the pages.

I get up and walk towards the window. The late winter sun is bouncing off the Thames, deceptive in the warmth it suggests.

It astonishes me that the thing I most want to run away from is also the thing that I feel so completely drawn to.

I stand there, staring out of the window until I feel my heartbeat settle. Nothing can change what I did, but perhaps by piecing together what really happened that night I can learn to live with it.

I turn around to face Rachel and Andrew.

'Yes,' I say. 'I mean the suicide.'

ALIA

Fifteen years ago

The last day of school before the summer holidays: it was something I had been looking forward to since even before term started, but now that it was here, I felt strangely nostalgic.

'Are you going to go and see your parents?' Noor asked as the final bell rang and the class erupted in a chorus of hoots and exclamations.

'Things are still volatile in Turkey,' I said, shaking my head. I threw my backpack over my shoulder and picked up the stack of books I'd borrowed from the library. All fiction. 'I'm staying here.'

'Won't you get bored? I couldn't stand six whole weeks in Delhi,' she said as we walked out of the classroom and joined the hordes of students crammed into the corridors. One of the many things I'd had to get used to was the strange way the school year was structured in India, with the summer break falling right in the middle of term. This meant a summer full of homework and test prep, but I suppose it was better than having nothing to do. Someone screeched and I turned to see a young girl frantically fanning her chest. I followed her glare across the corridor from where a group of junior boys were throwing water balloons at girls as they passed by. They were clearly bored of upskirting already.

'Their brains are even smaller than the memory chips in their phones,' Noor said, steering me so we were out of the line of fire. 'I'd invite you to Shimla, but Abbu said it's family only this time.'

I rolled my eyes as we circled a group of girls posing for a picture, Sabah beaming at the centre. A little further, I saw Dhruv waiting for me by the gates. My boyfriend. Just the thought made me smile. 'I'll be fine.'

The summer felt endless. The Delhi heat, which I had been enjoying in the spring, became unbearable, climbing up to a high forty-eight degrees. I spent most of my time holed up in my room with the old air con turned on and lights switched off. A week after school let out, Dhruv and his family flew to Europe on holiday. Even Saloni jetted off somewhere posh with her cousins. Every now and then I spoke to Addi on the phone, and I even went to see a film with her one afternoon, lured by the promise of a chilled cinema and popcorn, but other than that, I stayed in.

I stayed in and refused to think about my parents who couldn't even be bothered to pick up the phone and talk to me, let alone take me on holiday. They liked to pretend they were terribly important, even though we all knew that as aides to the ambassador and his wife, they were really just well-paid servants.

I was lying in bed lost in the ordeals of the March sisters when the phone rang.

It was Noor.

'We came back early,' she said, her voice sounding at once really far away and extremely close. I could hear the faint echo of 'Wannabe' in the background.

'How come?' I spoke into the phone, fiddling with the cord till the sound evened out.

'Abbu had to work. Something about the arrests in Kanpur.'

I knew about the arrests in Kanpur. Everyone did.

There had been riots raging for days. What had started with a group of college students handing out flyers and leaflets about an AIDS awareness programme had quickly turned into communal violence when a Hindu extremist group attacked a bunch of Muslim volunteers over accusations of antinationalism, a term that seemed to stretch across everything from homosexuality and sex outside marriage to generally having and voicing an opinion. In response, the police in Kanpur had arrested four of the twelve college students, all of them Muslim, which of course only led to more outrage and retaliation, and eventually a curfew in Kanpur. In a matter of three days, dozens more arrests had been made as rioters took to the streets setting cars and buses aflame, thrashing buildings and beating up anyone they saw.

'Is Javed Uncle going to Kanpur?' I asked, aware that Hindu–Muslim riots fell under his remit as the Minorities Minister.

'Yeah. *And* he's taking Faraz. I wish he'd let me tag

along,' Noor whinged and I laughed. I hadn't realized how much I'd missed her. 'Anyway,' she said, 'are you coming over or what?'

The last two weeks of the summer slipped by and before I knew it, it was time to go back to school.

As usual, I was spending the night at Noor's.

As usual, Sabah had not been invited.

'So, will they put up the shortlist next week?' I asked.

'Uh-huh,' Noor said, not giving me anything. She was bent over her sketchbook, filling it with quick, feathery strokes. I craned my neck to see what she was drawing, but she twisted away.

'I'm sure you'll be on it; you'll make a better Head Girl than her anyway. I saw her with Vineet at the cinema the other day. They looked nauseating.'

'Good for her.'

'Yeah, apparently they're a thing now.'

Something passed over her face but before I could prod further, Noor flicked on the TV.

I'd heard bits of gossip over the summer so I knew that Sabah and Vineet were officially dating. He'd invited her over to his farmhouse a few times but she came up with a new excuse every time. Apparently she wanted to make him wait till they'd been together at least a year. He's not sticking around, Addi had said, the dating guru with even less experience than me, but thinking about how Vineet had drooled at Saloni at the party, I was inclined to agree. Plus, there was a rumour going around that he'd been seeing someone else on the side.

I was dying to dissect this theory with Noor but I could tell she was preoccupied. Instead we watched Ross and Rachel argue on screen and munched on *murmure* until it was late enough to go to bed.

I woke up, as usual, at dawn. I slipped out of bed, careful not to wake Noor. I eased the door shut and crept downstairs in the dark, my feet finding their way instinctively into the kitchen. I flicked on the light and got the milk out of the fridge, humming to myself as I pulled things out of cupboards and lit up the stove.

With its curving staircases, marbled halls and dozen or so bedrooms, Noor's house was large enough to get lost in. Yet somehow, it was in this house that I felt most at home, most visible.

I was watching the bubbles break on the surface of the saffron-coloured milk when I heard movement behind me. I could tell by the heavy sound of the footsteps that it was Noor's father.

'You're up early.'

I flicked the gas stove off and turned around. 'I couldn't sleep. You?'

'This is my time to think. You'll realize how seductive it can be when you grow up, the lure of a few hours to yourself.'

'I can go . . .'

'No, it's fine. Stay.'

I poured my *kesar* milk into a glass while he made a cup of tea for himself.

'How were the holidays?'

'Good. I painted my room,' I said, blowing at the milk. 'And read loads of books.'

'Anything interesting?'

'Classics mainly. *Little Women*, some Jane Austen,' I said.

I didn't feel the need to mention the Sweet Valley High books I had been devouring.

He nodded quietly and we stood there for a few minutes, sipping on our drinks, me sitting at the kitchen table and him leaning against the counter facing me.

Once again I had the strange feeling that he could see right through me.

'What's troubling you?' he asked when the silence had transitioned from companionable to awkward.

'Nothing.'

I continued blowing at my drink, now tepid.

'Alia?'

'School starts next week,' I admitted.

'You seem to have settled in well.'

'And we've got the Oxbridge trip coming up.'

He nodded deeply. 'Yes. It's quite an expensive trip, isn't it?' He paused, as if he was weighing up his words. 'Alia, are your parents—'

'I don't think it's expensive.' I'd managed to pull together some more money over the holidays, but it was still nowhere near enough to cover the cost of the trip. If there was one thing I hated more than being poor, it was people *knowing* that I was poor.

'Things are different here. I miss London,' I added, surprising myself with my honesty. I was so desperate to go on this trip partly because I wanted to go back to London. Even if it was just for a day, I wanted to lose myself in the busy streets and packed tubes. I wanted to be invisible again. Yet as I stood in front of Noor's father, all I wanted was to be seen.

'Of course you do.' He smiled a sad little smile. 'Did you know my ancestors are from Sindh? When my grandfather moved to India after the partition, he had to leave everything behind, his property, his business, his friends, and build a new life here from scratch. He moved to the camp that Nehru had set up near Purana Qila and eventually managed to buy a small shop in old Delhi. He used to sell spices during the day, and after the shop closed every night, they would all sleep there. My grandparents, my father, my uncle and my two aunts. Six people stuffed into a room that was smaller than this kitchen.'

I glanced around the room trying to picture it. I had a mental image of the sardines my mum used to buy from the corner shop, packed tightly in a tin. I pushed the image, and her, away.

'My father and my uncle never went to school. But they learned, and they hustled. They expanded that shop into a business, moved into a house, sent their kids – us – to school. But throughout my childhood, I was very conscious of how hard my father worked just to provide us with the basics. Anything my brother or I wanted, we had to earn. So all this, it can still feel overwhelming, vulgar almost.'

I opened my mouth to say something but no words came out. He was looking at me in that peculiar way that he had and in that moment, I could sense how much he cared, how *deeply* he cared.

'When I look at you, I see that same energy that I had when I was your age. Noor, Faraz, even Sabah to an extent, they expect everything to be handed to them, but you . . . you're not like that. You don't wait for things to happen to you. You work for them. And I know how hard it can be to be surrounded by kids who don't have to think about money or opportunities or plan their future. But you know what, it doesn't matter. You are brave and resourceful and smart. And in the end, everything is going to work out for you. I can feel it.'

The conversation – so random yet so kind – baffled me. I found myself blinking furiously to hold back tears.

'Now, before my crazy daughter comes looking for you, off you go, *jaan*.'

Jaan. I hung on to that word. I had only ever heard him call Noor that.

Jaan.

Life.

ALIA

Fifteen years ago

Upstairs, Noor was snoring softly, hands tucked beneath her head, the duvet pulled up to her chin. She always slept like that, coiled tightly into a small ball as though she was trying to hold a world of secrets inside her. I watched her for a moment before tiptoeing into the bathroom with my book.

The bathroom was a mess. Pots of make-up were littered around the sink and there were clothes strewn across the sparkling marble floor. She was so used to having someone clean up after her, I sometimes thought Noor felt obligated to make a mess just to keep her army of maids and servants busy. I tidied the sink and wiped it before putting my book down.

I pulled my nightie over my head and twisted in front of the mirror to look at my neck. The label had been bothering me all night. My skin had turned a deep red where I had rubbed it raw. I applied some lotion – Noor's – and then picked up a T-shirt that Noor had thrown over the bathtub and held it up in front of me. I slipped it on, the fabric soft, pillowy.

I looked like a caricature of Noor, little more than a cheap imitation. My face, slim after weeks of track practice, looked drawn instead of chiselled. My hair hung limp around my face and my skin looked ashen under the glare of the overhead lighting, the dark circles under my eyes pronounced after months of sleepless nights.

I rolled up the sleeves of the T-shirt so they finished just above my elbows and pulled my hair away from my face into the kind of messy bun that Noor favoured. I sucked my cheeks in and looked at myself in the mirror. Better.

I sprayed some of her perfume on my neck and behind my ears, breathing in that intoxicating smell. I was years away from being able to identify notes, but even back then, I knew it was the way the delicate floral notes conflicted with the darker woody ones that made the scent so seductive, innocence flirting with danger.

I twirled in front of the mirror. Something was still missing.

Her *hijab* was sitting on the shelf, neatly folded into a small rectangle, the deep scarlet jarring against the all-white bathroom.

Like a single drop of blood on a white skirt.

Just the thought gave me goosebumps.

I couldn't, could I?

I picked it up, letting the silky fabric slither through my fingers.

It wouldn't hurt to try it on.

It wasn't like I was stealing anything.

I placed the scarf carefully on my head, twisting the

fabric around my face the way I'd seen Noor do hundreds of times.

I tucked my hair into it.

I rearranged the folds of fabric.

When I was done, I let my eyes meet the reflection in the mirror.

I pouted. I tilted my head and smiled. I traced the outline of my lips with my finger.

I could have sworn I was looking straight at Noor.

A week after school started, the headmistress summoned me to her office. She told me that I had been selected for the sponsored spot on the Oxbridge trip.

'The cost of the trip, the programme fees and all incidentals will be covered by the scholarship,' she said, handing me my deposit back.

'I didn't know there was a scholarship,' I said, confused. I had pored over the school's financial aid guide for days. I had spent hours begging the accounts office to let me spread the cost of the trip across the year. There was definitely no scholarship like the one Banerjee had just described.

'Well, there is now,' she said, somewhat gruffly, before showing me the door.

I walked out, thick wad of cash in hand, silently thanking my not-so-anonymous benefactor.

Perhaps I could have the kind of life I'd always dreamed about.

ALIA

I can hear them through the door, the jokes and chatter leaking through the conference room into the corridor where I'm waiting for my cue.

I hear Omar's voice behind me and I step to one side, flattening myself against the wall. It takes me a few seconds to recognize the couple he's escorting. Divya's parents. I force my lips into a small smile as they pass through and the guard steers them into the conference room.

I wait till the door has closed safely behind them before turning to face Omar.

'What are they doing here?' I whisper.

'They wanted to be here,' Omar says. His words are delivered nonchalantly but he refuses to meet my eye.

He nudges me along the corridor towards the conference room where more than a dozen journalists are waiting for me to make a statement.

'I will not make a spectacle of that family. This is not a political move.'

Omar looks straight at me then, a hint of pity in his

eyes. There is an edge to his voice when he speaks, and his words, spoken in his usual matter-of-fact tone, cut right through me.

'It's election year,' he says, holding the door to the conference room open and ushering me inside as flash-bulbs go off in my face. 'Everything you do is a political move.'

Saeed is on the phone to me even before I've stepped off the podium.

'Drop this.'

I'd expected masked hostility. His candour catches me off guard.

'Saeed *ji*,' I say, adding on the perfunctory *ji* to his name, a sign of the respect I absolutely do not have. 'I'm not sure—'

'How dare you go after my son?'

'You have a daughter, don't you, Saeed *ji*?' I say, keeping my voice low.

He doesn't acknowledge my question, just like I had known he wouldn't. Because something like this would never happen to someone like his daughter.

'My son did not rape anyone.'

'I didn't say he did,' I say. 'All I've said is that the boys should be questioned. This is about due process.'

'Listen to what I'm suggesting.'

I wait.

'No matter how hard you push, my son and his friends will not go to jail. We both know that. Drop this and I will make sure the girl's family is looked after and that your position is secure.'

'My position is already secure,' I say, but my words sound hollow and he picks up on it.

He scoffs. 'I know you relied on Javed a lot, but I did not realize you were this obtuse,' he says. There is a stillness to his voice, a calm that riles me more than outright anger would have, and yet it's this version of him that I feel most comfortable with. I slip out of the conference room and back into the corridor.

'You've lost the Muslim vote,' he continues, 'and without our support . . .'

He doesn't need to finish that sentence. Uttar Pradesh has a large Muslim electorate and the Indian Muslim Congress controls nearly ninety per cent of those votes. Without the alliance, I wouldn't just be risking my future; I would be risking the party's chances of winning a majority in the general election.

And yet, this isn't just about winning an election. It's about getting a young woman justice.

'Have you ever made a mistake, Alia?'

Noor's face floats in front of my eyes. I don't say anything.

'Because I'm going to find every mistake you've ever made and I am going to use it. We all have skeletons in our closet. Keep this up and I'm going to drag yours out for all the world to see.' His voice grows louder, more confident. 'At worst, my son made a big mistake. There are ways to make amends without destroying his life. I'm sure you can understand that.'

I maintain my silence.

'And if you can't, just remember that I will do whatever I have to to protect my child.'

SABAH

Pushing open the front door, I'm transported in an instant to my childhood. Running home after my Maths tuition, or ballet lesson, the smell of my father's cooking and the lilting sound of my mother's favourite Fleetwood Mac album greeting me even before I'd stepped through the door. I feel my mother's kiss on my forehead as she opens the door to let me in, an unopened bottle of chilled white wine in hand. I hear my father call out to me from the kitchen, his back to me as he stirs a sauce, apron on, shirtsleeves rolled up. I see myself toss my bag on the floor, chattering non-stop, filling my parents in on my day while setting the table.

It was a happy home.

The wind sucks the door shut, rattling me out of my thoughts.

I drop my bags in the hall and wander through the house, opening doors and peeking into rooms at random, refamiliarizing myself with the spaces I had once inhabited with ease. My mother left most of the furniture and art behind, but without the clutter of everyday life, the house feels haunted.

I trail a finger over the kitchen counter, one of the many habits I've inherited from my mother. It's spotless. The cleaner that Savita Aunty sent over in preparation for my arrival has done a fantastic job. Even though the house has been empty for nearly a decade, there's not a speck of dust in sight and thanks to the bergamot diffusers in every room, a pleasant smell fills the air. An elaborate care package sits on the dining table. I reach for the note nestled in between a bunch of bananas and a box of Assam tea.

Wifi's all set up and I've stocked the fridge with some essentials. Pop over for a cup of tea once you're all settled in. Welcome home, darling. Savita

I drop the note on the table and send Ma a quick text to let her know I've arrived. I picture her looking at it a few hours later as she starts her day, strong black coffee in hand, sunlight streaming through the French windows in her San Francisco apartment.

My parents shipped me off to a boarding school in London two weeks after the funeral. Even though the true extent of my involvement never became public knowledge, the scandal, and the gossip it generated, made living here impossible. My father's business as a financial consultant to Delhi's elite took a direct hit and he left for Mumbai soon after. My mother, on the other hand, tried to assimi-late back into her old life for five years before deciding she was done. I woke up one morning to an email from her saying she had decided to relocate to her company's head offices in San Francisco. Exactly 8,380 miles from my father. They never divorced, never split the assets, but their lives had split the day they realized I wasn't quite as innocent as they thought I was. The move itself didn't come as a surprise but the associated guilt did.

Another thing I had broken.

The therapist they'd forced me to see afterwards would say my own romantic life, or lack thereof, had to do with my guilt about the failure of my parents' marriage but as with all her other theories, she would be wrong.

I pick up my bags and head up the stairs, pausing for the briefest of moments before pushing the door to my old bedroom open.

My stomach seizes. Like the rest of the house, my room has hardly changed at all. My favourite cushion still rests on the bed, the bedside table still holds the cuckoo clock I had bought in Switzerland, the desk my parents had built for me still takes up a whole wall. But it is the corkboard above the desk that draws me in. It's covered with pictures, timetables, motivational quotes, remnants from my old life that show a girl I barely recognize anymore.

One by one I remove everything from the board, laying things out in neat piles until the board is completely empty. Save for one photograph.

It's a picture from the picnic to Lodhi Gardens. Noor, Vineet, Mohit, Alia, Saloni and I are lying on the grass grinning up at the camera like there's nothing to fear in the world. In the photograph we look innocent, teenagers having fun, yet we all had a part to play in what happened to Noor.

I pull out the schedule that my production manager,

Jenny, had pressed into my hands as I was leaving. Andrew and Rachel had signed off on the pitch almost immediately after our meeting and within a matter of days, a budget had been allocated and timelines agreed. I've been given four weeks to complete the preliminary interviews and prepare the pitch deck for the networks. I'd have been thrilled at the outcome if I wasn't terrified of the job I had to do, investigating the people who had once been my closest friends.

I take the piece of paper I've been obsessing over for weeks now and pin it up next to the photograph, the looping handwriting on it as familiar as my own.

Details from that night have been etched in my memory. Some of them facts, but very few, very scattered, so the picture has never completed itself and I know there are parts missing. Crucial parts.

Noor died of a single gunshot wound to the head.

Her father found her, and the note she left behind.

Vineet was the last person to see her alive. When he was questioned, he said Noor probably thought it was easier to commit suicide than to embarrass herself and her family any more than she had already done.

Noor was buried the next afternoon but long after the *imam* sang and her body was lowered into the ground, the questions lingered.

Questions that I have pushed aside for years.

Until now.

ALIA

Fifteen years ago

It felt like we were on a film set.

We had been in Oxford for nearly a week and I still couldn't wrap my head around the sheer beauty of the city. With its gothic spires and ivy-clad buildings, it felt as though the university was drunk on its own splendour, every cloistered arcade and crenellated tower revelling in its own history. And yet, despite the history and tranquillity there was also a sense of anticipation.

It was as if a part of me knew that something important was going to happen there, with me at its centre.

I leaned back and closed my eyes as shafts of sunlight cut through the apple trees, bathing the garden in golden light.

It didn't take long for me to realize that although our school had been at pains to advertise the Oxbridge programme as educational, in reality it was little more than a fancy prep-school version of summer camp, albeit one that would give us an edge when it came to university admissions season next year. Instead of hiking and swimming, we spent our mornings in oak-panelled classrooms learning about Politics and International Relations and our afternoons on excursions around town. After a morning spent debating the role of religion in politics, we were sprawled out in the Fellows' garden waiting for our faculty chaperone, Agarwal Sir, to join us so we could go on a walking tour through the old town.

I let out a small belch, the acrid taste on my tongue reminding me of the lasagne I had practically inhaled in the dining hall earlier that afternoon. I glanced around, mortified, but to my relief, no one had noticed.

Noor was busy flirting with our student guide for the week, Simon, an Economics student with deep brown eyes and the kind of chiselled jaw that I'd only ever seen in posters. Ankit, who was clearly in love with Noor, was pretending to be in conversation with the awkward boy from the Science stream, while sneaking glances at Noor. And Sabah was busy training her latest minion, a girl whose pigtails would've been reason enough for Sabah to write her off in Delhi, but she didn't have many options here.

I let my eyes gravitate back towards Noor as I sipped on the orange juice I had snuck out of the buttery. She was leaning in towards Simon, talking quietly, her head almost touching his. I watched him nod along for a moment, before saying something that made Noor throw her head back in laughter. Next to them, the other student guide, a mousy blonde called Michelle, rolled her eyes.

I caught Sabah looking at me when I finally tore my eyes away from them. I stared back, undeterred, as Sabah pulled her earphones out of her ears and wrapped the cord up neatly around her iPod.

I could sense another jibe coming. The school had put up the shortlist for the Student Council last week, pitting Noor and Sabah squarely against each other, and it had been a constant stream of snide comments and passive-aggressive insults since then. I'd kept out of it – Sabah was not someone you messed with if you wanted to survive at Wescott – but I would be lying if I said I wasn't happy about this new animosity between them. For months I had felt excluded. There was so much history there it didn't leave room for anyone else. Now, I finally had a shot at a real friendship.

I lay down on the grass and went back to my dog-eared paperback.

I had barely started reading when I heard Sabah's voice. 'Simon, perhaps you could tell us something about the college while we wait? You know, since you're supposed to be our guide and all.'

I propped myself up on my elbow to look at the scene unfolding before me. The college porter had bored us with a long talk about the history of the college the day we arrived. Sabah had asked a million questions.

'Um – yeah, of course,' Simon faltered before launching into the history of the college and explaining the role it had played in the religious disputes of the sixteenth and seventeenth centuries.

Noor scowled at Sabah and came over and sat next to me.

'She's just jealous,' I said, setting my book down.

Noor shrugged it off but by then I could read her face well enough to know when she was upset. She rolled her shoulders.

'Did you manage to get hold of your parents?'

'Um, yeah. Yeah, I did,' I lied.

I'd told her I was going to call them this morning when I went to the Porters' Lodge after breakfast. Honestly, though, I didn't see the point in ringing home every day. I'd called Nani to let her know we had arrived safely on the first night, and as far as I was concerned, that was enough. Noor, on the other hand, spoke to her parents every single day. Each night, one of the student guides would knock on our door and Noor would follow her to the lodge. She was usually gone for the best part of an hour and when she returned she would relay her entire conversation to me in minute detail. I couldn't decide whether it made me feel angry or jealous.

'How are they?'

'Good. Or as good as they can be, I guess. There's still a lot of tension in the city so they are stuck in the embassy most of the time. That's why they haven't been able to visit either.' The lie was only small and I almost convinced myself that that was the reason I hadn't heard from them. But they had been stuck at the embassy in London throughout my childhood as well. There had been no tension in London, no active danger. They just preferred the glamour of hanging out with the ambassador's family instead of spending time with their own.

'Do you miss them?'

I shrugged.

I sat up and brought my knees up to my chest, hugging them tight until I could feel every muscle in my back expand. I was not going to let my parents ruin this trip.

'A couple of the other girls are having a movie night in the common room later. *Pretty Woman*,' I said, resting my chin on my knees. There were seven other groups on the same programme but since each school got to tailor its own schedule, we only ever saw them after hours. 'Fancy it?'

'*Fancy it?* You are *so* English!' Noor grinned, eyes sparkling as her gaze travelled back to Simon.

Sabah cornered us at breakfast the next morning.

'You need to be careful,' she said, with not even a hint of friendliness.

'Of the croissants? Aww, thanks,' Noor replied.

'Do you really think people don't see you sneak out every night? You can get into some serious trouble if the school finds out.'

'Oh yeah? And how are they going to find out?'

'Look, I'm just trying to—'

'Ruin our summer with your obsession with the rules? You aren't Head Girl yet, Sabah,' I said, finding my voice. 'Nor will you ever be,' I added, bumping my shoulder against Noor's.

She looked at me, eyebrows raised. 'It speaks.'

'Leave her be,' Noor said. 'Did your minion forget to save you a seat, Sabah? Sit,' she added, her voice chirpy. 'I'm sure we can make some room for a tiny little thing like you.'

'Thanks,' Sabah smiled down at Noor, 'but I'd rather eat in the toilet than sit next to traitors and social climbers.

Don't tell me I didn't warn you,' she said to me before flipping around and walking away.

We were supposed to be sleeping but we weren't. We were reliving the day, dissecting it minute by minute, obsessing over the tiniest details and glossing over the bigger picture.

That's how it went every night. We spent our evenings wandering the city or watching movies in the common room and our nights staying up long after lights out, telling each other things we would never dare to utter out loud in the day. There was something bewitching about it, being so far away from the world any of us knew, so disconnected, so *free*, from her life of privilege and mine of wanting. The feeling lifted me up and carried me; it made me feel like we were the only people in the world.

We spent hours talking, every hatched plan and whispered secret bringing us closer, cementing our friendship. That's when I told her that I had lied about Chris and she told me that she had lied about her string of boyfriends. That's when I learned that Saloni had once kissed a bus driver and that Yash sometimes came to school with vodka in his water bottle.

We spoke about things that mattered and things that didn't and with every secret that Noor shared, I felt closer to her. They had trusted Noor with their secrets and Noor trusted me. That knowledge made me feel special, warm in the glow of her attention.

'I still can't believe Dhruv's gone back to that conniving

little bitch. You're so much prettier than her,' Noor said, flipping onto her stomach.

I didn't want to admit it but I was slightly relieved. After a few weeks of dating, the charm of being Dhruv's girl-friend had faded; the idea of doing all the things he expected of me started feeling nauseating rather than exciting. I'd barely seen him over the summer and after school started, I ignored him often enough that the whole thing just sort of fizzled out. I was secretly quite happy when I heard that he'd gone back to Niv. This wasn't something I could say out loud, though, not when he was considered the prize senior, not when I had so willingly played at being his girlfriend for weeks. I decided instead to act magnanimous.

'Who cares? I hope they're happy together.'

I smiled what I thought was a sad but generous smile.

'I could never let it go that easily.'

I looked up at the ceiling. Her words, spoken carelessly, left me feeling ridiculed. I would turn sixteen in a few months and you weren't supposed to be sensible at sixteen, were you? You were supposed to be jealous and heartbroken and head over heels in love.

'At least I'm not looking the other way while my so-called boyfriend gets it on with someone else,' I said. 'Vineet and Sabah,' I said, elaborating when Noor gave me a confused look. As perceptive as she was about everything else, when it came to Sabah, it was as though Noor couldn't see what was right in front of her.

'You heard about that?'

'Who didn't? Not like she'll ever do anything about it,' I said. 'She's all but married to Vineet.'

Noor scoffed.

'What?'

'Nothing,' Noor said, but I knew all she needed was a little coaxing.

I turned on my side to face her. 'Tell me,' I begged, grabbing her hand and tugging at it playfully.

'Don't you trust me?' I asked, when Noor didn't respond.

'Of course I do,' Noor said, sighing slightly. She flipped onto her side so we were face to face, our foreheads kissing, our breath mingling. Her fingers grazed mine. 'You know we went on that camping trip last year?'

Did I ever. I couldn't get them to shut up about it.

I nodded along encouragingly as Noor proceeded to tell me what had really happened on that trip. By the time she finished, my head was spinning. I could hardly believe my luck.

Sabah wore her virtuousness like a bulletproof vest.

But there was a chink in every armour, and I had just found hers.

ALIA

Fifteen years ago

'Let's go,' Noor said.

'Where?' I asked. It was our last night in Oxford and I was curled up in bed, still exhausted from the send-off lunch the college had organized for us.

I dragged myself out of bed. Noor was standing by the door, wearing jeans and a white T-shirt that she had knotted up to reveal a taut triangle of skin. She had left her hair loose – with no parents to please and Agarwal Sir unlikely to report back, she had no reason to bother with the *hijab*.

'Anywhere that is not the common room. Sabah's taken over movie night,' she said, rolling her eyes, the room her theatre and me her admiring, if captive audience. She liked to put on a show, behaving at all times as if a spotlight were shining on her.

'Can I borrow this?' she asked, picking up my raspberry lip balm and dabbing it on before I had the chance to answer.

We wandered out of the college and through the cobbled lanes until we were standing on Magdalen Bridge.

Dappled sunlight danced on the water, casting patterns

that seemed to shimmer and slide every time I moved my head. I held up my camera and took a picture. The riverbank that had been lined with sunbathers earlier lay bare now and except for the odd punt that sailed past, the river was still.

If only for the night, Oxford was ours.

For the first time in what seemed like forever, I felt a sense of deep calm, a conviction that things were going to work out. There was something else too, a flutter of something that I couldn't quite put my finger on, but it left me feeling warm and fuzzy.

We climbed down the short flight of steps and walked along the river until we found a grassy stretch.

'I wish we could stay here forever,' Noor said as we sat down side by side, matching denim jackets spread out beneath us. 'No parents, no rules, no *Faraz*. You're so lucky you don't have siblings.'

'Why do you hate him so much?'

'I don't hate him. He's annoying, that's all. You know he went to Sameer's house and threatened to smash his car if he called me again. I mean, seriously? I went out with him *once*. We barely even held hands.'

'He's just looking out for you. It's sweet.'

I leaned back on the grass and looked up at the sky through the cobweb of branches. Sameer was the captain of the football team and one of the more notorious seniors at Wescott, the kind of boy who spent every weekend with a different girl and somehow still came across as charming. Even though he was only seventeen and still under legal driving age, he drove to school every day. Rumour had it that the back seat of his car had seen more action in a year than all the motel rooms in Surajkund put together.

'It's embarrassing.'

'Will you see him again?'

I looked at her. She had that look she got from time to time, like she was slipping away. I knew Noor had been seeing someone off and on for a while, but not once had she given me the details. I wondered if it was Sameer.

'Maybe.'

'Does Faraz have a girlfriend?' I felt emboldened enough to ask.

'Interested in my brother, are you?'

'No,' I burst out, heat rising up my neck. 'I'm just curious.'

'Relax, I'm joking.'

'He was dating this girl from his college,' she added, 'but her father found out and, like, completely lost it. He rang Abbu and told him that if Faraz even looked at her again, he'd kill him.'

'That's insane. Have you met her?'

'Nope. But I've seen her picture. Faraz had a photo tucked away in his history book. She's not even that pretty.'

I couldn't begin to imagine a love like that, a feeling so intense that everything else paled in comparison, but I'd had enough ambiguity and detachment in my life to know that that's what I wanted – the kind of love that you'd risk anything for. The kind of love that was so whole that you could crawl inside it and live there.

'Maybe he doesn't—' I sat up when I heard a rustle behind us. 'Did you hear that?' I whispered.

We both got up without a word, our hands laced together. For a moment, I felt like I was the heroine in an adventure novel and it sent a delicious tingle of excitement through me, the element of danger only adding to the thrill.

We crept along the bank, whispering and giggling as it became clear what the sounds were. We stood listening for a minute, then Noor pushed the leaves apart and we peered through the gap.

I moved closer to get a better look, ashamed by that want yet unable to turn away.

The couple was facing away from us. The boy, or perhaps the man – I couldn't really see his face, was lying on the grass, jeans pulled down to his ankles in a pool of inky blue denim. The woman was on top of him, glossy blonde hair thrown back, hips thrusting in sync with her moans, one strap of her creamy white sundress pushed down to reveal a naked breast. My knowledge of sex until then had been limited to what little I'd seen in romantic comedies and the raw, animal-like sounds they were making startled me. It was horrific, yet I felt compelled to watch, my feet refusing to do what my brain commanded.

After a few seconds, the wrongness of what I was doing hit home, and I backed away, dragging a madly giggling Noor with me.

'Now that's a picnic that went *very* well,' Noor smirked. She pointed to their picnic basket and, beyond that, to the empty punt.

Before I knew what was happening, Noor picked up the open bottle of Prosecco and ran over to the river.

'You know how to swim, right?' Noor asked when I had caught up with her. She grinned and took a long swig from the bottle.

For a second, I thought she was going to insist we strip down to our underwear and leap into the murky water but Noor could never be that predictable.

She unhooked the chain that was holding the punt and jumped in.

'Are you crazy?' I mouthed, twisting to see if the couple had realized we'd stolen their Prosecco yet.

'Get in,' she replied in an excited whisper.

This was insane even for her. We'd been punting earlier that week. Noor, Sabah and me forced into one punt while the boys chose to attend a tech seminar instead. We'd all had a go at it, but that was in the daytime with an instructor and mandatory life jackets, in a boat that we hadn't stolen.

She stepped onto the slatted decking at the bow and grabbed the pole, her hands positioned exactly how the instructor had shown us.

'Don't tell me Alia Sharma is scared of a little adventure,' she said, looking at me like I had disappointed her. The punt was already drifting away. 'Come on.'

'You're crazy,' I repeated and then jumped in, making the narrow boat rock from side to side.

Noor let out a ripple of laughter as cold water splashed into the boat, soaking us both to the ankles.

I picked up the paddle and settled onto a damp cushion

as Noor dropped the pole into the riverbed and pushed back until the boat moved, gently, imperceptibly forward.

She stood up straight and repeated the whole thing again and again, letting the pole slip down into the water and then leaning on it until we were gliding along almost seamlessly.

'Wow,' she said, a little out of breath. The delight in her voice was infectious and I cheered her on as we sliced through the river.

'Smile,' I said. I lifted up my camera and looked at her through the lens, the golden evening light on her face, the watery landscape behind her, tall trees and dense undergrowth hemming her in from both sides, casting dark green shadows over the glassy water.

The breeze picked up as we approached a curve in the river and I watched her struggle for a moment, her forehead scrunched up in intense concentration as she tried to hold the punt steady.

Just as she got the boat back under her control, the wind pushed us forward, her curls whipping up a storm around her face.

'This is amazing,' I shrieked, my words broken and breathless, my hair tangled, my eyes wet.

Later, as we stumbled back through the meadows, she turned me to and said, 'We don't need parents, or school, or boyfriends. This is everything.'

I pressed my forehead to hers and closed my eyes. We were so close I could hear her heart beating. Our lips grazed as I spoke, an irrational warmth sweeping through me.

'This is everything,' I whispered back.

I didn't realize until much later, until I had ruined it all, that the warmth I had felt that night was what belonging felt like.

ALIA

The problem with having it all? You worry, you fret, you panic. You live in a state of near constant anguish, just waiting for someone to pull the rug out from under your feet. Every achievement, every smile, every victory reminds you of how in one moment, everything can change. The fear of losing it all never leaves you, yet you have no choice but to switch off, push yourself, carry on.

Fear makes multi-taskers of us all.

As expected, my stance on the DU rape case has ruffled more than a few feathers and I spend the next few mornings locked in closed-door parliamentary meetings and after-noons visiting senior party members and campaign donors, alternating between seeking assurances and doling them out, trying to pre-empt the havoc Saeed threatened me with. I don't make it into the office until late in the week. The change of pace jostles me.

'Everything all right?' I ask Omar as he follows me into my cabin. I motion to him to close the door. The office is noisier than usual, phones ringing, staff talking across the room.

He switches on the TV in response.

Faraz is on air, live from a women's refuge in my constituency – one of the first ones I'd set up after being sworn in as the Women and Child Development Minister. He's walking through the compound, the building a little dilapidated after five years and multiple budget cuts, talking to the reporter about living conditions, upkeep and funding, all areas that are directly under my remit, both as the WCD minister and as the elected MP.

It's little more than a pre-election awareness segment but it leaves me feeling uneasy. Women's rights have always been the linchpin of my campaign strategy.

'Has he made any comments about the alliance?'

'Not yet,' Omar says. Faraz never organized the intimate reception he had promised for the INP and judging by his speeches and appearances over the last week, he has no intention of doing so. It hits me once again how naive I've been. I let myself get swept up by my emotions. In my rush to support Faraz I hadn't stopped to consider that his policies might not align with his father's. There was a reason why Javed Uncle hadn't handed over the reins of the party to Faraz, why he'd always kept him behind the scenes.

'I've put feelers out about the nominations this morning,' Omar adds, reading my mind. We both know that it's only a matter of time before Faraz dissolves the alliance and announces his own plans to run. 'I also ran the numbers. If he dissolves the alliance, he will split the voters three ways, between the Muslim Congress, the INP and the opposition.' He lifts his shoulders, as if to say that much is obvious. 'Traditionally, we'd expect the split to be religion led in favour of the Muslim Congress.'

I nod, waiting for him to finish.

'But we're seeing a shift in the female vote – across the board – possibly because of your position on women's issues: triple *talaq*, rape, harassment.'

'You mean my position on the DU rape?' I say. It's juvenile, but I can't help it.

Omar gives a brief nod before continuing. 'My guess is that Saeed and Faraz are working together. Saeed's tackling the Muslim votes—'

'And Faraz is going after the women,' I finish.

Omar nods, handing me a copy of the projections. 'Assuming the caste arithmetic stays the same, this election is going to be swayed by the female vote.'

I can't help but smile as I take this in. An election that's decided by the female vote. Even if I lose, that's got to count for something. I hand the sheet back to Omar. 'Tap a source in Faraz's team. I want to know when he's planning to announce.'

'Already done. We should have some intel within the next few days.'

I sit down and flick through the folder of briefing notes on my desk, thicker than usual. I stop when I get to the weekly report from the sexual harassment helpline.

Less than a week after I stood up in Divya's defence, there's been a spike in the calls received by the helpline. It's no surprise that the men accused are mostly ones in power. I grimace as I read through the accounts – everything from workplace harassment to rape. Yet there is comfort in the fact that I've created a safe space, a sense of confidence in a system that has let victims down for decades. I feel my spine straighten as pride flutters through me. I close my eyes.

I did this.

Almost instantly Noor's face flashes behind my eyes and the flutter morphs into something darker. I feel myself shrink as my brain reminds me of the other thing I did.

The thing that might destroy me if I let it.

I snap my eyes open and force myself to focus on what Omar is saying.

'I've organized some interviews and panel discussions for you over the next few weeks. It will help us build visibility in the lead-up to the nomination.'

'Thanks,' I say, turning back to the folder in front of me.

I look up when Omar continues to linger. 'Anything else?'

He shifts his weight.

'Omar?'

'We're going to need more than just media appearances to win this election.'

I raise my eyebrows. The insinuation isn't lost on me but I let him carry on.

'I know you're friends, but Faraz doesn't exactly have a spotless history. We can start gathering—'

'No,' I say.

I run a clean campaign. Always have, always will.

*

'So, are you going to tell me?' I say as Niv heaps pasta on a plate and hands it to me.

'Tell you?' she says, twisting away to open a bottle of Italy's finest and carefully pouring the wine into two long-stemmed glasses.

'About your new man?' I say, my tone teasing, friendly. I'd tried to apologize to Niv about my behaviour the other night, but she'd waved my apology away, skipping right past the awkwardness to welcome me in.

'There's nothing to tell,' she says. There is something artificially flippant about her tone. It gives her away.

I fix her with a look, just enough to give her pause. It works.

'Okay, fine.' She sighs, pushing her spaghetti around. 'There is someone . . . from work . . . but it's complicated.'

'Complicated how?' I ask. I break off a piece of bread and dip it into my plate, lopping up some of Niv's gorgeous pomodoro sauce.

'Just, you know . . . it's still very new and I don't know if it's going to lead anywhere.' She reaches for her wine, gives it a swirl. 'And he's not *exactly* single. Yet.'

I feel a shiver of anxiety as the scene I'd witnessed earlier in the week flashes before my eyes. I brush the thought away. Niv would never do that to me. And anyway, I reason, if she was having an affair with my husband, she'd hardly be sitting here talking to me about it.

Right?

'Anyway,' she says, eyeing me over the rim of her wine glass. 'I heard Sabah's in town.'

I rush to cover my reaction with a gulp of wine. I wait till my heartbeat settles. When I speak, my voice is casual, unconcerned.

'Oh really?'

'She's here for work, apparently. A documentary,' Niv says. 'Neighbourhood gossip,' she adds by way of explanation.

Sabah and Niv are neighbours, or they used to be. Though Niv moved out years ago, her parents still live in the house where she grew up which means we occasionally get titbits of gossip about Sabah from the neighbourhood grapevine.

'Do you think she'll be at the reunion?' Niv asks and I shrug. Considering her history with the school, I'd skip it if I were her.

Unless.

'What's the documentary about?' I ask, hoping Niv won't question the sudden pivot in the conversation, or the slight tremble in my voice.

Niv lifts her glass and drains it in one long swallow. She places the glass on the table, a single drop of wine dancing along the rim before trickling all the way down to the tablecloth, the stain spreading slowly, a blotch of dark red on the creamy linen.

When I look up, Niv's eyes are fixed on me.

'Your guess is as good as mine.'

SABAH

I start the way I always do: with the family.

'It's good to see you,' Faraz says, pulling me into a hug as I step out of the car.

'I'm so sorry I couldn't come sooner. When I heard about Javed Uncle . . .' I trail off, not knowing how to finish that sentence.

'Thank you,' Faraz says, squeezing my arm.

'Looks like you're doing a lot of work here,' I say, looking around as we circle the fountain and walk up the front steps. There are at least a dozen tradesmen scattered across the grounds, cleaning out the fountain, trimming down the ivy, pruning the bushes.

'I thought it was time we laid the bad memories to rest. This used to be a happy place,' he says. 'And the renovation gives Ammi something to focus on. You remember how much she loved working in the gardens.'

I nod. Faraz has always been thoughtful like that.

'How is she?'

'Oh, you know. It's hard. She seems to have developed a bit of an obsession with online courses and she hasn't left the estate since . . . I guess everyone deals with grief differently.' He shakes his head. Smiles. 'She's been looking forward to seeing you. She always had a soft spot for you, didn't she?'

Guilt softens my edges and for a moment I forget why I am here. Neither of us are strangers to the horror of a sudden death. People always assume it's easier than a long drawn-out illness. They're wrong. The shock, the disbelief, the stabbing pain. It blinds you every time you remember what you've lost. I search for something to say, some way of reassuring him, but there is none.

'And you were always jealous,' I say instead and he winks, relief spilling into his face. 'Congratulations on the new position, by the way.'

'Congratulations on the latest award,' he counters, before adding, 'Ammi's on the terrace.' Without either of us leading the way, we walk along the wraparound porch and climb down to the back garden.

When I first called Faraz about the documentary, I'd expected a certain amount of resistance, a period of cajoling – after all, the Qureshis had consistently refused to talk about Noor for fifteen years – but he had been surprisingly willing. Keen, almost. His only request had been that I interview his mother in his presence. He was worried it would be too much for her and I'd happily obliged.

The terrace, as the Qureshis have always liked to call it, is an elaborate sunken garden at the back of the house. I remember watching it being dug up and as the memory lingers, I can practically see Fatima Aunty standing there, shouting out instructions to a bunch of gardeners and landscapers as they installed arches, paved looping paths and planted rose bushes.

I trail Faraz as we walk silently along the concrete path and descend the stone steps to the terrace. The gardeners haven't touched this part of the estate yet and the air of dilapidation only adds to the charm here, a faded grandeur that will play well in front of the camera. We step through an ornate arch and make our way towards the edge where I can see Fatima Aunty stooped over the rose bushes.

She straightens up and turns to face us. I was expecting her beauty to have faded, but she is still as striking as ever. With her delicately lined skin and pale cream *hijab*, she looks almost aristocratic.

'Sabah, *jaan*,' Fatima Aunty says, cupping my face. She leads me towards the white wrought-iron table in the corner, as a maid appears with tea and a platter laden with dates and almonds.

'I'll be right back,' Faraz says, frowning at his phone.

'He's been so busy,' Fatima Aunty says, her eyes on Faraz as he paces a few feet from us, talking quietly into his phone. 'He should really be at the party office, but he refuses to leave me on my own.'

'I was so sorry to hear about Javed Uncle,' I say when her gaze slides back to me.

Fatima Aunty nods but doesn't say anything and I sit in silence while she pours tea into two delicate china cups. Time flies past as she quizzes me about my life in London and asks after my parents, our shared history peppering the conversation as we catch up.

I notice the light changing and busy myself with setting up my camera. I very rarely film research chats – there is the risk of the final interview looking rehearsed if the contributor knows what questions to expect – but I am hoping that I will be able to use footage from today's conversation as part of the sizzle reel. Pitch decks are great for communicating narrative arcs and listing assets but the real selling point for any documentary is its emotional impact, and nothing demonstrates that better than a trailer-style sizzle reel featuring the key contributor.

'Thank you for agreeing to do this,' I say, slipping into work mode once Faraz is back. 'I know how hard it is to talk about everything that happened back then.' I direct my words towards Fatima Aunty. She had never been comfortable in the spotlight, often staying home with Noor instead of attending political rallies and events with Javed Uncle. 'Try to forget about the camera and just think of this as a regular conversation with me.'

I ease into the interview, asking Fatima Aunty about what Noor had been like as a child, pretending I didn't remember what her favourite films were or how every Friday had to be pizza night.

Her voice dries up when we get to the later years.

'Do you still think about her?' I ask, cautiously.

Fatima Aunty doesn't say anything. I am about to repeat myself when I notice her hand trembling as she sets her water down. I look away. She heard me.

'Every day.' Her voice is quiet. 'You know, people skirt around it, they worry about reminding me. What they don't realize is that losing a child . . . like that . . . that's not something you can forget.'

I nod, urging her on.

'It was my job to protect her, to keep her safe, and I –' She pauses and as I realize what's coming next, my stomach twists. 'When the news broke and all the papers started attacking her . . . I should have stood by her . . . and I didn't. It was so selfish of me . . . I keep thinking about how scared she must have been, my girl. My baby girl.'

There is anguish in every word. I glance at Faraz but he is looking down, his hands clenched in his lap, and for a moment I consider backing off. But then I think of the piece of paper pinned up on my corkboard and some of the steely resolve that I had relied on during the Harriet Clarke documentary reappears.

'What do you think happened that night?'

'I don't know. We can never know. That's the hardest part. But I don't care if she held the gun to her own forehead. It was that boy. He stole the light out of my Noorie's eyes.'

ALIA

Fifteen years ago

Is there anything more dangerous than a bunch of bored teenagers?

Halfway through the winter term, the headmistress called a special assembly for our class. There had been an incident involving firecrackers on the fire escape in our block. It seemed it was a Wescott tradition for the year eleven students to set off fireworks on school grounds both as a mark of respect for the graduating class and as a reminder to the school authorities: you can't control us.

The school had all but come to accept it and from what I was told, the perpetrators usually got off with a day or two's suspension. This time, though, the boys from our class had taken it up a notch. They had used an incense stick to set off a *ladi*, a string of five thousand interconnected firecrackers, in the stairwell behind our classroom. The *ladi* went off for a good twenty minutes and caused one of the windows to shatter. Pieces of hot glass crashed down from the fourth-floor window and hit one of the janitors. He had to have eighteen stitches. This was before the days of CCTV in schools, and thanks to the slow burn of the incense stick, the culprits were long gone by the time the *ladi* started going off. There was no way for the teachers to know who set it up. It was borderline genius.

Of course, most of us knew. Orchestrating something of this scale took meticulous planning and a serious amount of cash and we had all contributed in one way or another.

Noor and I shuffled in with the rest of our class, the floorboards creaking under the weight of anxious footsteps as forty-something students filed into the auditorium.

'What do you think she'll do?' I whispered to Noor as we slid into the second row next to Mohit and Yash. Sabah was in the front row with Vineet, Addi and Saloni. The school had put up the schedule for the Head Girl interviews the day before and that had brought with it a fresh round of under-the-breath insults and angry snares, which, terrible as it was, made for a refreshing change from all the in-jokes and shared history that they used to laud over me. Since Oxford, Noor and I were the ones with the in-jokes and for the first time, I felt like I was on an even footing.

'There's not much she can do. Banerjee likes to call these things every once in a while to remind us that she's the headmistress.'

'Yeah, but someone got hurt.'

Noor looked at me like I was crazy. In this world, maids and janitors existed to make our lives easier but their value was in their invisibility.

'Don't worry about it.'

From the aisle our homeroom teacher shot us an irritated look and held a finger up to her lips.

Noor waited till she had turned her wrath on another group of gossiping students and then leaned in towards me, giggling. 'Here we go,' she whispered as Banerjee started speaking.

'I know you all think you can get away with anything but let me remind you that this prank has caused serious damage. You're lucky that the janitor only had to have a few stitches, or we'd be looking at getting the police involved. I've warned you before and I'm warning you again – I will not tolerate vandalism.'

Banerjee paused and I snuck a sideways glance at Noor. She was sitting straight in her chair, her face set in a blank expression. Around us, the others had occupied a similar stance. Noor was right: it was obvious that they had all been here before. The thought was comforting and I allowed myself to relax until Banerjee started talking again.

'Letters have been sent out to your parents informing them of the damage you have caused and the action the school will be taking. I will find out who is responsible for this and when I do, the concerned students will be expelled and the rest of you will get suspensions.' She paused, letting her words sink in as the warning rippled through the room. 'Unless you come forward yourselves. Your choice. You have until Friday.'

I felt my breathing quicken. I absolutely could not have a suspension on my record.

As we filed out of the room, I could sense that the mood had changed. Banerjee's warning had had more of an impact than Noor had thought it would.

Outside, Sabah was standing in a huddle with Addi, Saloni, Vineet, Mohit and a few of the rowdier boys from our class. She beckoned us over.

'So we're agreed? No one says anything,' Sabah said.

Everyone nodded.

'We could all get suspended,' I burst out.

No one spoke. I saw a glance pass between Sabah and Noor and an almost imperceptible nod as Noor took over.

'Not if we stick together,' Noor said, gripping my arm.

'I don't know, she sounded pretty serious,' I said, looking around the group for some support. None came.

'Banerjee loves issuing warnings,' Sabah said, echoing Noor's words from earlier. 'You think she'd *dare* suspend any of us?'

I didn't say anything. I didn't have rich and powerful parents waiting in the wings to come to my defence. I wasn't untouchable like them.

'Alia's *obviously* not going to say anything,' Noor said, her hold on me tightening as she turned to me for confirmation.

I swallowed, feeling myself cave. Without Noor, I would go back to being a nobody and we both knew it.

'Obviously,' I said.

I almost convinced myself. But as the week wore on and Banerjee piled on the pressure, my panic grew. These kids could risk anything, I couldn't. A suspension would mean I'd lose the financial aid I relied on to go to Wescott. It would make getting a scholarship to go to a good university impossible. It would cause so much pain to my grandparents who had done nothing but support me.

And a comprehensive in London was all well and good, but going to a state school in India would be the end of my prospects.

It would seal my fate as a nobody.

I didn't even dare think about what my parents would say.

We all knew it had been Yash and his cousin, Tanmay, who climbed into the stairwell and lit the match. In the end, I did the only thing I could. I wrote an anonymous note and slipped it under the headmistress's door before classes started on Friday.

Both boys and their parents were called in to the headmistress's office after school the following Monday.

'I can't believe someone grassed on them,' Noor said.

We were gathered in the school's car park waiting to find out what had happened. The buses had long gone and other than the handful of drivers waiting to take their charges home, we were the only ones there.

'I wonder who it was,' Sabah said, looking at me. She leaned into Vineet as he draped an arm around her waist.

'Yeah,' I said, 'it's a pretty shitty thing to do considering we were all involved.'

'I just saw them,' Addi said, panting as she joined us. 'Tanmay said Banerjee was threatening expulsion, but Yash's father offered to pay for a new indoor swimming pool. They've been let off with a week's suspension. Off the record.'

'Well played,' Vineet grinned. 'Nothing like a wad of cash to set things straight. Do you need a lift home, babe?' he asked Sabah, pulling her close.

I saw something flicker across Noor's face briefly before she rolled her eyes and turned to me, her finger looped around the gold pendant necklace she always had on. 'Told you it would be fine,' she said. 'My place?'

SABAH

I nip into the house under the pretext of using the loo before the long drive back. Almost automatically, my feet find their way up the stairs and along the corridor until I'm standing in front of Noor's room. Even though I know what to expect, a gasp works its way out of me as I push the door open. Though most of the old furniture is still there, the room has been stripped of anything even remotely reminiscent of Noor. It occurs to me that in keeping my room exactly as I left it, my mother was holding on to some invisible thread of hope that one day I might return. There was no such hope for Fatima Aunty to hold on to.

My legs gravitate towards the window seat that Noor and I had spent hours cuddled up on as little girls, our tiny legs tangled together as we whispered secrets. As we'd grown, the space, too small to fit us both, had taken on a different significance. I lift the cushion and run my hands across the wooden panelling, feeling the bumps and grooves under the fresh paint until my fingers find what they're searching for. I run a finger along the plank on the far right and slip my nail under the edge. I ease it upwards, revealing a small cavity in the woodwork. The ingenuously titled Hiding Place, where Noor stored everything from Valentine's cards and miniature bottles of alcohol to her diaries.

I know it's a long shot but I plunge my hand through the opening anyway, stretching my fingers to feel along the inside, the wood rough against my skin. It doesn't take me long to realize there's nothing there. I'm about to pull my hand out when my finger brushes against something, a piece of metal wedged in the small gap between the wooden panelling and the wall. I curl my fingers around it and tug it out.

It's a pendant necklace. A gold sparrow hanging off a flimsy chain that has turned reddish with age. One of Noor's favourites.

A few days after the funeral, Javed Uncle had asked me to come over to help him clear out Noor's stuff but my parents had thought it morbid, the idea of clearing out my dead best friend's room or, worse, keeping something of hers for myself. I slip the necklace on and tuck it underneath my top. A talisman.

Standing in front of the mirror in the hotel toilets, I take a moment to compose myself. I take a deep breath. Pull my shoulders back. I undo a button on my top, check my reflection, spot the curve of Noor's pendant resting against my chest, do it up again.

It is ridiculous that I'm nervous about seeing him, that despite what he did, I still *care*.

I feel that old niggle of resentment rise up my throat and I push it back down.

I'm the one lying now.

I cringe as I think of the phone call a few days ago.

'Vineet,' I'd crooned down the phone, my voice silky. 'It's Sabah. I'm in town for a few days and I wondered . . .' I'd paused there, leaving him hanging for a long moment before continuing. 'Well, I wondered if you wanted to meet up. Coffee, maybe?'

It was a cheap trick, but it worked.

He'd suggested lunch, probably so he could avoid any awkward questions from his wife. That's what savvy men do – have the illicit meetings over lunch and play the doting husbands over dinner. I should know.

I run a hand through my hair as the hostess at La Piazza leads me towards a table at the back. I resist the urge to flinch as I spot the man who looks only slightly like the boy I'd swooned over as a teenager.

'Sabah,' Vineet says, getting up. 'My God, it's nice to see you again.'

He's wearing a suit. Anonymous, black, boring. His tie is askew, the top button of the predictably blue shirt undone.

I feel my spine lengthen as I look over the menu.

I steal glances at him as we order, taking in the receding hairline, the slight hint of a belly, the heavy gold wedding band. I cover up the slight shudder with a laugh as he tells me about his kids.

After twenty minutes of bedtime rituals and cartoon

characters, I work the conversation around to Noor. Vineet's face pales over his carbonara.

'Why are you bringing this up now?' he says, motioning for the waiter to bring us more wine.

'I guess I'm just curious. We never really spoke after that night.'

'*You* never spoke. I called you nearly every day for weeks afterwards. I even turned up at your house to try and talk to you.'

I nod. I try to explain how quickly things had escalated at home. My parents had practically shuttered me in, I tell him. He doesn't sympathize.

'You could have called, emailed. You just disappeared. I didn't even know you'd moved to London until two months after you'd gone.'

'I'm sorry,' I sigh. 'I'm just wondering, you were the last person to see her. You were with her hours, if not minutes before. What happened? Did you go inside with her?'

Something passes over his face, a hostility that I'd forgotten he was capable of.

'*What happened?*' He sets his fork down with a clang. 'Do I need to remind you why I had to take her home? Fucking hell! After what you did to her . . .' Every word feels like an assault and I shrink back, my whole body clenching in retaliation. He must see what it's doing to me, because he stops. His face softens. 'She was messed up, Sabah. She could barely walk straight. I had to stop the car twice so she could throw up. But she seemed fine after I gave her some water. She told me she'd call me the next day. I dropped her off and I went home. If I'd known what she was about to do . . .' He shakes his head. Smiles as if the whole thing was nothing more than an embarrassing but harmless teenage indiscretion. 'Anyway, why am I talking about all this when I'm sitting next to Hollywood's finest? Tell me, what are you working on next, or is it a big secret?'

His words fall into a silence as I take a slow sip of my water. I look at him across the table, waiting for it to hit home. I'd debated it for days before finally concluding the only way I'd be able to have this conversation with Vineet was under false pretences. After news of Noor's suicide broke, I had been heartbroken but Vineet had been persecuted. Even though, or perhaps because there was no official investigation, Vineet had become the focus of suspicion and intense public outrage. The country needed someone to blame and as the spoilt son of a property magnate, he made for the ideal suspect. He'd spent years battling the media, his lawyers throwing out injunction after injunction. Being upfront with him would mean throwing away any chance of a conversation and even if I couldn't interview him for the documentary, I needed to see him, to hear him talk about that night so I could lay my suspicions to rest.

'Oh, you've got to be kidding me,' he says, when realization finally dawns. He throws a wad of cash on the table, acting as if my little trick can even come close to what he did all those years ago. As he jerks his seat back, I am reminded of the boy I knew, full of teenage bravado and cockiness, traits that feel repulsive in a thirty-one-year-old man.

'I'd forgotten what a manipulative bitch you are,' he says before stalking off.

As I sit there alone, finishing my salad, the niggle of doubt I'd felt earlier reappears, only this time I'm not thinking about my duplicity.

I'm thinking about his.

ALIA

Fifteen years ago

Nothing happened for about two weeks. We had the midterms coming up and I spent most afternoons studying or helping Noor with her pitch for the Head Girl interview. Yash and Tanmay served their time and came back to school cockier than ever. It seemed as if the entire thing had just blown over.

We were in the cafeteria cramming for the Maths exam that afternoon when Sabah strode in.

'You bitch,' she hissed, leaning over the table to look at Noor.

'Sabah, I –'

I looked at Noor as she stood up, confused at this sudden escalation of the cold war that had been waging for weeks. 'What's going on?'

'You keep out of it,' Sabah spat at me before turning to Noor, tears brimming in her eyes. 'How could you? Of all the things you've done to me . . . you're supposed to be my best friend.'

'Sabah, just let me explain, please.'

'Go on then,' Sabah stood back, arms crossed in front of her. 'Explain.'

'It happened only once. We were drunk and stupid. We were talking about you—'

'Is that meant to make me feel better?' Sabah interrupted, her voice rising above the din of the cafeteria. 'That you were talking about me while you were making out with my boyfriend.'

A bomb going off in the middle of the school would have caused less disruption. Heads turned as the entire year eleven student body turned to look at us.

Well, to look at Noor.

From the corner of my eye, I noticed another disruption. Vineet was pushing his way through the cafeteria towards us.

Noor stepped closer to Sabah and held her lightly by her shoulders. 'I'm so, *so* sorry, Sabah. It was a mistake. You have to believe me, I never meant to hurt you.'

'I don't have to believe anything.' Sabah pushed her away. 'Was it not enough to screw every senior in school? You had to go after my boyfriend.'

'It wasn't like that—'

'Sabah, it's not her fault,' Vineet jumped in. 'We—'

'We?' Sabah shrieked. 'I'm done with you. Both of you.'

'Do you want to talk about it?' I asked Noor after Sabah stormed off with Vineet chasing after her, making heads turn the other way.

'There's nothing to talk about,' Noor said, sitting down and flicking through her book.

'Those rumours in the summer,' I said, only just working it out. 'You were the one Vineet was seeing?'

She sighed. 'We were just hanging out as friends to begin with . . . but then . . . It was a mistake.'

'What about Sameer?'

'He has his uses, but I don't like him like that.'

I nodded, not sure how to respond to that. I thought of the pimpled boy who had acted as Noor's personal porter the entire time we were in Oxford. He had had his uses too.

'You think I'm a bitch,' she said, mistaking my silence for judgement. 'Go on, you can say it.'

'No, of course not,' I said, though of course I was judging her. Best friend's boyfriend . . . who could resist the high horse when it came to something that scandalous and that cliché? 'But I don't understand. Why him? You can have literally anyone you want.'

'Clearly, I can't,' she scoffed. 'Look, if I hadn't been so drunk, I wouldn't have let myself act on it. I would never do anything to hurt my friends . . . you know that, right?'

'Yeah,' I said, picking up my pen and absent-mindedly scribbling an equation into my notebook. 'Wait – what do you mean act on it? Do you, like, *like* him?'

'*No.*' Noor made a face. 'I have standards.'

We had PE after the exam and the whole class emptied out quickly, relieved at the prospect of an afternoon of mindless laps and long jumps after three hours spent battling advanced trigonometry.

I laid my gym kit out on the bench. I had mastered the art of changing in a busy locker room without revealing more than an inch of skin than was necessary years ago. I pulled on my leggings underneath my skirt, and then started the somewhat more complicated dance of swapping my button-down school shirt for a vest top.

I was lacing up my trainers when Noor burst in. She had been summoned to the headmistress's office right after the Maths exam, presumably about the Head Girl interviews.

'How'd it go?' I asked her, but she walked right past me to where Sabah was standing, surrounded by her usual posse. I followed her. The group parted to let Noor in and I caught a glimpse of Sabah standing there in nothing but a silky white bra and matching knickers. Spotless. Pristine.

'You think you can just throw me under the bus?' Noor yelled.

'I did no such thing.'

'You told Banerjee I brought the fireworks to school!'

Sabah smirked but said nothing. She busied herself with pulling on her light pink leggings.

'She's already taken me off the Head Girl shortlist,' Noor continued. 'And she's talking about a suspension.'

Sabah made a show of twisting the drawstring on her leggings into a neat little bow.

'Come on, Sabah, it was one kiss and I apologized.' Noor sighed. 'This is serious. You know what Abbu's going to do.'

Sabah turned to face the locker as she unhooked her bra. She took her time changing into her sports bra and vest. It felt like a piece of theatre, the showdown between the wife and the mistress, while the audience waited, hearts thumping, to see who would come out the winner.

'Sabah!' Noor yelled when the silence had become excru-ciating, even for the rest of us.

Sabah turned around slowly. 'You're right,' she said, her voice pragmatic, measured. 'This is serious.'

I felt myself relax a little, relieved to hear something, anything other than Noor's panicked voice.

'If you think you can make out with my boyfriend and I won't do anything, it's *really* serious.' She took a step towards Noor and slanted her head to one side, her profile lit up by the beam of sunlight leaking in through the skylight. A modern-day Medusa. 'A kiss might not matter to someone like *you*, but it means something to me.' She slammed her locker shut. 'You had it coming.'

'Fine,' Noor said. She took a step back. 'Fine,' she repeated with an overtly casual shrug. A slow smile was spreading across her face 'If this is how you want to play it, from now on, all bets are off.'

Noor spun around and marched away from the group before Sabah had the chance to respond, leaving all of us staring at her open-mouthed.

She was halfway across the room when she paused. 'Oh, and FYI,' she called out, without bothering to turn, 'it wasn't just the one time, and it definitely wasn't just a kiss.'

SABAH

The lamp casts a spotlight across my desk as I work through the case from the beginning. I wade through pages and pages of archived articles, news clippings and interview transcripts, pulling out the most relevant extracts and pinning them up on the corkboard in front of me, mapping out the sequence of events. The box of family photos and videos that Faraz sent over is sitting on the floor ready for me to unpack but I am too wired to be able to focus on that particular task.

I'd expected a certain amount of hostility from Vineet, but it's the slipperiness of his reaction that is bothering me. He had looked stricken, panicked almost when I asked him about that night, but then laughed it off a minute later. And then there was the detail about the bottle of water and the fact that Noor told him she'd call him the next day. After everything that had happened, why would she say that?

I push my chair back and stand up, a thought forming in my head. Every teenage girl has a secret life, but I'd always believed that Noor's secrets and mine were knotted together inextricably just like our histories. We had been inseparable, spending hours analyzing every little crush, dissecting every conversation, poring over every tiny thing that happened in our overly dramatic lives. I thought I knew her better than I knew myself and yet I hadn't seen it coming. Not the kiss with Vineet, not the stuff with Alia, none of it.

And if I had missed that, what else had I missed?

I set my plate on the kitchen counter and slide the phone towards me.

I draw my face into a smile. 'Jenny. Hi.'

'I wanted to touch base and see how you were doing.' She sounds a bit breathless and I am reminded of how young she is. Young and overeager.

'I'm fine,' I say, trying to keep the exasperation out of my voice. Jenny had insisted on doing a full risk assessment before the trip, as if I was heading out into a war zone, not my childhood home. Though perhaps going to a war zone would have been easier than my lunch with Vineet had been. I think about the next interview on my schedule and my shoulders stiffen.

'Amazing. You had the ex-boyfriend yesterday, didn't you? How did that go?'

I flinch at the categorization.

'Good. The interviews are coming along well.'

'Are you able to send me a copy of your notes? Just something to give us a bit of flavour over here,' she says, adding, 'You know how Andrew likes to be kept informed.'

Her nervous giggle hops and skips across continents to irritate me.

'I'd rather wait till I've completed all the interviews. I don't want to lead you all down a path I don't end up pursuing,' I say, knowing full well how much that will annoy her. The path had been set, as evidenced by the corset-tight schedule she'd put together for me.

There is a long pause as Jenny comes up with a response.

'Um, sure, okay,' she says, finally. 'So I can see the next interview is scheduled for tomorrow afternoon. Would you mind dropping me a text afterwards, let me know how it goes?'

I'd mind very much.

I glance at the clock. It's just past eight but if I leave now, I might make it.

'Sabah?' Jenny's voice crackles in my ear.

I slide my uneaten dinner into the bin.

'Actually, Jenny, there's been a change of plans. I'm heading out for an interview just now, but I do need to speak to Dan before I go. Can you put him on?' I speak quickly, leaving no room for her to interrupt.

There is a short pause while Jenny tries to figure out whether or not it's worth telling me off for meddling with her schedule. She must decide to let it slip because I hear a few short beeps and then Dan's voice hollers down the phone.

'Sabah! How's it going?'

I smile. I've always liked Dan. Not only is he one of the best archive producers I know, he's a genuinely nice guy and one of my few friends at the company. I spend a few minutes complaining to him about Jenny before I get to the point.

'And there I was, thinking you'd rung to hear my dulcet tones,' Dan says before going on to explain that he's sent requests out to all the big archive agencies for the footage I'd asked for. 'I should have the clip log ready for you in a couple of days.'

'Great.'

'I've got to be honest, though,' he says, 'I'm not having much luck with the Delhi police. I've filed the right to information request but they just keep bouncing me around. I'll try ringing them first thing tomorrow, but I think you might have to sort this one out on the ground.'

I groan. I should have expected this really. 'It's just classic Indian bureaucracy at play. I'll probably have to hound them down physically before they release the files.'

He laughs down the phone. 'Okay, I'll let you go do your thing. Let me know how it goes.'

'Dan?'

'Yeah?'

'Did you say you were good with computers?'

'Not as good as I am with the ladies but I know my way about.'

'Oh, fuck off,' I say, smiling.

'What do you need?' he says, his tone serious, reminding me that he's one of the most strong-nosed researchers I know. Even though it was outside his remit as archive producer, he'd spent weeks tracking down old suspects' information for the Harriet Clarke documentary. More than that, I know I can't do this alone and I trust him.

'Depends,' I say. I take a breath. 'Can you keep a secret?'

ALIA

The room is packed, heaving with overexcited volunteers and party members, thrilled at the prospect of being in the same room as so many senior MPs, chests swollen with pride over the fact that they've been invited to the annual conference. It's all a big song and dance, a show we put on to get the volunteers energized before an election, passing on irrelevant titbits of information here and there, letting them believe they're privy to the party's campaign policy while holding the real strategy close to the chest, to be revealed at the most opportune time to just the right person.

I feel a flicker of irritation as I move through the crowd. Arjun was supposed to accompany me tonight, but he cancelled at the last minute without so much as an explanation, though if I were to guess, I'd say it had something to do with the photos of the dinner with John that had turned up online. There had been a minor scandal when Arjun won the tender for supplying solar panels to the Commonwealth Games Village in 2009 – his first big break. Even though I was a newly elected junior minister at the time, and Arjun and I hadn't been married then, our relationship had irked his competitors and the entire project had been clouded by rumours of political corruption. Entirely unsubstantiated claims, which disappeared as soon as they had emerged, but just the whiff of a scandal was enough to damage a young company. It had taken years for Arjun to repair the damage. Over the past few weeks, some of those rumours had started cropping up again, courtesy, no doubt, of Saeed, and once again it had put Arjun on edge.

I spot the party president standing at the front of the room, surrounded by a group of reporters, party workers and other MPs. I weave my way through. I'd met with him less than two weeks ago, talking him through the constituency's vote share and reminding him of all the work I'd done over this last term. I'd rattled off statistics – employment, education, crime; the numbers were better than ever before and though the nomination list wasn't due to be publicly released for several weeks, I'd left happy, confident that I'd get the unofficial nod from his office within the next few days. That had been before I made the mistake of supporting Faraz's bid for party presidency. Before I publicly supported the DU rape victim. Before Saeed's son was arrested and the rumours about Faraz dissolving the alliance started doing the rounds.

I am halfway across the room when I notice the woman making her way towards me. As I catch glimpses of her face through the crowd, I feel myself contract. I want to turn away, pretend I haven't seen her, but my legs refuse to move and before I know it, she's there, standing in front of me. Sabah.

The crowd that was irritating me just a few minutes ago seems to disappear as I stare at her, startled to see that fifteen years have not left any mark on her whatsoever. Her face is slimmer, her features sharper but she has none of the fine lines that seem to have cropped up on my face almost overnight. Her hair is just as glossy as it was in school, her eyes still as bright as they were when I first met her.

It seems impossible, but she is as beautiful as ever.

A few moments pass as I try to match the features of the woman in front of me to the girl I once revered, whose actions had dictated my choices over that one short, fateful year.

The memories that I've been keeping boxed away tug at me, demanding to be let out. That year should have been the best one of our lives. It should have been three sixteen-year-old girls falling in love, having their hearts broken, making mistakes and laughing them off.

It should have been three girls having fun.

Instead we lied, we schemed, we cheated.

We hurt and got hurt, and in the end, we ruined each other.

It's been fifteen years since that night. To anyone looking, I have moved on. I have travelled, I have built a life for myself, but in all the ways that matter, I am still there, listening to the fireworks sizzle through the stillness of the Delhi winter. I am still there, breathing, talking, laughing, looking the other way while fifty feet from me my best friend's life spins out of control.

As my eyes finally meet hers, I realize that she is still there too. She nods, slowly, imperceptibly, and even though I have been expecting this encounter, waiting for it almost, I take a step back, startled by the strength of the thing that binds us together.

It hangs between us, like a dead weight, and in an instant, all my worries about Arjun, about the election, about Faraz evaporate. I'm drawn back to what we did.

To her.

To Noor.

ALIA

Fifteen years ago

Noor wasn't suspended – her father's position on the school board made that eventuality impossible – but she did get pulled off the shortlist for the Student Council, which all but guaranteed Sabah's stake on Head Girl.

Even though things seemed to have gone relatively well, Noor was upset. I could sense an outburst coming but I could never have predicted what happened next.

Within a fortnight of the argument, Sabah and Vineet broke up. The halls were abuzz with what had gone on, but with both Vineet and Sabah refusing to talk about it, we were all left to speculate. Half the school thought Noor and Vineet were secretly dating, the other half thought he was still hankering after Sabah and using Noor to make her jealous.

'Sabah's so frigid, can you blame him?' Addi spoke into the phone. 'To be honest, I was surprised when Vineet and Sabah got together in the first place. She's way too much of a goody-goody for him.'

'That's not what I've heard,' I say, thinking back to one of my midnight conversations with Noor.

'What do you mean?'

'Oh, nothing. I guess I just don't get what the appeal is? He's cute but there's something about him that gives me the creeps.'

'You say that about pretty much every guy in school,' Addi laughed. 'Anyway, I'm staying out of it. At this rate, one of them is going to self-destruct.'

With Sabah out of the equation and Addi and Saloni hedging their bets, I planted myself firmly by Noor's side.

Bit by bit I moulded myself, adapting my personality to fit around Noor, to be who she needed me to be, not quite Noor but an almost perfect mirror image, the eager-to-please understudy. I spent most afternoons and all weekends at her house, preferring the chaos and drama of her world to the emptiness of mine. I had been lonely for so long that my friendship with Noor and the position it bought me within her family became my anchor and my lifeline. It was a friendship that swallowed me, that made the days so busy, our secret world so consuming, there was little room for anything else to exist.

It was a friendship that helped me forget who I was and focus on who I could be.

But it was a friendship that wasn't without its secrets. Noor was skittish, irritable. She'd be her usual, chirpy self one day, and withdrawn and restless the next. There were moments when I could see her retreating into herself, her face vacant. She stopped sketching altogether. She spent ages on her phone, but every time I asked her who she was texting, she clammed up.

I could sense that something had happened with her parents. I could feel it every time I went over to her place. Her parents were gracious towards me, but their dynamic with Noor had changed. There was a wariness there, which I hadn't noticed before, and the intimacy that had made me feel jealous earlier seemed to have disappeared altogether. More than once, they asked if Sabah would be joining us, which of course only got Noor's back up and made me even more desperate to take Sabah's place.

Noor's mood swings got more extreme but I never forced her to tell me what was going on. I trusted that she knew what she was doing, and my job as her best friend was to help her get away with it. And with the two-week winter break fast approaching, there were opportunities aplenty.

'There's a crafts fair on at Ansal Plaza. Should we go for that and then head to the bowling alley?'

'A film, bowling, a trip to the museum,' Noor said, mimicking me. 'It's the last day before the holidays, for fuck's sake. Can you at least try to be interesting?'

I tried not to let her words get to me. Sometimes best friends were mean to each other. Everyone knew that.

'What do you want to do then?'

'I don't know,' she moaned. 'I am so sick of this.'

She picked up her phone and started texting. I sat silently, trying to read her face as the texts went back and forth. I stared at her, convinced that she was secretly chatting with Sabah, moaning about how boring I was, both of them biding their time before announcing to me that this whole year, my friendship with Noor, it had all been nothing but an elaborate ploy, something to keep them both entertained before they went back to being best friends. I tried to shake some self-respect into myself.

'We're going out,' Noor said, finally looking up from her phone. She looked me over, sizing up the outfit I had squeezed myself into that morning. 'You need to change.'

'Wait here. We'll be a few hours,' Noor said to her driver as we climbed out of the car.

I followed Noor into the restaurant and back out the other side, a trick that no longer surprised me.

'Taxi,' she yelled out, hailing a cab as she slipped off her *hijab* and pulled her skirt up a few inches. 'Ready?' she asked, flashing me a quick smile.

The taxi slowed as it turned into the narrow lane and bumped along next to overstuffed rickshaws and bikes. The party was at a farmhouse in Sainik Farms, Delhi's poshest neighbourhood built entirely on illegal farmland. I'd been to the country club there with Noor's family once before. Noor, Fatima Aunty and I had spent the evening sitting by the pool and munching down *paneer pakoras* and French fries while Faraz and Javed Uncle met with a group of men in the library. There was something odd about the place and when I mentioned it on the drive back, Javed Uncle had laughed, impressed with my obser-vational prowess. Because the neighbourhood, spread over several hectares, was home to some of the country's most influential politicians, bureaucrats and businessmen it had never been demolished, but the government drew the line on providing infrastructure and utilities to an entirely unregulated area. The result was a neighbourhood that felt at once excessive and unkempt. Poorly lit dirt tracks led to sprawling farmhouses with in-house cinemas and swimming pools, BMWs jostled for space alongside battered bicycles, there were fridges full of champagne and expensive wine but chauffeurs had to be sent out on twenty-minute milk runs before tea could be served. The overall effect was illicit, tantalizing, and deliciously dangerous.

Here was a neighbourhood that existed outside the normal laws.

The taxi slowed down as we approached our destination. The driveway was packed with cars. Music and laughter spilled out of the building, the party in full swing though it was still early.

'Fifty rupees, madam,' the taxi driver said, looking at us in the rear-view mirror.

I placed my bag on my lap, protecting myself from his prying eyes while Noor counted the cash out.

'Want me to wait?' he asked her in Hindi and Noor shook her head.

'How will we get back? There aren't any taxis here,' I said as we slid out of the car.

'We'll get someone to drop us or something. Relax, will you?' she said, walking up the short set of steps and heading straight in.

'Come on,' Noor said, impatiently. She twisted to grab

my hand and I let her pull me through the tightly packed room towards the back of the house.

I'd been to plenty of parties with Noor, but this felt different. The room was thick with smoke, giving everything a haziness that made it seem ethereal. Music pulsed through the floor and sent shivers up my entire body. Across from us, a couple was pressed up against the wall, arms draped around each other as they kissed. In the corner, two girls in barely there dresses were perched on the pool table, slim legs dangling as boys circled them, making suggestive jokes as they attempted to manoeuvre their cues around them.

'You made it,' Sameer yelled over the music as he broke away from a group of boys to hug us. He twirled a lock of Noor's hair around his finger as he took in her appearance, his eyes lingering on her cleavage. 'You haven't brought your crazy brother with you, right?'

Noor flashed one of her dazzling smiles. 'Nope, he's in even more trouble than I am,' she said.

Faraz had got into a fight at his university last week, something to do with another student calling him a Muslim terrorist. His anger was entirely justifiable; the damage he did to that boy's face, and to his own prospects in the Student Union election, not so much. It had worked out well for Noor, though. Her parents were so angry with their son, they had little energy left to deal with their daughter's comparatively minor transgressions.

'This way,' Sameer said, pointing to the double doors leading out into the garden.

Noor and I followed in his slipstream as he hustled

through the crowd and led us to a small table on the decked patio. He lit up a joint and passed it to Noor before heading back inside to get us some drinks.

He returned a few minutes later with a stocky boy in a sweat-drenched T-shirt and baggy jeans in tow.

'Here you go,' Sameer said, setting down two frothy glasses in front of Noor and me. He pulled his chair close to Noor's and slipped an arm around her shoulders. 'This is Karan,' he continued, introducing us to his friend. 'I told him you wanted to party.'

'That's why we're here,' Noor said in a voice that sounded unnaturally chirpy.

We had barely picked up our drinks when Karan produced a little plastic bag from his pocket. I looked at Noor, shocked at this sudden turn of events.

Sameer and Noor leaned in as he shook out four tiny white pills and pressed one each into their hands.

'Alia?' Karan asked, laying one sweaty palm on my thigh. I brushed it away.

I wasn't naive. I knew Noor smoked weed sometimes and that there were drugs at nearly all the Wescott parties. I had seen groups of people disappearing into the bathroom enough times to work out what they were doing but up until that moment I hadn't allowed myself to consider the possibility that Noor was one of them.

'Oh no, not for her,' Noor said. 'Alia's a good girl.' She was smiling, which only made the words feel sharper.

I took the pill from Karan's outstretched palm.

'What is it?' I asked no one in particular.

'E,' Karan said. 'I mean, ecstasy.'

'I know what E is,' I bit back.

'Only if you want to,' Sameer said.

Noor nodded. 'It's totally up to you.'

'I'm not—' I started.

'But no party poopers allowed,' she winked, cutting me off. I watched as she opened her mouth and placed the pill on the tip of her tongue.

I understood then that it had all been a test, the mood swings, the parties and now the drugs – she was testing me, trying to see how far I would go to hold on to my spot as her best friend. The answer was as far as it took.

I took a big gulp of that lovely sugary drink and then did exactly as she had done.

We had reached that point in the night when the room felt overcrowded rather than bustling, when the smoke in the air felt suffocating rather than decadent. Every time I blinked, the room shifted, every detail simultaneously pin-sharp and disorientating. Noor and I were dancing, arms thrown around each other as 'Mr Brightside' played in the background.

'I feel sick. I need the bathroom,' I spoke into Noor's ear.

'I'll come with you,' she said.

I shook my head. 'I'll be fine. Back in a sec.'

I untangled myself and headed into the hall but the bathroom was occupied. The couple from the deck had decided to move things up a notch.

I wandered through the maze of rooms looking for

another bathroom. By the time I found one and then went back to the party, Noor was nowhere to be seen. I tried not to panic as I went from room to room looking for her. She was not dancing in the centre of the room, not bent over the pool table insisting she knew how to play, not even outside smoking and laughing with the boys.

I marched over to Karan. He was sitting at the same table as earlier with a group of boys I vaguely recognized from school.

'Where is she?' I asked, my tone accusatory.

He didn't say anything, just wiggled his eyebrows as he tried to pull me onto his lap.

'Get your hands off me.' My scream was met with a burst of rowdy laughter and whistling. I pushed him off and walked away, searching instead for Sameer.

I found them in an upstairs bedroom.

'There you—' I started, relieved to have found her until I realized what I was looking at.

Noor was passed out on the bed, her skirt hiked up all the way to her hips, lacy pink knickers exposed. Sameer was crouched on the floor, bent over the bedside table.

The surge of anger that rushed through me left me startled. If I hadn't been so terrified, I could have killed Sameer.

'What the hell are you doing?'

Sameer turned around, revealing two thin lines of white powder on the table. 'Want to join in?' he slurred.

'Noor,' I said, walking over to her.

She mumbled something incoherent before closing her eyes again.

I yanked her skirt down and pulled her into a sitting position. Her eyes snapped open with the sudden movement. 'Alia, I don't – I don't feel good.'

'I know, I'm here now,' I said, helping her up. 'Let's get you home.'

Outside, the driveway was packed with cars but I couldn't find a single person willing to give us a lift home. I couldn't blame them. One look at Noor would be enough for even Mother Teresa to back off.

I sat down on the porch and tried to get my brain to work. It would be impossible attempting to hail a taxi outside, but maybe I could call for one. I rummaged through Noor's bag and pulled out her phone, trying to remember the number for directory services.

I shrank away from Noor as two girls in high heels swayed towards her. One of them crouched down and peered at Noor, laughing as she said something to her friend before disappearing inside.

'Are you okay?'

I turned to see an older boy leaning against the door frame smoking.

'Yes, I –' I said. 'No, actually. I need to get my friend home. Do you know if there are any taxi companies here that I could call?'

He looked at Noor and then at me. 'That might not be the best idea,' he said, not unkindly. 'Isn't there someone you can call?'

He was right, I thought, remembering the way the taxi

driver had leered at us on our way to the party. I ran through the options in my head as I scrolled through the contact list on Noor's phone. I could call my granddad, of course, but I couldn't bear for him to see me like this. Noor's parents were out of the question as well. I lingered on Faraz's name, but I was scared to think how he might react when he found out that we had been here with Sameer, when he found out what I'd seen in that bedroom. There was only one option, really. As much as I resented her, when it came to Noor, I knew that she was the only one I could trust. I scrolled further until I saw Sabah's name and pressed call.

SABAH

I'm the one who breaks the silence.

'It's nice to see you,' I say, giving Alia an awkward half-hug.

I look her over. Even in her politician's *sari*, she's an haute couture, high-end version of the scholarship kid I'd known in school. Her face has the sheen that can only come from regular facials and expensive skin creams, diamond solitaires twinkle in her ears, and her hair, though worn simply down her back, has subtle highlights that catch the light as she moves. And then there is the ring on her finger. A glittering, two-carat statement in itself.

If life has treated someone well, it is Alia Sharma. Though judging by how quickly and completely she had ingrained herself into Noor's life and later the Qureshi family's, this transformation isn't down to pure luck or hard work. This is a modern-day Cinderella and she's anything but innocent.

We end up in the hotel's coffee shop.

'So, how are you?' Alia says, settling back into the chair, the nervousness I'd noticed earlier replaced by an easy smile. The practised politician. I play along as we slip into the usual niceties, acting as though this unplanned visit is nothing out of the ordinary. We skip over the fact that there is a conference next door where she is probably required and as she asks me about my work and my life in London, I find myself pulled in, unable to resist. I'd vote for her, I think at one point and I have to remind myself that her charm is entirely manufactured, designed to hide the crude social climber lurking underneath.

I realize that I've spent the past hour answering questions instead of asking them and I switch gears. I repeat the pitch I'd sent to her office, going over the timeline and expected release date.

Alia nods, a slight frown punctuating her features. 'Who else is involved?'

'The Qureshis are on board,' I say and she nods. 'I'm also planning to interview Saloni, Addi, Yash, Niv and a few of the teachers from school.'

Something crosses her face at the mention of Niv but she doesn't press for details and I don't offer any. I pull out my notebook and skip ahead to the reason I'm sitting across from her. Noor had already been drunk by the time I saw her that night, but Alia had spent the entire afternoon with her.

'How did she seem that day before the party? Did you notice anything strange?' I ask.

A memory arrives. Me, earlier that day, telling Alia to go to Noor. Telling her exactly what to do.

'She was upset. Tetchy,' Alia says. 'I guess, after everything that had happened, it was understandable.'

'Did she say or do anything out of the ordinary?'

I can see that she's waiting for me to say more, to explain why fifteen years after I used her to get to Noor, I'm asking her to explain how it played out. I consider telling her the truth but the words dry up in my mouth.

I don't need anyone to tell me how much of this is driven by my own guilt, how my desperation to find someone to blame is really just a way to come to terms with what I did all those years ago.

What I made Alia do.

Alia closes her eyes for a long moment. When she finally looks at me, I can see the tears shimmering in her eyes. It strikes me that despite how I feel about her unscrupulous path to the top, I can't fault her when it comes to Noor. She worshipped the ground Noor walked on. That was a large part of why I could never stand her, why I took every opportunity I could find to belittle her. 'She took ages getting ready. She had no idea what we had planned. She thought –' Alia says, her voice breaking at the mention of our betrayal. 'She wanted to go to that party, Sabah.'

My voice, when I finally get it to work, is barely a croak. 'Why?'

'She wanted to see you.'

ALIA

Fifteen years ago

'How could you be so stupid?' Sabah asked, jumping out of the car and going straight to Noor.

'Noor,' she said, sitting down next to her. 'Noor, wake up. What did she take?' Sabah asked me.

'She smoked a joint, and then there were some pills. Ecstasy. She was fine. I went to the bathroom and when I came back, she was gone. Maybe she did some coke. I don't know.' I was blabbering. Now that Sabah was here, calm, controlled Sabah, it was as if I could finally allow myself to feel scared.

'Alia, get a grip,' Sabah said, without turning to look at me. She pulled out a bottle from her bag and splashed some water on Noor's face. 'Can you hold her hair back?'

I crouched down behind Noor while Sabah forced her mouth open. Their touching was thoughtless in a way that I couldn't understand and yet desperately craved.

'I need you to puke now, okay, Noor?' Sabah said, slapping her lightly. 'Can you do that?'

Noor nodded and let Sabah stick a finger down her throat.

★

I pushed my seat back and closed my eyes, listening as Sabah called Noor's parents from the car and explained that Noor and I were at her house and that we were just going to stay there seeing how late it was. There was a practised ease to Sabah's actions that unnerved me despite my own sorry state.

'Of course not, Uncle,' she spoke into the phone. 'Honestly. I can wake her up if you want?'

She paused to listen to what Noor's father was saying, before adding, 'No, I know. It's nothing like that. She just fell asleep watching a film . . . you know how she is. Alia's here as well.'

I twisted to look at her in the back seat. Noor had her head on Sabah's lap and Sabah was stroking her hair while she assured Noor's father that his daughter was fine. I watched Sabah finish that call, then make another one to her own mother to let her know Noor and I would be staying over.

'She does this every now and again. It got really bad last year. That's why her parents sent her away before the school year started,' Sabah said softly after she hung up.

'Sent her away . . .' I said slowly, my brain processing what Sabah was telling me as the memory of Niv threatening Noor on the first day of school reappeared. 'Like, to a rehab centre?'

'Singapore,' Sabah nodded.

I turned around, my eyes fixed on the road ahead. It didn't make sense to me. I knew that Noor thrived on drama but she had *everything*. Why would she risk it all for a few hours of escapism?

'I tried to warn you,' Sabah said. 'She's not all light and sparkle, Alia. There's a darkness inside her that someone like you can never understand.'

I woke up to the sound of Noor and Sabah whispering. It was early, really early, the light filtering through the window milky instead of the warm, orange light I'd come to associate with Delhi winters. I turned on my side, the pull-out bed Sabah and I had made up for me creaking as I moved. I opened my eyes a sliver. I could just about make out Noor and Sabah on the double bed across the room.

'If I'd known you were struggling again, I would've—' Sabah was saying.

'You would've what? You knew. You're the only one who knows what it's really like and you – you just abandoned me. Faraz is being a prick as usual and Abbu's threatening to send me away.'

'I don't think he would—'

'Of course he would. All he cares about is how I make him look,' Noor sighed. 'I didn't have anyone to talk to.'

Noor's words made me flinch. She had *me*.

'I didn't realize things were so bad,' Sabah said. 'You seemed fine . . . and I was angry, but you know I'm always here if you need me. Why didn't you say something?'

'After what I did . . . I just – I'm so sorry, Sabah. I don't know what I was thinking. Our friendship means much more to me than a boy,' Noor said, her voice breaking.

'I'm sorry too. I shouldn't have ratted you out. I was being petty.'

There was a pause in the conversation and I adjusted the duvet, inching closer until I was at the edge.

'Can we just pretend the last six months never happened and go back to being us? I've missed you. Plus, Faraz has started seeing this new girl and we *need* to bitch about her.'

Sabah laughed. 'Tell me everything.'

I listened to Noor babble on about Faraz and his new girlfriend, telling Sabah things she had not even mentioned to me.

It felt as though someone had pulled my heart out of my chest and was squeezing it until there was nothing left.

I closed my eyes and let the sunlight dance on my lids. I tried to count in my head all the things she had told me that Sabah didn't know about.

Less than a handful.

'Say you'll forgive me?' Noor said when she had finished recounting the saga that was Faraz's love life.

'There is nothing to forgive. We're sisters.'

ALIA

It's one a.m. and I'm wide awake. I curl onto my side, the sheets a tangle around my waist, my skin hot and clammy despite the cool November night.

I squeeze my eyes shut and try to will myself back to sleep but my brain draws me back, again and again, to the conversation with Sabah and, of course, to Noor.

For years I have managed to keep Noor boxed away, every thought, every memory folded away in the furthest corner of my brain for those rare moments when I felt strong enough to face her. Thinking about her hurt. A lot. And with no answers forthcoming, the only way I knew to survive was to push her away.

Denial. That's always been my go-to tactic.

But the truth is that these days Noor is never far from my thoughts. I see her every time I watch a teenage girl throw her head back in a delighted ripple of laughter; I hear her every time someone utters the word 'seriously', their tone dripping with sarcasm; I smell her every time I get a whiff of that intoxicating perfume. The same perfume that I'd smelled on Sabah last night.

Arjun thinks it's unhealthy, this fascination with what he assumes is nothing more than a gruesome chapter of my life, so brief it was over even before it started. The way he sees it, the past belongs in bittersweet anecdotes and photo albums that you occasionally stumble on and quickly put away.

I wonder if he would look at things differently if he knew the gory details of what happened back then, if he knew what I did and, more importantly, what I didn't do. I had never intended to lie to him, but I couldn't exactly come out and say it, so I held back, letting him paint his own picture, a composite of the little that I told him and the things that he'd already read in the papers. Somehow, I came out blameless in this version, and that became the baseline of the narrative that I would rely on years later to make my political debut.

Every time I wake in the night, my skin clammy, the sound of those fireworks echoing in my ears, all I want to do is tell him. I picture waking him up and explaining to him why it bothers me so much, why after all these years, the same questions still haunt me, why the guilt sometimes feels so heavy, it seems like it might crush me. But any new account I give him would need to be preceded by a confession and when it comes down to it, I buckle. I keep it to myself, the secret getting heavier every year, and the questions becoming darker as I run through the sequence of events again and again, trying to fill in the blanks and figure out just where I fit into it all.

Trying, more than anything, to find an alternate narrative

that might lessen my guilt, that might help me convince myself that there was nothing I could've done to help her. But my brain argues back. Every single time.

I try to distract myself by thinking about the campaign instead, but Saeed's threats and Faraz's disloyalty eclipse any deliberations of election strategy. I flip onto my side and edge myself closer to my husband.

He turns and drapes an arm around me, murmuring lightly in his sleep, instinctively sensing my need to be held. As he pulls me in, it's all I can do not to bury my face in his neck and tell him everything.

This guilt is mine and mine alone.

Morning arrives eventually. I drag myself out of bed and into the office. Door closed. Steaming cup of coffee in front of me. I try to focus on the draft bill on my desk but my brain keeps deflecting, taking me back to overheard conversations and tightly held secrets, Sabah's calculated words and Noor's nervous laughter.

A knock at the door forces me out of my thoughts.

'I've got the reports that you asked for,' Omar says, placing a file on the desk. I give him a blank look. I can't even remember what it was that I asked him to bring me. 'The shortlist for the sexual harassment committee,' he adds.

I had asked him to get me in-depth profiles for all the women on the shortlist. They're all great candidates, women known for their brilliance and professionalism, but it is their integrity that I care about the most.

As if I'm one to speak.

Show me a woman who has shattered a glass ceiling and I'll show you the ghosts she carries with her.

'I'll look at it this afternoon,' I say, turning back to the Excel sheet in front of me. When I look up a minute later, Omar's still hovering.

'Yes?'

'It's not on the news yet but Saeed's son has been cleared,' Omar says. 'He has an alibi, apparently.'

I raise my eyebrows.

'He was with his parents on the night of the . . . death,' he says, stumbling over the word.

My hand tenses around the handle of the coffee mug, the dark swirl of liquid trembling as my grip tightens.

I look at Omar. Fury looks the same on everyone.

We both know it was murder.

We both know there is nothing more we can do about it.

'The other boys have alibis as well. And since there was no rape kit . . .' He trails off, the meaning behind his silence unmistakable. 'We should expect some backlash from Saeed,' he adds.

The anger and frustration twist into a dark knot in my throat, a roar building inside me. Saeed will turn this into a political play, Divya will be forgotten and her rapists, her *murderers*, will roam free, safe in the knowledge that they are untouchable. It happens every single day and that is the fucking problem.

My face tightens into a mask as I walk out of the office without a word, but underneath it all, my heart is screaming.

SABAH

'Why?' Alia demands, her voice hurtling in before she's even stepped through the door.

There is an odd, frantic energy to her and I move aside to let her in. 'What—'

'Why are you making this documentary now? And don't you *dare* give me that random anniversary bullshit again. You haven't looked back in fifteen years.'

I consider her for a moment. The girl who had transformed herself into a near replica of Noor, who had all but moved in with the Qureshis, who had been nothing but a nuisance to me for the entire time that I had known her. She is without doubt one of the most successful women in the country now, yet there is a sadness about her. I can see the same guilt and shame in her eyes that I have lived with for years. I have not been able to escape the destruction of that night, and as I look at her, I realize that there's been no closure for her either. Noor's death had left us both devastated and, yes, we had both nursed our wounds in entirely different ways, but it occurs to me now that we are both searching for answers to the same question.

Noor had trusted her. Perhaps it's time I did too.

'Come on,' I say, walking quickly up the stairs.

She follows me into my bedroom as I go to my desk and unpin the piece of paper that I've been obsessing over for weeks.

'This was sent to me,' I say, holding it out.

I can see the recognition in Alia's eyes as she catches a glimpse of the handwriting on the page.

Her hand trembles as she reaches for it.

Her eyes skim over the sheet, quickly at first, then back again a second time.

'This is –' She struggles to keep her voice under control.

'A page from her diary, yes.'

She thrusts the paper back at me and takes a step back, tears streaming down her face.

'This is why,' she whispers and I nod, the unspoken words humming between us.

Almost automatically, my gaze is drawn back to the page, Noor's hold on me just as strong even after fifteen years. I reread the words I now know by heart.

and that's what scares me the most. I know I've done some terrible things but I'll fix them. I'll apologize. I'll do whatever it takes to make things right. I'll even start praying, for real. But I don't know if that will be enough. What if the next time I'm not so lucky? What if the next time I shout for help, there's no one there to hear me? I am so scared. I don't want to die. I really, really don't want to die.

Alia's eyes are on me when I look up.

There is so much about Noor's words that doesn't make sense, but then Noor had always loved her secrets and that year, for the first time in years, the keeper of her secrets hadn't been me.

I need to say it, I realize. I need to know that Alia is seeing the same thing as me.

'This means—' I start but Alia beats me to it.

'This means Noor didn't kill herself,' Alia says. 'She was murdered.'

In the beginning, I had been obsessed with finding out what had happened that night. Despite the note, despite what my parents, my therapist and even the police thought, I couldn't bring myself to believe that Noor had committed suicide.

But aside from my own suspicions, I had nothing to go on, not a single piece of evidence that suggested foul play. Nothing to suggest that the gnawing feeling in my stomach wasn't just a manifestation of my own guilt. I pushed it aside, told myself I was being crazy, buried the questions that kept cropping up deep underneath coursework and therapy and the daily slog of living a life that was shadowed with shame.

I promised myself I wouldn't look back.

Until I received that email.

It was one of hundreds in my tips inbox. No subject, no text, just an unknown email address and an attachment. If it hadn't been for the events earlier that day, Andrew's ultimatum and the ever-growing stack of unpaid bills, I would have assumed it was spam and deleted it without a second glance. But that night I was feeling desperate enough for a lead into a story that I clicked on the attachment.

And as Noor's handwriting appeared on my screen and I realized what it meant, that desperate need to uncover the truth reappeared. I had never believed that Noor had killed herself and with that email, I finally had something to back up that feeling.

But I had nothing to go on, except an uneasy feeling that it had something to do with Vineet.

That's when the idea for the documentary began to take shape. It was the perfect excuse to come back and ask questions, to try and close up the holes that appeared every time I ran through a theory in my head. Moreover, it would be enough to keep my job safe.

Alia's voice pulls me out of my thoughts. 'Omar can speak to the commissioner, but it might take a few days. Can you wait?'

I nod. I might have been away for fifteen years, but I haven't forgotten how difficult life in India can be without the right connections. And after a week of trying and failing to get hold of the police files through the official route, it seemed silly not to ask the cabinet minister sitting across from me for help.

'Who do you think sent it?' Alia asks after she's finished the call. We are sitting on my bed, an empty Domino's box between us, reenacting a scene that had played out count-less times before, just without Noor this time.

'It came from an unknown address,' I say, thinking back to my conversation with Dan earlier that day.

'The sender used a VPN so all I can tell you is that it originated in Asia. I can't even pinpoint a country, let alone get you an IP address. Whoever sent this did not want to be found,' he'd said.

'What about—'

'Patience, Khan,' Dan had laughed down the phone, before going on to explain how VPNs work and, more importantly, how Trojan Horses work. He had a plan. I'd drafted a response to the original email and Dan had sent it out along with said Trojan. It was a long shot, but if it worked, he'd be able to trace the exact GPS location from where the email account was accessed.

'So as long as this person,' Alia says now, waving her hand, 'clicks on your email, your friend will be able to trace their exact address?'

'In theory. But it's a long shot. I sent two emails before I even came to India and I haven't had a response.'

Alia lets out a long sigh.

'Even if you find out who sent it, what does that actually tell us?' she says, reading my thoughts. 'I went to help Javed Uncle clear out her room but it was too painful. In the end, his staff went through all her things. Most of it went to charity, I think. Anyone could have found her diary.'

Alia draws her knees up to her chest and wraps her arms around her legs and for a second, I'm reminded of the gullible teenager I'd first met.

'If I'd known she kept a diary . . .' she says, her words laced with regret.

'Noor loved her secrets,' I say. I leave the fact that I had always known about her diaries unsaid.

A small act of kindness to make up for everything else.

'Now what?' Alia says after a few minutes.

'Now we find out what really happened that night.'

ALIA

Omar is pacing in my cabin when I walk in.

'Five of our donors are backing out of their commitments,' he says, before I've even had the chance to sit down.

I close my eyes. 'Saeed. Are any of them salvageable?'

Omar shakes his head. 'There's more. He's been saying that we're embezzling state funds. The nutrition supplements tender. I've had two reporters ring this morning.'

I sigh. I'd advocated for the nutrition supplements scheme to ensure women on low incomes were getting the supplements they needed for free. The supply contracts had gone to a Delhi-based business after the usual tender process. I hadn't realized until months later that the company belonged to an old friend from Cambridge, not that there would have been anything legally wrong with it even if I had known.

'So we open our books,' I say. 'They won't find anything.'

Omar looks at me for a long moment, as though he's weighing up whether or not to be straight be with me.

'We can't do that,' he says finally. 'It doesn't matter whether our books are clean or not, that kind of scrutiny just before an election will scare any remaining donors off. If there is even a whiff of a scandal, we can kiss our funding goodbye.'

'Okay, so what do we do?' I look him square in the eye. More than half of the allegations that get thrown around before an election are false, but that doesn't mean that they aren't damaging.

'What does Saeed want?' Omar responds with his own question. And I know what he's thinking – what can we offer him to kill the rumours? How can we negotiate so that I'm up against just Faraz, so that it's a fair fight?

The biggest currency a politician has is image and I'd ruined his. This isn't about his son anymore, it's about his ego and the only thing that will pacify him is a public apology. But it will also discredit everything I stand for.

'You could rescind your statement,' Omar says, but the conviction with which his words are usually spiked is absent. He knows that rescinding my statement will cost me the female vote.

'Absolutely not.'

'Saeed isn't going to stop and we can't win an election without funding.'

I rub my forehead. I haven't come this far to let a Saeed-sized hiccup get in the way. An image of Noor bent over her sketchbook appears and I blink it away. The solution is an obvious one yet it isn't one I want to immediately reach for. Between Arjun, his parents and his cousins, more than half the donations for my first election had come from the Mehta clan, but that money came with strings attached and

I'd sworn I'd never ask them again. It's easier to owe your career to strangers than to your in-laws.

I glance at the calendar in front of me as an idea begins to take shape. Just because I don't want to take Arjun's money doesn't mean I can't use his connections. After all, he's been using mine for years.

I turn back to Omar. 'How much do we need?'

I'm in the bedroom getting dressed when Arjun walks in.

'You look nice,' he says, dropping a kiss on my shoulder before heading into the bathroom. 'Going out?' he calls out.

I finish pleating and pinning my *sari* before following him in. He's standing in front of the mirror, razor in hand, a white ribbon of shaving cream still outlining his jaw. I feel some of the anxiety from the past few days lift as I watch him shave, the rhythmic movements soothing.

'I thought I'd come along to the industry awards tonight,' I say, leaning against the door frame.

'Are you sure? You don't usually like these things.'

I smile. It's typical of him to offer me a way out, but the five donors that had backed out had taken 60 per cent of the campaign funding with them. My phone calls this afternoon had helped, but I'm still out by 40 per cent. One evening spent socializing with Arjun's contemporaries could solve that.

'I'm sure it can't be that bad.'

He wipes his face clean and turns around to look at me, his eyes serious.

'I've already RSVP'd, though. Maybe next time?' He walks past me into the bedroom and starts getting dressed.

'I hardly think they're going to turn a cabinet minister away,' I say, a hint of desperation leaking into my voice. 'Come on, it'll be fun. Plus, I've barely seen you the past few weeks.'

Arjun doesn't respond, just busies himself with picking out cufflinks.

'Do you not want me to come?' I ask.

'No, of course I want you to –' he starts, then stops talking abruptly, focusing on threading the black and gold studs through his cuffs. The silence stretches on for a few seconds before he breaks it. 'Actually, you're right. I don't think it's a good idea.'

My breath tightens, as the suspicions I'd convinced myself were a result of my own paranoia resurface.

'Why not?' My voice comes out tinny, unstable.

'The Barclays contract is supposed to come in next week and with the rumour-mongers hovering right now, Niv thinks I need to create a bit of distance.'

'A bit of distance from your wife?'

That whips his gaze around. He closes the gap between us in two long strides.

'No,' he says. He grips my shoulders lightly, dark eyes fixed on me. 'That is not what I'm saying.'

It's my turn to stay silent. Truth is, I don't trust myself to speak.

'Come on, sweetheart. You know it's not personal. With the kind of stories that have been doing the rounds, Niv thinks I shouldn't be seen with you at an industry event. With the Barclays deal so close . . . it would be bad PR. You get that, right?'

Right.

ALIA

Fifteen years ago

I should have seen it coming but naive as I was, I believed that even though Noor and Sabah were friends again, nothing would change. The idea that I would be left behind, discarded, cast in my role as the outsider forever, didn't even cross my mind until suddenly, it was all I could think about.

I waited a whole week for Noor to call me back. One whole week of the winter break spent sitting at home, watching the days meld together, my whole existence soundtracked by the melodramatic daytime soap operas Nani liked to watch. One whole week of convincing myself that Noor hadn't called because she needed time to recover after the incident at Sameer's party. One whole week of staring at the phone, waiting, waiting, waiting.

I got sick of waiting.

It was New Year's Eve and Noor and I were supposed to spend it together.

I packed a change of clothes and slung my backpack over my shoulder. I tiptoed down the stairs and put my shoes on, shouting to let Nani know I was leaving when I was already out the door.

An hour-long rickshaw ride later, I was standing at Noor's door, puzzled by the darkened windows and the police car standing on the drive. The maid let me in, telling me to wait in the hall.

I crept towards the stairs, craning my neck to look at the first-floor landing but it was shrouded in blackness. I pulled my sleeves down and wrapped my arms tightly around myself. I had never seen the house so quiet or so dark.

Javed Uncle's voice turned me around.

'Alia?'

He was wearing a rumpled *kurta pyjama* and there was the shadow of stubble outlining his usually clean-shaven jaw. I peered at him, trying to work out if he was sick.

'What are you doing here?' he asked. There were none of the usual pleasantries, no offer of cold coffee or *paneer pakoras*. Behind him, Faraz popped his head out of the living room for a mere second before going back inside and quietly closing the door.

I could feel my muscles tense. Something was very, very wrong.

'I – Where's Noor?'

'She's in Goa with Sabah and her family. I thought you went with them.'

'No, I didn't know.' The words spilled out before I could stop myself. I looked at Javed Uncle but it didn't seem like he had noticed. His attention was seized instead by whatever was going on in the living room.

He kept twisting, turning to look at the closed door, silhouetted around the edges by a sliver of golden light.

'When is she coming back?'

'I don't –' he started. He ran a hand through his hair, threw another glance towards the living room. 'Sunday, I think.'

Sunday: the day before school started.

Also, Sunday: six whole days away.

'Look, why don't I get the driver to take you back home and you can see Noor at school next week?'

'Maybe I could –' I started, but I didn't know what the end to that sentence was. Maybe I could stay here till Noor comes back? Maybe I could spend New Year's Eve with you and your family? Maybe what?

When my own parents couldn't be bothered to spend time with me, why would anyone else?

Something flickered across Javed Uncle's face. It took me a long moment to realise it was pity.

Tinged with a tiny bit of disgust.

I hooked my thumbs around the straps of my backpack and pulled it tighter as Javed Uncle led me out of the house and into a waiting car.

It was only as we were driving past the police car that I realized that I'd been so lost in my own drama that I hadn't even asked him about that.

It wasn't until after the funeral that I realized that if I had to go back and pinpoint the day when everything changed, it would be that day.

Nana and Nani were in the living room watching TV when I got home.

'We've ordered some *chole bhature* from Nirula's,' Nani

said. 'Something special to see the New Year in.' She smiled.

I nodded. I couldn't decide what was worse, the fact that Javed Uncle could see how desperate and lonely I was or that my grandparents couldn't.

'The awards show starts in fifteen minutes,' Nani called out after me as I headed up the stairs.

I went straight to the phone, not even bothering to take my jacket off before dialling the familiar number.

'Hello?' I spoke uncertainly into the phone. They hardly ever answered.

'Yes?' I heard my mother's voice. I tried to tell myself she hadn't recognized me because of all the noise in the background. I could hear the sound of chatter over loud music, ice clinking in glasses, high-pitched laughter. I felt my heart sink. They were having a party.

'Mum?'

'Oh, Alia, it's you. What is it? Are you okay?' The impatience was palpable.

'I'm fine.'

'Where are your grandparents?'

'They're downstairs watching –' I started before changing tack. My mother didn't like prevaricating. 'Mummy, can I come and visit on my birthday? Next week,' I added quickly. I didn't know if she'd remember and I didn't have the courage to find out.

'Alia—'

'Just for a few days,' I pressed on. 'Please?'

The pause seemed to last forever. When my mother spoke, her voice was clipped. 'You have school.'

'Nothing much happens in the first week. And I can bring my books.' I spoke quickly, trying to use my swiftness to win her over.

'Maybe in the summer,' she said, the exasperation evident. She was eager to get back to the party. 'Now you have a nice—'

'Where's Dad?'

I heard her sigh down the phone. 'He's busy, sweetheart,' she said. 'Must go now. Happy New Year!'

My mother didn't like prevaricating. She liked speed.

She hung up before I could say anything.

I went downstairs after a few minutes. I'd seen my parents host dozens of such parties in London and I could practically see it: the dimmed lighting, Dad's record player spinning in the corner, the room crammed with my parents' friends, the über-rich expats, the bourgeois literati, the intellectuals and the diplomats. Even though my parents were just aides to the ambassador, they were ambitious and somehow they managed to surround themselves with the right kind of people – exotic creatures who were as interesting as they were important.

I spent New Year's Eve camped on the sofa with my grandparents, watching Bollywood's version of the Academy Awards and eating *chole bhature*.

When my grandparents asked me if I had thought of a New Year's resolution, I shrugged. I kept my eyes on the TV screen, watching confetti erupt over movie stars and celebrities.

I wanted that kind of power, that success that made the world stop and take notice. And as I climbed into bed later that night, I swore to myself that I would do whatever it took to get it.

Whatever it took.

ALIA

Fifteen years ago

'There you guys are,' I said, hopping over to Noor and Sabah after track practice.

I was still sweaty after the sprints and Sabah scrunched up her nose to remind me. They were sitting on the bleachers, Sabah's back propped up lightly against Noor's leg. There was no awkwardness in their posture; their bodies fit together automatically, folding around each other in another reminder of their long and twisted history.

I ignored her and looked instead at Noor.

It was the first day of school and the first time I'd seen Noor since Sameer's party. It was obvious that Sabah was trying to prise Noor away and I wanted to make sure Noor knew that I was still her friend. Her *best* friend.

'So what's the plan?' I asked Noor. 'I just need to have a quick shower and then I'll be good to go.'

Sabah pretended to study her trainers. She was the least sporty person I knew, but somehow always dressed for PE as though she was competing in the Olympics.

'We were going to go see a film. Sabah's cousin scored tickets to a premiere.'

'Oh right, of course,' I said, the bravado from earlier disappearing. I tried to keep the disappointment from entering my voice. No one likes a killjoy, as my mother liked to remind me often. I gave an ineffectual shrug. I smiled. 'I'll see you tomorrow.'

Sabah laughed, a high tinkle that punctured my bitterness. 'We got you a ticket, silly. Meet us at the gates?'

I hurried to the shower, unsure whether I was more relieved that I had been wrong about Sabah or excited that she was finally letting me in.

The days angled on. Between classes and track practice and gossiping in the cafeteria, I wormed my way back into Noor's and Sabah's lives, believing, really, truly believing, that I was one of them.

I needed this all-consuming friendship to be my real life so badly that I convinced myself it was.

'Isn't it your birthday next week?' Sabah asked, her voice leaking in through the flimsy cubicle. I heard the sound of a zip going up before Sabah yanked the curtain open and stepped out in a tight red dress with a zip all the way down the front. She smoothed the dress down and turned, looking at her profile in the mirror, frowning.

'Maybe with the heels?' Noor said, poking her head out of the adjacent fitting room.

Sabah nodded, before turning to face me, in my boring jeans and jumper combination.

'What are we doing?' she asked. 'For your birthday.'

Would it be an exaggeration to say that it felt like my

heart would leap out of my chest? No one ever remembered my birthday. Last year, I'd gone to see a film by myself, just so I didn't have to sit at home alone, pathetically waiting for my parents to realize what day it was.

'I'm not sure,' I said, trying desperately to keep my voice breezy. 'Maybe we could have a sleepover or something?'

'Seriously?' Noor said, stepping out of the fitting room. 'It's your sixteenth! We need to do something special.' She sat down next to me and started reeling off ideas while Sabah went back into the cubicle to change into her own clothes.

'Leave everything to me,' Sabah said later, looping her arm through mine as we waited for Noor to finish paying for her jumper. 'It'll be your best birthday ever.'

ALIA

Niv and Arjun. Niv and Arjun. The words – and the accompanying pictures – fill my head, whirling around relentlessly, giving me a headache. I try to fold the thoughts away and focus instead on the campaign funding spreadsheet in front of me, trying to use the very real threat of losing the election to quell my rapidly escalating paranoia about my marriage.

I've always been good at partitioning my life. Most people are, to a certain degree, but creating separate compartments in my brain is a particular skill of mine, and one that has served me well. I can deal with one aspect of my life and not have it spill over into another in any way. That's how I've managed to keep going for all these years. That's how I've managed to focus on my work instead of getting sucked into the past with Sabah. But as Arjun's words from last night pound against my skull, the compartments start to give way.

It feels as though every part of my life is disintegrating.

Faraz had been on another one of his constituency visits yesterday. This time to one of the crisis centres I'd set up for battered women. With the TV crews in tow, of course. He'd spent three minutes praising the good work the volunteers were doing before harping on for the next fifteen about the poor response time, lack of medical facilities and the absence of a multi-faith room. He didn't reiterate Saeed's allegations of embezzlement, but he didn't need to, just the insinuation is enough. It's another brushstroke in the picture he is painting of me – the MP who claims to be secular, incorruptible, but is really no more than a charlatan who is more concerned about her own ambition than serving her constituents. The worst part is, of all the things he could say about me, this is the biggest untruth.

When you constantly feel like an outsider, you work harder than ever to earn your place.

I've fought for every refuge, every crisis centre, every temple restoration and every new mosque that has been built in the constituency. Yes, there are improvements to be made, and larger budgets to be negotiated, and I could have done more – you can *always* do more – but the fact that Faraz might be able to repaint budget cuts into embezzlement to push me out is infuriating. More than that, it is unfair.

An image of Noor perched on her school desk appears and I tuck it away into the furthest corner of my brain. Almost immediately another image, this time of Arjun surrounded by a group of his friends, pops up and I do the same.

I push myself to my feet and step into the open-plan area directly outside my office, where someone has turned on the oversized TV we had installed during the last election campaign. Faraz is due to make the keynote speech at the Annual Indian Muslim Congress conference and, as expected, every news channel in the country is streaming it live.

'For too long our community has been ignored. We have been treated like second-class citizens, our ambitions squashed, our voices silenced. We've been used as stepping stones, called terrorists, told our commitment to our religion makes us a liability. We have been told we don't belong in the country that our ancestors sacrificed everything to build. My father created the Indian Muslim Congress because he believed we have as much of a right to be here as anyone else. He gave his whole life to the country, he fought for the rights of our community, he opened doors and created opportunities for us that never even existed before. He ignored personal vendettas so he could focus on serving the people.'

I glance around the large open-plan space. Everyone's eyes are glued to the TV, their careers inextricably linked with my own. I have got to win this election. If I don't, all the sacrifices, the long hours, the heartache – it will all have been for nothing.

'But the scales of justice are skewed in this country. Our mosques have been burned down, our sisters raped, our brothers falsely accused. No more. With this new wave at the Indian Muslim Congress, we will make sure we are represented in every local council, every state assembly, every ministry. We will strengthen the alliances we have spent years nurturing and form new ones. We will make sure minority affairs are a priority, not an afterthought. From now on, we will make sure every Muslim voice is heard. We will fight for our place, our dignity, our freedom. When power rests with a chosen few, if you're not ready to fight, the silence can kill you. Don't let fear keep you quiet. You have a voice. So use it. Speak up. *Bekhauf azadi*.'

Bekhauf azadi. Freedom without fear.

I slink back into my office as the camera pans to show the crowd – close to fifty thousand people – cheering and clapping. Somehow, despite the message of segregation, there is something inspiring about Faraz's speech. The call to arms is right on the pulse as well, I think, as I watch Facebook and Twitter explode.

This is Faraz's masterstroke.

Within moments, Omar is standing in front of me.

I know what he's going to say even before he opens his mouth, but I'm not prepared for him to be armed.

He hands me a thick folder. I merely have to glance at the first page to see what it is. Opponent research on Faraz. A desperate attempt to salvage my position by ruining his. I'd be surprised if by this point Faraz doesn't have a similar folder on me with a list of all my little indiscretions and an action plan to use them all to maximum effect.

I skim through it then hand the folder back to Omar.

'We can't use this.'

'Alia *ji*, this is not the time to be honourable.'

I walk to the window, barely listening to what Omar is saying. A group of drivers and watchmen are sprawled out on the back lawn, basking in the glow of the midday sun while they eat their lunch. In less than five hours, the same men will be scrambling to light a bonfire, huddling around it in their hand-knitted jumpers and monkey caps to keep warm. My first winter in Delhi, I didn't get it. I couldn't understand how it could be scorching hot in the afternoon only for the temperature to plummet in the evening. It took me a long time to appreciate the trick that the Indian sun plays on people, letting them relax in its warmth, lulling them into a false sense of security, before snatching it all away in a few short hours.

Omar is still talking when I turn to face him. He thinks I'm being naive. He's wrong.

I think of the file I keep locked away in my desk.

We can't use anything Omar's dug up because I've got something much better. A piece of information I've kept secreted away for years.

I'm just waiting for the right time to use it.

ALIA

Fifteen years ago

My birthday arrived in the usual way: with a building sense of apprehension in my stomach. But for the first time in years, the nervousness was caused not by fear but rather by excitement.

Sabah did not disappoint. Her cousin, the same one who got her tickets to the premiere at the start of term, arranged backstage passes for a Viva concert on the night of my birthday. Viva were meant to be India's answer to the Spice Girls. Their popularity faded as quickly as their cheap hair dye, but still, it was a concert and we had backstage passes. We were excited.

The concert didn't start until nine but Noor, Sabah, Addi and I were going to Saloni's just after lunch so we could all get ready together and if I'd deciphered all of Sabah's hints correctly, have some birthday cake.

I spent the morning primping. I'd used my birthday money to pay for a haircut at the new salon in South Extension. The stylist had set it in tight ringlets and as I tried on outfit after outfit, I smiled and tossed my hair, twisting every few minutes to catch a glimpse of my curls bouncing in the mirror. I decided on a black top with a deep lace-up neckline and a pair of bootcut jeans that, after months of track practice, sat teasingly low on my hips. I felt pretty, beautiful even. I packed it all into my backpack along with my nightie and an outfit for the next morning and sat down on the porch steps to wait.

Noor had said she would pick me up at four. She was already twenty minutes late, but then Noor was always late. I reminded myself that her erratic ways were part of her charm. After another twenty minutes had passed, I went inside and called her mobile – no answer – so I went back outside, certain that she would turn up any minute. I sat there, waiting, heart thumping, throat drying up, looking up every time a car passed, growing frustrated when none of them were her. Time passed, the street lights went up and my curls went down; my granddad came to check on me twice but she didn't show up. It was already six o'clock. We were due to leave Saloni's at seven thirty.

I felt the prickle of tears and I squeezed my eyes shut, pushing the tears back into my eye sockets through sheer will alone.

Crying was for the weak, my mother always said. In that at least, I agreed with her.

I considered calling Sabah or Addi, but that would mean admitting to them that Noor had forgotten to pick me up. It would mean admitting to myself that I was being edged out of Noor's orbit just as quickly as I had wormed my way into it.

I thought about going back inside, telling my grandparents that my only real friend hadn't bothered to turn up, crawling into bed and spending my Saturday night there, my bouncy new curls pressed flat into the pillow.

No way was I doing that.

I went upstairs and changed into the outfit I had so carefully folded into my backpack. I draped a sparkly scarf around my neck and then tried ringing Noor one last time. This time she answered.

'I thought you were picking me up,' I spoke into the phone.

The line crackled, and for an instant I wondered if I had got it wrong.

'Oh God. I'm so sorry,' Noor said finally. 'I was going to but my driver went MIA and I had to get a lift with Sabah. She said she'd send her driver back for you.'

I didn't say anything.

'She probably just forgot, you know what it's like.'

'Uh-huh.' She forgot to pick me up for my own birthday party? I did know what it was like.

Noor was forgetting that I was her best friend and Sabah was making her.

'I can send him for you now?' Noor said. In the background, I could hear laughter and the faint strains of Dido.

'No, it's fine,' I said, forcing my voice back under my control. 'I'll see you there in twenty minutes.'

I thought about my New Year's resolution and the secrets Noor had whispered to me in Oxford.

I hung up and called a taxi.

It was time to show everyone who Sabah really was.

'I can't believe you've invited Vineet,' Saloni said, pouting as she applied a thick layer of pink lip gloss. She smacked her lips loudly when she finished and handed the tube to me. She turned to face Sabah. 'Do you think you'll get back together?'

'I hope so,' Sabah smiled. 'I feel like something like this either destroys a relationship completely or makes it stronger, you know?'

Addi and Saloni nodded, the idea of the romantic fairy tale that Sabah loved to peddle far more seductive than the dirty reality of being a teenage girl. No one liked to admit they felt it: the desperate need to be liked, validated, but look underneath the strawberry lip gloss and the sparkly eye shadow and you'll find it there. Every single time. I was so sick of it.

'I'm so jealous, between the Head Girl appointment and Vineet, it's like all your dreams are coming true,' Addi said. 'I can't even get a boy to look at me.'

'Not dreams, plans. And maybe if you didn't try so hard,' Sabah said, giving Addi the side eye. 'There's nothing more off-putting than desperation.'

'Well, you deserve every bit of it,' Noor said, smiling at Sabah.

'I think it's incredible that you're both willing to forgive each other,' I said. 'I mean, especially Vineet.'

'Excuse me?'

'Well, you know, a kiss is one thing,' I said, 'but it must be hard for him to get past the fact that you slept with his best friend.'

'What did you say?'

'Mohit. Didn't you guys hook up at camp last year? It must've been hard for Vineet to –' I cast around the room, wide-eyed and innocent. 'He knows, right?'

I watched the expressions change on Saloni's and Addi's faces from surprise to disgust. I resisted the urge to smile at my handiwork.

'*You told her?*' Sabah shrieked, spinning to face Noor.

'I – oh wow, I didn't realize it was a secret,' I said, looking from Noor to Sabah and back again, my expression one of mortified remorse. 'I'm *so* sorry.'

'I bet you are,' Sabah said, her eyes narrowing into little slits. She let me wither for a moment before shrugging. 'Whatever, okay. It was a drunken mistake, and Vineet and I weren't even dating then. It's a non-issue. And for the record, he couldn't – you know,' she added with a wiggle of her eyebrows, 'so we didn't even get past the fooling-around stage.'

Noor snorted from across the room. 'Anyway, shouldn't we be doing shots instead of talking about missed car crashes?'

I smiled and sucked down the tequila shots Noor passed around, all the while seething inside, unaware that the crack between Noor and Sabah was widening.

ALIA

Fifteen years ago

After the concert, and my 'accidental' revelation about Sabah and Mohit, on the surface at least everything seemed fine. After a few days of harmless teasing, we all eased off Sabah. She didn't get back together with Vineet and my rebellion didn't split the group but there was an undeniable chasm of tension between Noor and Sabah. I slipped right into it to reclaim my position as Noor's best friend and for a while, everything was perfect.

Or so I thought.

The truth is, I was just a naive teenager who was years away from being able to unpick the manoeuvrings of the complicated game that was Noor and Sabah's friendship.

I settled into the empty chair next to Noor. We had been sent to the library to work on our history projects, but most of the kids from my class were busy working on something else altogether.

A few weeks into the term, The List had started doing the rounds. It was being passed around the library, the single sheet of paper tucked in between the pages of a Wren & Martin grammar guide, titles such as Hottest Girl and Biggest Charmer bristling against verb forms and complex tenses. I heard a loud guffaw, followed by the librarian's urgent hushing, and turned to look at the group of boys clustered by the bookshelves behind us.

'Jerks,' Sabah said, depositing a stack of books on the table before slipping into the chair across from me.

Noor rolled her eyes, agreeing.

'Speaking of,' Sabah started, 'what's up with Faraz? I haven't seen him since we came back from Goa.'

'He's in trouble again. Abbu's sent him to my grandparents,' Noor said, going back to the notebook in front of her, equations and formulae from the chemistry class eclipsed under elaborate doodles.

'Because he was driving?' Sabah pressed on.

'Don't be silly,' Noor said, barely glancing up.

I flicked open the history book I had picked out, trying to work out how the Indian account of colonial rule and the independence movement could be so completely different from the British one.

'That's not what I heard,' Sabah said.

'Well, he wasn't. Abbu's angry with him for hanging out with those boys.'

'They died, you know.'

This made me look up. 'Who died?'

'A couple and their two-year-old,' Sabah said.

I must have given her a blank look because she rolled her eyes. 'Have you been living under a rock?' she said. 'There was an accident on New Year's Eve. A bunch of drunk boys in a BMW crashed—'

'—into a Maruti with the family,' I finished, catching on. Nana had been talking about the case just last week. The BMW had been on the wrong side of the road, going well over the speed limit. The boys had been lucky, the airbag in the BMW inflating at just the right time; the family in the beaten-down Maruti not so much. The husband and baby had died instantly, but the wife hung on for a few weeks on a ventilator before giving up.

I looked from Noor to Sabah, eyes wide. 'Wait, was Faraz in the car?'

For a long moment neither of them said anything. As Noor and Sabah looked at each other, their eyes locked in silent combat, I got the distinct sense that a treaty was being negotiated.

I wracked my brains for the details of the case. The boys, both unnamed, had been let off with probation and a fine thanks to their underage status. But Faraz was over eighteen, so if he had been in the car . . . even with my limited knowledge of Indian law I knew that would most certainly mean jail time.

My mind flashed back to New Year's Eve, to the police car I'd seen on the Qureshis' drive, the strange atmosphere in the house that evening. I felt my legs tense up under the table. What had I walked in on?

'Are you crazy?' Noor said at the same time as Sabah said, 'Of course not.'

I looked at them, horror spilling onto my face.

Sabah broke the silence with an easy laugh. 'Stop it with the crazy eyes,' she said. 'Faraz was with us in Goa.'

I stared at her. I had seen Faraz that night. He had stepped out for a mere second before Javed Uncle had motioned for him to go back inside.

Sabah lying could only mean one thing.

I was trying to work up the nerve to challenge her when Sabah motioned to the girls on the adjoining table for The List and one of them leaned over and slid the Wren & Martin textbook towards us. Noor flicked it open. 'So predictable,' she said before scribbling on it herself and passing it to Sabah.

'This is accurate,' Sabah smirked, glancing through The List. I watched her add a few names before passing it to me. 'You might find this interesting.'

I looked at the sheet in front of me, my pen poised to add my own comments, my eyes lingering over Biggest Tease (Noor Qureshi), Biggest Flirt (Mohit Yadav), Biggest Creep (Ankit Agarwal), Hottest Girl (Sabah Khan) until they came to rest on the last title.

Tears pricked my eyes but even through the blur I could recognize Sabah's unmistakably neat handwriting. I could feel Noor's and Sabah's eyes on me. I blinked the tears away.

'This is so lame.' I tried to inject my words with sarcasm, but somehow they came out whiny.

I smiled and flicked the book shut, trying to focus on the conflict between Nehru and Jinnah, but the words were imprinted on my brain.

Biggest Fraud: Alia Sharma.

SABAH

Thursday morning. I am immersed in the first batch of archive footage that Dan sent through, forcing myself to sit on my hands as I watch grainy video clips showing panel after panel dissect what a group of teenagers got up to at parties, when my phone pings. I hit pause as I skim through the text from Andrew, then read it once again, hardly able to believe the words that have appeared on my screen.

I mentioned the doc to the Amazon series commissioner last night – he is VERY interested. Wants to look at a proposal within the week. Can you put something together? Doesn't need to be the pitch deck, even an outline will do – just communicate overall tone and narrative arc, maybe hint at possible foul play? Sizzle reel, if you can whip one up, will be brilliant.

I glance at the time, then do the mental maths to work out the time in London. Five a.m. Andrew's a late riser. Famously. For him to be texting me this early . . .

I try to quell the excitement that's bubbling within me. Amazon. They've been making big strides in the TV industry and Andrew's been trying to get the series commissioner to come in ever since they set up shop in London.

I type back quickly. From what I've heard, Amazon like to move fast and they pay well above the market rate.

Pre-empt likely?

His reply is instant.

Extremely.

I take a breath. I haven't hammered out the profit participation terms with Andrew yet, but even with a conservative royalty agreement, a pre-emptive bid from Amazon would be enough to wipe out all my debt, even pay my parents back. Plus, with Amazon's reach and distribution network, the viewership would run into millions.

I look at Andrew's text again, my eyes lingering on 'foul play'. I can see what he's trying to do. Ever since the multi-million-dollar success that was *Making A Murderer*, every distributor loves the unsolved mystery angle. Even the hint of foul play is enough to get the commissioners salivating. It's a better hook and as long as viewers tune in, it almost doesn't matter where the hints lead. I don't need him to tell me what a big opportunity this is.

I'll have something over to you by tomorrow.

I wait till I see the little blue ticks appear next to my message, then turn to my laptop. I open up a new document and start typing.

ALIA

Fifteen years ago

It wouldn't be a Wescott sleepover without a game of Truth or Dare.

Noor, Sabah, Addi, Saloni and I were sitting on the floor in Addi's room, still buzzing from the vodka Noor had smuggled in past Addi's mum.

I laughed along as we went through dare after dare, giggling as Saloni attempted to make out with a pillow and Addi wrote her name on the floor with her tongue.

I sat up straight when the bottle came to rest pointing at me.

Somehow, despite my carefully executed plan to sit opposite Addi, people had moved around during the game and I found myself staring at Sabah across from me. She cocked her head and smiled sweetly. If anyone knew how to add menace to even the most innocent gesture, it was Sabah.

I swallowed. I didn't think she knew anything humiliating about me, but then, this was Sabah. She was an expert at deploying words to cause maximum damage.

'Hurry up,' Sabah said, 'there are only two options.'

'Dare,' I said. I didn't really have a choice. I'd told plenty of lies since I started at Wescott and Sabah practically traded in secrets. I had no way of knowing what little nugget of information she had up her sleeve.

'Really?' Sabah raised her eyebrows. 'I didn't think *you* had it in you to surprise me.'

I laughed nervously.

Sabah pretended to think for a moment. She shrugged. 'Kiss Noor.'

'Excuse me?' My voice came out like a screech. I looked at Sabah to see if she was joking, but her eyes were fixed on Noor. Once again, I had the strange feeling that I was caught in the middle of some game that Noor and Sabah were playing, but I didn't know the rules.

'Truth,' I murmured.

Sabah tore her eyes away from Noor and looked at me.

'Doesn't work like that, Sharma,' Sabah said.

I felt my cheeks flame. I looked at the others but none of them would meet my gaze.

'This is stupid,' Noor said, putting me out of my misery. She reached out and spun the bottle.

I leaned back against the bed as the heat shifted from me to Noor.

'Dare,' Noor said, looking squarely at Addi across from her.

'Ooh, I don't know,' Addi said, rubbing her palms together.

Sabah leaned in and whispered something to Addi.

'No way,' Addi said, nervously laughing her off.

Sabah raised her eyebrows, the message clear.

'Come on. It's not like it'll be the first time, right?'

The atmosphere changed in an instant and I understood that their whole act of friendship was just that: an act. Sabah was still furious with Noor about letting slip her secret.

Addi mumbled something and left the room. Sabah slid over to her spot.

'Still want a dare?' she asked Noor, lips twisted into a half-smile.

No one else was playing anymore; it was just the two of them, Noor and Sabah.

Noor cocked her head to one side, pretending to consider it. 'Yeah, let's see what you've got.'

'I dare you to go down on *someone* –'

Noor scoffed.

'– from school, on school grounds.'

'Is that it?' Noor looked around the group as Saloni and I shifted uncomfortably, before letting her eyes settle on Sabah. She shrugged. 'Easy-peasy.'

ALIA

Fifteen years ago

No one expected her to go through with it. She could have laughed it off. She could have lied about it. She could have found a way to flip the coin, but Noor was not one to back down from a dare. On the following Monday, she stayed back after school, skipping the extra credit art class for a far more intimate and entirely different extra-curricular activity.

Had it been anyone other than Noor, that would've been the end of it.

But it *was* Noor, and that was just the beginning.

I could sense a frisson of excitement on the bus the next morning. Wescott's student population was obsessed with their Nokia 7650s, but even so, I had never seen people bent over their phones with such intense focus.

I slipped into my usual window seat then leaned forward to talk to the girl in front of me.

'What's going on?' I asked her

She twisted in her seat to look at me. 'You don't know?'

she said, eyebrows knotted in an expression that made me feel simultaneously belittled and enraged. 'I thought you were friends with Noor.'

'I am,' I said haughtily.

She shook her head, disgusted. 'You know what she did then?'

I stayed silent.

'Here,' she said, holding up her phone. 'Click play.'

I could hear the murmurs behind me, the boys whispering to each other but I refused to acknowledge them, my eyes focused instead on the video that had started playing on the phone.

It was a grainy mobile phone video, but somehow the grittiness made it look even seedier than if it had been a proper production. Noor appeared on screen, hair left loose, shirt unbuttoned, showing off a lacy white bra that had been pulled down to reveal one breast. She was kneeling in front of a boy, also in the Wescott uniform, his trousers pooled on the floor. I felt a wave of nausea rise up in me. Even though I had seen her with far less on than this, sitting on the bus looking at Noor in a video that had been made without her knowledge made me feel dirty. I couldn't see what she was doing but the grunts in the background told me where her hands were. She tossed her hair back, eyes unknowingly meeting the camera for a millisecond before she bent down and –

I pushed the phone back at the girl sitting in front of me, who had been watching me with interest, as if now that she had seen the video, the next best thing was watching my reaction to it.

'Have you seen it?' Addi asked as soon as I sat down.

'Yeah.' I twisted in my seat to face her and Saloni. Noor's seat next to mine was still empty.

'I can't believe she actually did that,' Saloni said.

'I know, it was just a stupid game,' I said. I glanced at Sabah. She was in her usual seat, bent over her notebook, as if this entire thing wasn't all her fault. 'I bet *she's* happy.'

'What are you—' Saloni started, but the homeroom bell cut her off.

Noor rushed in ten minutes later, her cheeks flushed.

'You've missed roll call,' the teacher said.

'Sorry, ma'am,' Noor replied, panting. 'I missed the bus.'

Noor made her way through the desks and slunk in next to me. I felt my stomach writhe as the murmurs from the back of the classroom drifted into my ears, nastier than anything I'd ever heard before. I squeezed her hand, unsure of what to say.

Did you forget to get on the bus because you were busy getting off?

I'm free after school.

I'll show you mine if you show me yours.

Oh yes, Noor, yes, just like that.

As homeroom gave way to Chemistry, then Maths and Geography, the boys carried on whispering, the silkiness of their murmurs making the words sound cruder than they were. I snuck glances at Noor. She had barely said a word all morning, keeping her head bent as she scribbled with a ferocity I had never seen before, furious strokes filling page after page with sketches. As the morning wore on, the whispers continued, nastier, sharper, anything to elicit a response. There was a note being passed around and by the third period, the whispers had turned to chants. Even Sabah looked embarrassed as the boys repeated the words from the video, filling the classroom with moans, chanting Noor's name as if they were in the throes of pleasure. They would start off every time the teacher turned to write something on the blackboard, their words too quiet for the teacher to catch but loud enough for Noor to hear.

Loud enough to rip Noor apart.

I nearly jumped with relief when the bell rang for lunch. I turned to Noor, trying to come up with words that might comfort her, but she was already out of her seat. I could feel the anger bubbling up inside me as I watched Noor make her way to Sabah. My fists clenched into tight balls. Of course, just like that they were best friends again. It didn't matter that it was Sabah's fault Noor was even in this position. Noor was crouched next to Sabah now, whispering, but Sabah was ignoring her. I flicked my notebook shut and crammed it into my backpack, ready to go and interrupt their conversation but before I had even finished zipping my backpack shut, I saw Sabah push Noor away.

'What a complete bitch,' Saloni said a second later, watching Noor's back as she got up and ran out of class.

'I can't believe she did that to Sabah,' Addi said, standing up. 'It's just—'

'What she did to *Sabah*?' I cut her off, outraged. 'What are you talking about?'

Addi took a small step back. 'I thought you knew.'

I shook my head.

Addi looked at Saloni. They were standing side by side now, backpacks slung over their shoulders.

'What?' I said, mildly aware that my voice was getting louder. Addi started to speak, then shook her head, as if the words were too difficult to summon. I grabbed my backpack and flung it over one shoulder. 'Just tell me.'

It was Saloni who spoke.

'The boy in the video,' she said, slowly.

I glanced at the group of boys huddled together in the corner, bent over a mobile phone. All familiar faces; boys who had claimed to be Noor's friends.

'Yes?' I said, impatience bristling against apprehension as something occurred to me. I looked at the group of boys again. Not him. Please not him.

Saloni had the hint of a smile on her face. I had never liked her, but in that moment, I hated her with a ferocity that surprised me.

I raised my eyebrows. 'Just tell me,' I repeated.

'It's Vineet.'

SABAH

The cafeteria is packed with faces that look eerily familiar. Women who have had their faces botoxed into near replicas of their teenage selves, men with pudgy middles wearing identical suits and slapping each other's backs as though they are still seventeen-year-olds. Though there are more than a few hundred people crammed into the room, the atmosphere is intimate and sentimental, with a heavy dose of irony thrown in.

The cameraman by my side isn't helping and as I snake my way through the crowd, I can see the gossip travel through the room in ripples, soft murmurs skimming over the starched white tablecloths and flickering candles, the trepidation and curiosity mingling with nostalgia.

I have never seen the appeal of reunions. Their only function seems to be to keep decades-old rumours and speculation alive, embers smouldering years after the fire has been put out.

'Just walk around and get some candid footage. I'm going to layer everything with voiceovers so don't worry about the audio,' I say to the cameraman before waving him away.

I stifle a yawn. I've spent the past thirty-six hours glued to my desk, trying to piece together a pitch deck and a sizzle reel using archive footage and the handful of interviews I've already conducted. I sent it to Andrew mere minutes before the commissioner walked in. That was three hours ago. No news is good news, I tell myself.

I force my face into a smile when I see Vineet approaching.

'Vineet,' I say. 'I'm sorry about how we left things.'

'Save it,' he says, thrusting a business card at me without even the pretence of civility. I glance at it. A smirk escapes. Gokuldas and Partners. Criminal defence lawyers. How completely predictable.

'Next time you want to catch up, call my lawyer,' he hisses.

My gaze drifts to his exceptionally pretty, incredibly gullible-looking wife, who is watching us from a few steps away, shifting her weight uncomfortably in her sky-high Manolos. I feel a pang of pity for her as Vineet spins around and curls his arm around her waist, steering her towards the group of men I'd once called friends.

The hand on my shoulder turns me around.

'Sabah?'

The features are softer, the face fuller, but the dimpled cheeks and impish smile I remember from school are still intact. My face breaks into a grin as Addi pulls me into a hug.

'Addi! I haven't seen you in ages,' I say, genuinely pleased to see her. 'Don't tell me you've moved back?'

Despite my sudden departure from school, Addi and I

had remained friends. We kept in touch online, following each other's lives on Facebook, but I had barely seen her over the last decade. She'd invited me to her wedding in Jaisalmer a few years ago but work had kept me away and since then she had all but disappeared. The last I'd heard, she had moved back to Bristol amidst enough family drama to get Netflix excited, but that's a story for another day.

'I wish. I'm here for a much-needed holiday. Well, if you can call it that,' she grins. 'It's just me with my sister and her baby girl. You remember Mia, right?'

I nod, vaguely recalling the chubby girl we'd all known as Addi's little sister.

'She's a new mum but refuses to accept any help. So I've dragged her here under the pretence of a holiday.'

'That sounds . . . fun?'

'Oh, it's super glamorous, if you like two a.m. wake-up calls and smelly nappies,' she says, laughing. 'How are you, though? I'm so sorry I never replied to your email.'

I shrug it off, glad that she brought it up herself. 'It sounds like you've had your hands full.'

'I'll do it, of course.' Addi slants her head, her gaze sliding off me. 'I keep thinking about that last night, after the party. I could see how drunk Noor was when she was walking into the house. It was obvious that she needed help but I just . . . I should have got out of the car. Maybe if I'd gone inside with her, we'd both have gone to bed, she wouldn't have—'

'Sorry, what?' The words spill out before I can clamp down on them. 'You saw her go into her house?'

'Yes,' Addi says, looking confused. 'Why?'

'I thought Vineet drove her home.'

'He did. I was in the car behind him,' she pauses. 'With Mohit.'

'*Mohit?*'

Addi looks at me as if debating whether or not she should continue this conversation. She had always been thoughtful and considered in her responses, never one to be hurried into an answer. I adjust my face, urging her on silently.

She sighs and pushes the loose strands of hair away from her face.

'I'm not proud of this . . . Mohit and I had been fooling around at the party and, well, he was going back to Vineet's and he asked me along.' She shrugs but I can see the colour rising to her cheeks. 'Anyway, Vineet said he had to drop Noor off first, so Mohit and I followed them. I saw her get out of his car and stumble through those massive gates.' Addi pauses to look at me, her brows knotted together, regret underpinning every word. 'She couldn't even walk straight. I should have got out to help her.'

My stomach clenches without my permission.

'Did you make any stops on the way?'

'I wouldn't call them stops, but yeah, we pulled over a few times so she could throw up. She was a mess, Sabah. Why?'

Out of all of us, Addi had always been the one with the strict moral compass. She wouldn't lie, not about this.

'Did you tell someone? Noor's parents? The police?'

'I told her father at the funeral and he said he would

contact me if the police needed a statement but I never heard back,' she says. 'But I guess it wasn't relevant anyway.'

'Right.' I take a sip of my drink as I try to slot this new information in.

'Anyway,' Addi says, 'Have you seen—'

I cut her off. 'What happened afterwards?'

'Excuse me?'

'After you went to Vineet's? I mean, could he have gone back to Noor's afterwards, or maybe you mixed up what you saw . . .'

'What are you really asking me, Sabah?' Addi's tone is light but her eyes don't leave my face.

I get straight to the point.

'Is it possible that Vineet went back to Noor's later?'

'And what, shot her?' The incredulity in her voice is genuine. 'Are you serious?'

I flinch at the bluntness of her words.

She sighs. 'I was too drunk to do anything, and anyway, seeing Noor like that – it sort of killed the mood. Mohit, Vineet and I stayed up all night watching movies. I was there when he got the call.'

I don't say anything. I can't.

Addi places a hand on my arm, her eyes softening.

'Look, I don't want to seem indifferent,' Addi says. 'After everything you both went through, it makes sense that you'd want to find somewhere to place the blame. But you knew her, Sabah. You remember what she was like, right? Before rehab. There's a reason no one was surprised.'

I am not one for melodrama, yet somehow I can feel

the blood gushing in my ears, drowning out what Addi's saying. I step away from her, mumbling something incoherent.

When Alia asked me who I thought killed Noor, I'd dodged her questions, telling her, and myself, that I didn't want to name names until I had something more than just a feeling to go on. But secretly, I have always believed it was Vineet.

Noor and Vineet had barely been speaking to each other at that point, so there could only be one reason why he had offered to drive her home. My theory for the longest time has been that he had tried something with Noor and when she fought back, he shot her. There were holes in this theory, of course, but holes I knew I could fill once I had a clearer picture. He could have coerced her into writing the note, he could have stolen a gun, he could have made it look like a suicide. There were endless ways to assemble this particular jigsaw.

But if Addi is telling the truth – and there is no reason for her to lie – then my theory about Vineet is wrong. It couldn't have been him.

I look around at the roomful of people I went to school with.

Old friendships have been reignited, if only for one night.

The group of girls – *women* – from the Science stream who Noor and I had always made fun of are standing in a tight knot at the front of the room.

The boys from the football team who had chased after us are assembled in a rowdy twist near the bar.

A few feet from me, Addi and Saloni are clinking glasses.

Further along, Vineet is in a huddle with Mohit and Yash.

We had all played a part in what happened to her. We are all here, alive, while Noor rots away in a coffin. The unfairness of it hits me with a physicality that defies logic.

My eyes come to rest on Alia standing alone with a drink in her hand. A few paces from her, Niv is dazzling the man I recognize as the old head boy.

Almost everyone in this room has held a grudge against Noor at some point.

And if Vineet didn't kill her, then who did?

ALIA

I glance at my watch. An hour in and I'm not sure I can do this any longer.

Wescott hosts these fundraisers masquerading as reunions every couple of years and usually I love attending. I am used to chairing national committees and attending meetings with the PM but there is a special joy in watching people who had once treated me as little more than Noor's and Sabah's sidekick spin cartwheels in my honour. But tonight, every conversation feels strained, tainted by the knowledge of how fragile my position is.

I feel an unexpected twinge of nerves as Sabah comes over and stands next to me. I haven't seen her since I burst into her house a few days ago, demanding answers. I wonder if tonight she will be more forthcoming, and I consider asking her if she's found any more leads but something stops me. When the present feels like it's going to swallow you whole, it can be reckless to focus on the past.

Especially if the past has the power to annihilate everything you've worked for.

'No husband?' she asks, conversationally.

Trust Sabah to find a way to unnerve me before we've even said hello.

'He's away,' I lie. Arjun and I hadn't spoken since our little spat last night. I'd pretended to be asleep when he got home from the awards and he pretended he could sleep through the disruption as I flicked on lights and opened and closed wardrobe doors in the morning. I hadn't even seen him at breakfast, choosing instead to eat in the office.

I know I am burying my head in the sand, but for now at least, it's the only way I can survive. I need to keep my single-minded focus if I'm going to win this election.

'Any news on the police files?' Sabah asks.

I let a passing waiter top up my wine before answering.

'We should have them in a day or two,' I say. 'The files are classified so we're having to take a slightly longer route. I've spoken to –'

I pause, distracted by the sound of loud laughter. I cast around for the culprits but instead I spy Niv.

I've been avoiding her all evening. My eyes follow her as she moves through the room with her usual grace, shoulders back, narrow hips swaying gently, her swimmer's body still intact after all these years. She slips behind a column with an almost imperceptible glance around the room. I take a few steps back, trying to find a better angle to observe her from. My breath catches in my throat as I realize the person she's talking to is my husband.

Arjun and Niv are close, too close. Niv has one hand on Arjun's arm and she is whispering to him urgently. As I watch, Arjun scans the room then steps even closer, his attention focused on Niv again.

I feel the world spin around me and for a second it feels as though I am falling, until the pressure of a hand on my shoulder grounds me. I don't turn around. I keep my eyes on my husband, willing him to look at me, to realize that I can see what he's doing.

He doesn't.

I can't tell if the feeling that sweeps through me is relief that I don't have to confront him or anger that even after all these years, he can't see me.

Niv says something and Arjun steps back, shaking his head.

Less than a minute later, he's standing next to me, apologizing for being late.

'I didn't think you were coming.' My voice comes out hard, brittle.

'Why would you think that?'

His dark eyes are searching mine, but I haven't got it in me to answer that. I deflect with a question of my own. I nod towards Niv, who's standing at the bar now, chatting to Faraz, glass of wine in hand. 'What was that about?'

'Oh, Niv didn't think I should – you know what, it doesn't matter,' he says, his gaze sliding off me and focusing instead on Sabah. He turns to her, his face breaking into a warm smile as he introduces himself, charming as ever. He chats to her easily for a few minutes before one of his colleagues pulls him away.

'I didn't realize Niv was friends with your husband,' Sabah says when he's out of earshot.

I force my voice back under my control. 'Family friends,' I say. 'They've known each other since they were little.'

'Oh.'

I can sense an ocean's worth of undercurrents rippling beneath that one word.

'What?'

'Nothing. I just never trusted her.'

Despite everything, I feel my sense of loyalty kick in. 'You barely knew her,' I say.

Sabah eyes me with a mix of confusion and pity. 'You aren't serious. She's your best friend and she hasn't told you?'

'Told me what?' I say, my patience wearing thin.

'Niv and I . . . we practically grew up together.'

I shrug. 'You were neighbours.'

'We were more than that. Noor and I thought of her like an older sister. We used to follow her around like puppies when we were little, trying to copy everything she did.'

I look at her, unconvinced. Niv is only a year older than us, the age gap hardly enough for her to play mentor or whatever Sabah is implying.

'A year can seem like a lot when you're six,' Sabah says. 'Anyway, the dynamic changed as we grew older, but we were still very close. Especially Noor and her.'

I can't quite piece this new information together. I think about that first day in the cafeteria. Noor and Sabah *hated* Niv.

'The year before you started, Noor found out that Niv

and Faraz had been seeing each other. For quite some time it turned out. Noor was furious. She'd been confiding in Niv for years and all along, she wasn't just her friend, she was her brother's girlfriend.'

I had never understood Noor's almost obsessive loathing for Niv but as I think about how possessive Noor was of her friends, how intense the rivalry between her and Faraz was, it clicks into place. For Niv to be involved with her brother . . . Noor would have seen it as the ultimate betrayal.

'What did she do?'

Sabah lifts her shoulders. 'What she always did. She sabotaged their relationship and things just kept escalating from there.'

I draw a breath.

Niv and I had been best friends for nearly a decade. We must have spoken about the Qureshis a million times. Why hadn't Niv told me any of this?

Sabah draws her face into a wide smile and waves at someone. I turn to look. Arjun is walking back towards us, flanked by a smiling Niv on his arm, her emerald-green silk dress swishing around her calves.

'Just watch your back,' Sabah whispers before she steps forward, arms open, ready to draw Niv into a hug.

ALIA

Fifteen years ago

Nothing that happened next was any different to what happens to every other girl in every other high school. But here's the thing: unless you've been *that* girl, unless you've walked the halls hearing the taunts and the whispers, unless you've crouched in the toilet trying to erase the sickening words scribbled on the walls, unless you've heard your best friend call you a whore, you have no idea what it feels like. You can't.

I didn't.

I told Noor I was there for her as the whispers and notes turned to outright bullying and abuse. I said I didn't judge her when half the senior class started bragging about having shagged her. I claimed I didn't hear the other girls talk about how they'd rather kill themselves than embarrass their families like she had. I promised her I would stay by her side, but in the end I abandoned her. I had to. It wasn't sudden, brought on by the flurry of urgent whispers that followed her wherever she went. It was slower, more painful. I hung on as long as I could but ultimately it was easier to nod along, to join in instead of trying to defend her and damage my own fragile position in the process.

I have never regretted anything more.

I stayed close to Noor the first couple of days, determined to prove to her that I was on her side no matter how bad things got. I looped my arm through hers as we slipped out of the classroom during lunch break a few days later and chattered mindlessly, trying to ignore the groups of girls whispering and boys whistling and making obscene gestures at her as we walked past.

A group of boys who I recognized from Sameer's party stopped us as we pushed through the corridor.

'Hey, girls, fancy a threesome?' a boy whose name I didn't even know said as his friends laughed rowdily.

'Come on,' I said to Noor, trying to nudge her away, but she was frozen in her spot. I followed her gaze further down the corridor to where Vineet was standing surrounded by his usual gang. My eyes met his for the briefest of seconds before he looked away, leaning back on the railing and laughing at something Mohit was saying.

I looked around but I already knew there would be no teachers in sight. They retreated to the staffroom at lunchtime.

'Move,' I said to the boys who had clustered together in a tight circle, barricading us. We would have to push through them to get past. I looked sideways at Noor, whose face had gone very, very still.

'Don't be like that,' the boy said. 'We all know Noor's up for it, and you'd never say no to Noor, right?'

Till a week ago, these boys would've been ready to fall at Noor's command, a flick of her hand and a teasing smile enough to get her whatever she wanted.

'I bet they get it on at their famous sleepovers,' his bespectacled friend spoke, flushing with pride as his words provoked a fresh round of laughter from the others.

'How about a live show just for us?' he continued, stepping so close that I could smell the *samosa* on his breath, the faint smell of onion and potatoes making me feel sick as I felt something twist inside me. 'We can pay, if that's what you want.'

I was trying to come up with a retort when I felt a shock of pain run through me. I flipped around, furious, but the boys were standing in a tight knot, surrounding us completely and it was impossible to tell who was responsible for the stinging pain that had spread across my bottom and the even sharper sting of shame that accompanied it. I gripped Noor's arm tighter and pulled her as I tried to push past the boys but she remained rooted to the spot.

'Noor, come on,' I hissed, desperate to get away, but she didn't move, her eyes fixed on the floor. The feeling of helplessness rose through my chest, choking me.

I saw the way they were looking at me, the way their eyes flicked over my face for half a second before moving down, tracing the curve of my breasts. I felt sick, violated, surrounded by boys who only wanted one thing.

I knew when it came to it there was one thing I was not willing to risk for Noor.

I tried one last time to pull her with me, and then I let go, gasping as I elbowed my way out and the group closed around her.

When it came down to it, instead of standing by her, I chose me.

When the boys crowded around, drool practically dripping from their mouths, I chose me. I ran.

I threw one last glance back at her before I ran down the corridor, away from them, past Vineet and his friends, past Niv and Dhruv, past the teacher who was looking at me suspiciously and the groups of girls who were shaking their heads, the boys' laughter and taunts following me all the way to the cafeteria.

I spotted Sabah holding court at her usual table. I ignored the prying eyes as I rushed through the room, panting as I plumped myself in the corner, praying that Sabah wouldn't ask me to leave.

She didn't.

She simply raised her eyebrows and continued talking, allowing me to fade into the invisibility I had spent months trying to escape.

Noor walked up to the table a few minutes later. I noticed her eyes, red, raw, and I forced myself to look away, trying not to think about how I had deserted her.

'Sabah, can we talk?' she said.

'Sure,' Sabah shrugged.

'Privately.'

'You can say anything you want in front of my friends.

I *trust* them,' Sabah said, looking around the table and gracing us with an indulgent smile.

Noor sighed, but didn't argue. 'I didn't mean to hurt you, Sabah. I didn't know he was—'

'Recording you?' Sabah cut her off, the hurt leaking through her voice. 'So once again you're sorry you got caught, not that you did it. Do you even care –' She took a breath to steady her voice before she spoke again. 'I can't keep doing this. He's not my boyfriend any more and you're not my friend, so you two can set up your own porn channel for all I care.'

'Noor, maybe you should leave,' Addi said softly, inching closer to Sabah and draping an arm around her shoulders.

Sabah looked at me, defying me to say something, jump to Noor's defence, but I kept quiet. I understood that it was time to choose between Sabah and Noor, and in that moment I chose Sabah.

I chose me.

'And never come back,' Saloni added.

Noor flinched but didn't say anything, the shock on her face evident. The girls who used to buzz around her like bees were now acting as if they were too good for her. Her eyes rested on me but I pretended I couldn't see the silent appeal, the desperation.

'Sabah, please, I'll do anything . . .'

'Clearly,' Sabah replied, sitting up straight. She brushed Addi's arm away and leaned forward on the table, her eyes focusing in on Noor.

'At least we could all see how much you enjoyed it,' Sabah said, pausing for a second before she added. 'But then, that's what sluts do, right?'

The day stubbornly dragged on. I kept my head down, pretending I couldn't hear the whispers that started every time the teacher turned her back, acting as if I hadn't seen the note that was being passed around the classroom, a connect-the-dots kind of sketch of Noor that left little to the imagination. I snuck glances at Noor when I knew she wasn't looking and when the final bell rang, deafeningly loud and desperately welcome, I slipped away without a word. Shame and guilt scorched through me, but neither was enough to burn down the sense of self-preservation that had cropped up sometime between having my bum pinched and realizing I still had a place at Sabah's table, as long as it was without Noor.

A small crowd had gathered around the snack shop outside school. It was always busy after school, with kids pushing to get to the front to buy a *masala bunta*, some Cheetos or a bar of ice cream before jumping on one of the hundreds of school buses that lined the street. But the crowd today was buzzing with the kind of excitement that could only mean one thing: a fight.

'How dare you go near her?' I heard someone yell as I elbowed my way to the front. My heart stuttered. I knew that voice. Faraz.

Vineet was standing alone in a small clearing amidst the crowd, shifting from foot to foot, hands held up in front of Faraz and a few other boys, all older and probably from Faraz's university.

'Look, man, I didn't do anything she didn't want me—'

'That's my sister, you son of a bitch,' Faraz snapped.

Faraz lurched forward, his body a blur. One moment, Vineet was standing in front of him, the next he was splayed out on the ground, knocked back with a single punch. I saw Mohit push through the crowd across from me and then step back as soon as he realized that Faraz had brought company.

'Faraz, calm down—'

Faraz's foot on his stomach cut Vineet off.

'Did you think you could do anything you wanted and I wouldn't find out? You arrogant –' He stopped, breathing hard. 'You are going to pay for this. I'm going to make sure of it. My *father* is going to make sure of it. No one messes with a Qureshi.'

I felt fear ripple through me as I spotted Noor pushing her way to the front and, almost instinctively, I stepped forward.

'What the hell are you doing?' Noor yelled, running to Vineet to help him up.

'Get away from him. I'll deal with you later,' Faraz said.

He grabbed her arm and dragged her a few feet away towards the road to his waiting car.

'Let go of me,' Noor screamed, struggling under his grip.

'Shut the fuck up and get in. You've caused enough embarrassment already,' Faraz snapped, shoving her in and slamming the door shut.

'Make sure she stays there,' he said to one of his friends, who nodded and took position by the car door as if he was guarding a convict.

The entire crowd held its breath as Faraz strode back to Vineet, who had just about managed to get up. Faraz grabbed his collar and lifted him up, their faces inches apart.

When Faraz spoke his voice was calm, but loud enough for all of us to hear.

'If you even *look* at her again, I'll snatch your eyeballs out. Got it?'

ALIA

Fifteen years ago

The most effective way to destroy your competition is to whip up a scandal and then disengage, to deny them the drama and the validation of a response, to let them simmer in their own misery until they have no choice but to self-combust. You'd think I would have learned that in politics, but the truth is, there is nowhere better to learn the rules of power than at school.

The other thing I learned?

Things have to blow up before they can blow over.

Noor didn't come back to school that week, or the next, and with no one left to bully, the gossip died down to the odd comment here and there. A new transfer student had started that week and when people found out that she had been on a TV show as a child, by the time the weekend rolled around, the focus had shifted almost completely from Noor.

I knew as soon as I woke up that something was wrong. The house was silent for a Saturday, no whirling washing machine, no strains from the TV, no pressure cooker going off. I tiptoed downstairs, still in my pyjamas. I could hear hushed voices coming from the dining room and I crept up to it.

The door was open. I looked in.

Nani was sitting at the table, head bent low over a newspaper. Nana was standing at the window looking out.

I pushed the door open and they both turned to look at me.

'Come in,' Nana said.

I sat down at the table next to Nani. It was clear that she had been crying.

My stomach twisted uncomfortably.

'What's—'

Nana held up a hand silencing me mid-sentence. His face was blank, his expression so cold it took my breath away.

'You are not to see Noor or any of those girls again,' Nana said.

'But—'

'And no more parties or after-school activities. You'll go to school and come straight home. We can decide what to do next when your parents get here.'

'My parents?'

'They're flying in for the weekend.'

'I don't understand. What's happened?' I asked, hating the sound of my voice, so shrill.

He threw a bunch of pictures on the table. Photos from the trip to Oxford, from the concert, from all the parties I had been to in the last year. Photos that showed me smoking and drinking. My backpack lay open in the corner.

I was so terrified I forgot to be angry.

The silence stretched on, so thick it felt like I would choke.

'Nani,' I said, trying to appeal to my grandmother.

'I don't know what to say to you,' Nani said. She took a deep breath and my insides flipped. 'Do you take us for complete fools, Alia?'

The photos showed a side of me that they had never seen before but even so, their reaction was extreme.

I looked from her to Nana, trying to figure out what had prompted the only two people in the world who had ever loved me to distrust me enough to search my bag, until my eyes fell on the newspaper on the table. I twisted it towards me.

My breath caught in my throat. It was horrible enough as it was, but to find out about it from my grandparents, for them to know what really happened at those parties . . .

Video featuring Wescott girl rocks the nation.

I skimmed through it. The video had been so widely shared among school and college students in Delhi, someone in Hyderabad, a complete stranger sitting a thousand miles away from Wescott, had decided to put it up on an online auction site. Noor's name hadn't been mentioned, but the fact that her father was a minister was.

I had never felt shame that deep.

I watched in agony as Nani scraped her chair back and got up.

There were a million things I wanted to say – sorry,

please don't be angry with me, I didn't do anything – but all I could do was stare as they walked out of the room and, once again, I was left completely alone.

I realized even before I made it to the classroom on Monday that this time the gossip wasn't going to die down.

I walked into the locker room after track practice to find a group of senior girls huddled together in a fierce knot of chatter. I backed into one of the shower cubicles but I needn't have worried. They were so busy slandering Noor they didn't even notice I had walked in. I leaned my cheek against the frosted-glass door and listened.

'My mum said she's being expelled.'

'And Vineet?'

'Probably, but it's not so bad for him, is it? He's not the one half the country's jerking off to. If he hadn't admitted to it, no one would even know it was him.'

'No, but it's not fair. He's the one that put the video out there.' Somebody sounded uncertain.

'Well, she shouldn't have done it in the first place if she didn't want people finding out.'

'She didn't know she was being recorded.'

'Actually, I heard that she did,' someone said, in a tone that was so cavalier, it could only be Saloni.

'No way. Who told you that?'

'Mohit.'

'And Vineet told Mohit? That's a reliable source.'

'Either way, it's her own fault for trusting him.' Saloni,

relishing the gossip, as always. 'I wouldn't be caught dead in a situation like that.'

'Only because you haven't been on a date in the last century.' There was a ripple of laughter and I found myself flinching at the sharpness of the words.

Slut if you do, prude if you don't. What was a girl supposed to do?

'She's back on the drugs too, you know. I saw her at Sameer's party last year – high out of her mind. It's no wonder the boys think they can get whatever they want from her.'

'Her parents must be mortified.'

'I heard this might cost her father the election.'

'I'm surprised they haven't sent her back to rehab already. What an embarrassment.'

'As if they'd take her back,' someone sneered.

'What do you mean?'

'My sister has a friend who was at the same centre. She said that Noor wasn't discharged early. She was thrown out. Apparently she was messing around with another – what do you call them – resident? Inmate?'

'I thought she was at a girls-only facility.'

'She was,' came the conspiratorial reply.

The pause stretched on for a beat too long.

'Bullshit.' Someone called it, finally.

'She probably just snuck in some weed or tried to seduce a doctor or something.'

'Maybe. But I've heard sluts don't discriminate.'

Another flurry of giggles.

'I heard,' someone said, 'that something happened between her and Alia.'

'You don't mean . . . ?'

'That's what I heard.' The same voice again. 'In Oxford.'

'I can't say I'm surprised. Alia made up a fake boyfriend, you know. Dave or Chris or something.' I'd know that haughty voice anywhere. Sabah.

Noor told her?

I felt something inside me snap. I swung open the door and marched out, ready to obliterate everyone that was out there. I wasn't the only one with secrets.

I stopped dead in my tracks when I saw who was at the centre of the group.

Niv whirled around to look at me and I understood in that moment that she was only doing to me what I had done to her.

'Alia. Oh no. You heard everything,' she said, her voice flat, devoid of even the slightest hint of regret.

ALIA

I spot Niv as soon as I get there. She's sitting at a table right by the edge of the terrace, her face turned out towards the huge green expanse.

I feel the resentment rise up my throat as I thread my way towards her, circling the golfers laughing over beers and looping around the society wives exchanging tips on the city's best manicurists while their children get fed by their nannies on separate tables.

I'm all too familiar with Delhi Golf Club's particular brand of elitism. Membership is a privilege that no amount of money or influence can buy. I've been on the waiting list for eight years now. Niv, however, has had a family membership for years, an heirloom more precious than her grandmother's diamonds. Usually, I love spending Sunday afternoons here. The food is good, the views of the green and the old Mughal monuments brilliant and Niv's company always welcome, but today everything about it exasperates me.

'I'll have the mezze platter,' I tell the waiter, without so much as a glance at the menu. 'And the Sauvignon Blanc,' I add, after a pause. I'm feeling rebellious.

'Small or large?'

'A bottle,' I say.

His eyebrows twitch for less than a second before he turns to Niv for her more respectable order but his message is clear: you don't belong here.

'Friday was fun,' Niv says, skipping our usual topics and going straight for the Wescott grapevine, fresh for plucking after the reunion last week. She doesn't moan about her mother or question why I had insisted on lunch at such short notice. I know she noticed the tension between Arjun and me at the reunion, but she doesn't ask me about it. She's trying far too hard to avoid talking about him and I find myself wondering how much she knows about the inner workings of my marriage. I wonder if he talks to her about me when they're working late, if they have their own whispered secrets woven through the shared history that predates me.

'Did you read the article about Sabah's documentary?' Niv asks, stabbing her fork into a piece of salmon and slicing a small piece. 'I'm a bit wary of the whole thing.'

'Why's that?' I'd seen the piece in the papers this morning. Apparently the documentary had been bought for a high six-figure sum, but what interests me more is Niv's objection to it.

Niv takes a sip of her Bellini and tilts her head to one side, thinking. 'Because I don't get her angle on it. She tells everyone it's a simple retelling, but then there's all that stuff about a suspicious death and foul play in the press release . . . I just don't trust her, I suppose.'

I raise my eyebrows. *I just don't trust her.* The exact same thing that Sabah had said about her. And yet, if there is a liar here, it's Niv. I think back to her stunt at school. At the time, I'd felt sorry for her. How damaged does someone have to be to pretend they'd been cutting their wrists? I'd thought. But for the first time now, I can see it for what it was. The damsel in distress. A ploy, the oldest one in the world, to attract the boy she wanted.

'Scared all your secrets will come out?'

Niv looks at me evenly. 'No, but if I were you, I would be. Sabah's got a special skill for twisting the truth.'

I look into the distance, studying the golfers on the lawn, their brightly coloured polo shirts and sun visors standing out in contrast to the lush green grass.

'Is Arjun staying on at his parents' tonight?' Niv asks between bites.

Arjun had left for his parents' house early this morning. It was all very last minute. His mum had called just after six to tell us his father had had a fall and dislocated his shoulder and Arjun had left soon after, eager to see his dad. It's disconcerting that Niv knows about this less than six hours later.

I draw in air, telling myself to be calm, logical, but I don't have it in me.

'You tell me. You seem to see him more than I do these days.'

'Excuse me?'

'You asked him to stay away from me. His wife.'

Niv sighs and puts her fork down. 'I was worried you'd misunderstand that. The firm is getting a lot of heat right now. As are you. And I don't know how much Arjun's told you, but he's been under a lot of pressure. If this Barclays deal doesn't go through . . . The project with John . . . it was a mistake. We're overstretched.'

Arjun hasn't told me any of this and hearing it from Niv only makes me bristle more. Secret confidences, burdens shared, that is how it starts, and Niv knows that better than anyone.

'And that's supposed to justify you meddling in my marriage?'

'Stop being so—'

'What were you arguing about at the reunion?'

'Alia –' she starts then stops. I realize that my voice has risen above the din of the terrace. I also realize why she insisted we meet here instead of at her house like I'd suggested. She wanted to make sure that I didn't create a scene.

For once, I don't care.

She places a hand on my arm. I jerk away.

'What? Suddenly you're out of words?'

Several beats of silence pass.

'Are you accusing me of sleeping with Arjun?' she hisses. 'Are you?'

'Of course not! How can you ask me that?'

'I don't know, Niv, it's pretty hard to trust someone when you find out they've been lying to you the entire time you've known them.'

I ignore the little voice inside my brain that calls me a hypocrite.

'What are you—'

'Sabah. Faraz. The fact that you pretended you barely even knew Noor. Would you like me to go on?'

'Jesus – is that what this is about? It was fifteen years ago, Alia. We were kids.'

'Why didn't you tell me?'

'Because there was nothing to tell. We were friends, then we weren't.' Niv sighs, then continues. 'Noor and I . . . we had a complicated history. She loved being the centre of attention and she could be so charming when she wanted to. I loved her. I treated her like a little sister. But she could also be cruel, Alia. Even you can't deny that.

'When she found out that Faraz and I were together, instead of talking to me about it, she started spreading rumours – nasty rumours – about me. She would write these mean little notes and stick them up on the school noticeboards. It was stupid, kiddish stuff but it was embarrassing. I didn't realize it was her until months later.'

'Why didn't you tell me all this? Why lie?'

'Because I didn't want to go into it. It's ancient history and you knew the most relevant parts anyway. Noor was a bitch.'

I wince at the tone. 'And she had it coming? Is that what you're saying?'

Niv has the presence of mind to look shocked, hurt even. 'No. But she doesn't automatically become a good person because she died. And I'm not sure what it is that Sabah's after, but if I were you, I'd steer clear of her.'

'It's funny, that almost makes it sound like you have something to hide. Where were *you* the night of the party?'

It takes a second for my unspoken accusation to land and when it does, Niv jerks backwards.

'How dare you?'

I stand, shockingly unbalanced on my feet.

'Stay away from my husband.'

I start to walk away but not before Niv's delivered her parting shot.

'You know, you've become so paranoid you can't even see who's on your side anymore.'

SABAH

My phone hasn't stopped ringing all morning.

I had heard of lightning fast pre-empts, of deals that raked up hundreds of thousands of pounds in advances alone, but nothing could have prepared me for the reaction from Amazon.

Less than forty-eight hours after Andrew pitched it to them, Amazon sent in their opening offer, a figure so ridiculously high that I'd had to ask Andrew to repeat himself twice on the phone, certain that I'd misheard him. I needn't have bothered. An hour after we accepted the offer, the contract landed in my inbox complete with the exclusivity clause and the release schedule that I'd insisted on.

Exactly fifteen years after she died, the story of Noor's life and death will be streamed in 200 countries across the world.

There are more than a thousand likes and comments on my Facebook post linking to the announcement on Deadline. There are thirty-four unread texts and eighteen voicemails on my phone, messages of congratulations, people I haven't seen in years telling me how proud they are of me.

I should be happy. I should be celebrating. This is exactly the reaction that I wanted. Hell, it's more than what I wanted. It's the perfect follow-up to the Harriet Clarke documentary and yet with every congratulatory message that I receive, my heart sinks a little bit further. I have run through the case sequentially dozens of times, I've interviewed everyone involved, I've pored over photographs and watched hundreds of hours of archive footage and yet I have no new leads and my only theory has been completely debunked. If I can't use this documentary to find Noor's killer, to prove to the world that she didn't commit suicide, then all I'm doing is using my best friend's death to pay off my debts. I am exploiting her family's pain to save my floundering career.

This is how I imagine a leech must feel.

I wonder if I got it wrong. Maybe Noor did commit suicide. Maybe the diary entry is nothing more than another example of Noor being dramatic for drama's sake.

My thoughts are jumbled.

My memories of that year have become so distorted, so muddled up with my own guilt, I'm no longer sure of anything.

I think about what Addi said, what my mother has been saying for years.

Noor was an addict with a depressive streak. She had been bullied and shamed and pushed to the edge until she cracked.

What if the only reason I've been so convinced that Vineet had killed her, that *anyone* had killed her, was that it was easier to believe that she had been murdered than to think that my stupid, childish actions, brutal in their imagining, relentless in their execution, could have been enough to tip her over the edge? What if the only reason I have been hell-bent on proving she was murdered is so I can assuage my own guilt over what I did?

My phone lights up with yet another congratulatory message and I distract myself, taking my time typing out a response.

Here's the other thing; the thing I don't allow myself to even think about. Believing that Noor committed suicide means finally saying goodbye. It means letting her go and focusing on the mess that is my life instead of obsessing over her death.

But maybe that is exactly what I need to do. I'm thirty-one. Save for the occasional Tinder hook-up, I haven't had a real relationship in more than ten years. I live alone in an apartment that I haven't even bothered to fully furnish. I have plenty of colleagues but no friends.

Perhaps I should look at this documentary as a chance at catharsis.

I look at the webpage open on my laptop.

Amazon Studios Grabs True Crime Docu-series From Sabah Khan & Arch Films in Pre-Emptive Buy

This contract is everything I've ever dreamed of.

I decide I should at least try to celebrate.

I head downstairs into the living room and put some

music on. I order a takeaway meal, then open a bottle of red wine and sit down at the table. I raise a glass.

To me and my ghosts.

I pass out on the sofa, letting the wine lull me into the kind of sleep that wipes everything out and leaves you feeling like the earth has shifted on its axis when you do finally emerge. I twist myself to a sitting position and roll my shoulders to ease the pain that is making itself known, every muscle and nerve ending in my back objecting. I reach for my phone to check the time, but it's dead, the battery worn out after a night of multiple notifications. I put it on charge and make myself a cup of strong black coffee as I run through my mental checklist.

Jenny's rescheduled my flight back to London so I can attend the initial meeting with Amazon next week, which means that instead of a fortnight, I now have three days to finish the preliminary research and figure out what really happened that night.

I gulp my coffee down then run upstairs and go straight into the shower.

Everyone who knew Noor believes that she committed suicide. Almost immediately after she died, there was a narrative that was set. The narrative of a troubled girl who was bullied by her friends, exploited by the media and persecuted by the nation, and looking at it from that slant, I can understand why the idea that she killed herself is so appealing. It's tidy, the narrative picking up the strands of underage sex, drugs, toxic friendships and tying them up in a neat, cautionary bow. But if there's one thing that I've learned, it's that real life is never this neat.

I get dressed and go downstairs to get my phone. Though there have been several tell-all books and documentaries about Noor, the police files have never been published. I think of some of the most high-profile cases from the past two decades – the Noida gang rape, the Arushi-Hemraj double homicide, the Ryan School murder; there are countless examples of the Indian police botching crime scenes, misplacing evidence, falsifying statements. Alia had said that the files were classified due to Javed Uncle's position on the cabinet, but what if the real reason was more sinister?

I send Alia a quick text before systematically checking my messages and voicemails.

It's another twenty minutes before I get to Dan's voicemail. I listen to him go on about Amazon for a while before he says the word Trojan and I sit up, alert. He explains the process his hacker friend used, talks about VPNs and IP addresses before uttering the words I've been waiting to hear: he's sent me an email with the GPS coordinates.

The location of the person who sent me Noor's diary entry.

My fingers fly over my phone as I find Dan's email and enter the coordinates into Google Maps. I pinch the screen repeatedly to zoom out.

My insides twist into a tight knot as I realize what I'm looking at.

My hand goes automatically to the gold sparrow resting against my chest. It's ironic really. It's the first place I looked, and the first person I ruled out.

I look at the white speck surrounded by acres of green.
The house I know so well.
I slump back in my seat.
The email came from the Qureshi house.

ALIA

School hurt without Noor there, more so because in a weird way, she was everywhere, around every corner, in every classroom, at track practice, in the cafeteria. Everywhere I went all anyone was talking about was what she had done and all that was reminding me of was what I had failed to do. I was the cowardly one. I was the one who had walked away yet somehow it felt like she had abandoned me.

Over the next week, things got even worse. Noor and Vineet were expelled. No amount of family money or influence could get them out of this, not with the whole country watching.

By the time the police sprang into action and shut down the website, the video had been downloaded over a million times. Not only had it become national news, everyone from my granddad's golf friends to our milkman had seen it. Everyone was talking about it.

There was no way of knowing how many people shared it privately, but what I understood was this – Noor and Vineet were never named. People knew who it was, they knew whom to slander, because they watched it. The unfairness of it all left me reeling.

Vineet had been walking around telling everyone that Noor had known he was recording the whole time. I'd even heard him tell someone that she was the one who sent it out, not him, and it was all I could do not to go and kick him in the guts myself. Noor, on the other hand, hadn't said anything at all. It was almost as if she had dropped off the face of the earth and yet all anyone was talking about was her.

The school launched an official investigation into the social lives of our class. No one knew what it was they were hoping to find, but we all knew there was plenty that we needed to hide.

I waited to see if anyone would find out what I'd done, if I'd get punished, but knowingly or not, I hadn't done anything that was technically against the rules. The school assumed that I was the impressionable new girl who had found herself in Noor's vice-like grip. Everyone was so concerned that I had been damaged by my friendship with Noor; they never even stopped to consider that I might have been the one inflicting the damage. So I got away with it, and for a while at least life continued.

After two weeks of angry silence, and an awkward phone call with my mother, who in the end couldn't be bothered to visit, my grandparents un-grounded me out of pity. But it was obvious that the relationship I'd had with Nana and Nani was gone. They had seen who I really was and like every other person in my life, they had decided they didn't like the real me.

Sabah had allowed me back into the fold, but barely. I had been demoted to my old seat.

I found myself missing Noor with a desperation I had not known before. Her madness, her chaos, her house, her family, her father. But more than anything else, I missed the camaraderie, the sense of belonging that I had never known before.

I missed having friends and I wanted back in, no matter what the cost.

I walked over nervously when Sabah summoned me after homeroom a few days later.

'We were just talking about the leavers' ball next week.' Sabah smiled sweetly. 'You are going, aren't you?'

'I don't know,' I said, trying not to get overexcited about what sounded like an invitation. Perhaps Sabah had finally decided to forgive me.

'You should come. It'll be fun,' she said.

Next to her, Saloni nodded enthusiastically.

'Okay,' I said.

I allowed myself a small smile as I turned around and trudged back to my seat.

'Oh, and Alia,' Sabah called out after me. 'Make sure you bring Noor.'

Over the next week, I called Noor every day, left messages, wrote her a letter. I apologized a million times over but she refused to talk to me.

I knew how important it was for me to make this up to Sabah. I had seen what she could do, what the boys at school could do. As much as I wanted to go to the leaver's ball, turning up without Noor would come with consequences.

I had resigned myself to the fact that I'd have to skip the ball altogether until the night before the party, when Noor finally called me back.

'I was getting sick of listening to you whine in your messages,' she said.

'I wanted to apologize. I just – with all those boys surrounding us, I panicked. I'm really sorry,' I blurted out.

'Are you?' Noor sounded bored.

'Of course I am. School's shit without you.'

'Oh, gee, I feel terrible for you.'

I sighed. 'Sorry, that was stupid. I miss you.'

'Me too,' she mumbled. 'What's going on at school?'

I filled her in on everything: the new girl, the new rules, Sabah's tyranny, Banerjee losing it over bathroom graffiti. I really had missed her, I realized as we spoke. She was the only person who saw the real me and never judged me for it.

'How are things with you?' I asked her cautiously, after the gossip from school had run dry. Though the story about Noor and Vineet's video had moved away from the front pages, the country's reaction to it had prompted a bunch of talk show specials. Noor's father was in the news almost daily, with his rivals using the riots in Kanpur as an excuse to pressurize him to resign, and the last I'd heard, Faraz had been suspended from college for beating up a bunch of boys who allegedly asked him for Noor's nightly rates.

'Shit. Ammi isn't speaking to me. Abbu looks like he

wants to kill me whenever I see him, and Faraz has just completely lost it. They're sending me away.'

'Where?' I asked. Even with her father's connections and all the money in the world, I doubted any school in the city would take Noor. I'd heard Vineet had just about managed to get into a school in north Delhi, not surprising perhaps since his father owned the building.

'Somewhere so far away that they can forget I exist. Sometimes I think it would be easier if—' She cut herself off.

'Are you okay, Noor?'

'Look, I don't need you psychoanalyzing me.'

'No, that's not –' I started, but that's exactly what I had been doing. I twisted the cord around my finger. 'What are you doing tomorrow? Should I come over after school?' I asked, trying to keep the desperation out of my voice.

'Aren't you going to the leavers' ball?'

'Yes, but . . . are you going?'

'I don't think anyone wants me there,' she said. Noor hadn't exactly been uninvited but it had become pretty clear that she wasn't welcome at any of the Wescott parties anymore. 'Plus, I'm grounded for life.'

'Since when do you do what's expected of you?'

Noor gave a short, dry laugh. 'Actually, you're right,' she said. 'Come over.'

It cost me an hour and 150 rupees to get there and all the while I kept telling myself I was doing this as much for myself as for Sabah. I missed Noor. I wanted to see her. That much at least was true.

'What's going on?' I asked Noor. I'd seen TV vans parked on the drive and I could hear loud voices filtering through from the living room.

'Abbu's having a press conference so all his stupid *karyakartas* are here. They talk so much shit, it's unbelievable.'

'Where's Fatima Aunty?' I asked. Something about the way Noor was sitting alone in her room didn't feel right.

'Visiting my grandparents. It wasn't enough to shut herself in her room, she needed a whole city between us.'

I felt my throat constrict as Noor told me how her mother had told her she couldn't even bear to look at her anymore, how her father kept his eyes trained on the floor when he spoke to her, how Faraz had been vacillating between spouting quotes from the Quran to ignoring her completely, how he walked around so angry that she was scared he would implode.

'Have you spoken to anyone from school?'

'No,' she said, looking everywhere except at me. It hit me then how completely alone she was and it made my guilt feel even heavier. 'The only one I want to speak to is Sabah, and she refuses to even pick up the phone.' She spoke matter-of-factly but I could see the tears bristling in her eyes.

'Are they still talking about me?' she asked after a few minutes.

'A bit,' I waffled, the lie twisting around my insides, tying them up in a tight knot. 'It'll pass, though . . . you know what it's like, they'll tire of this and move on to something else in a few weeks.'

'I think you and I both know that this isn't going to die down anytime soon. I just wish I hadn't been stupid enough to trust Vineet.'

Noor was sitting in the window seat, lit up by the late afternoon sun. There was something so unsuspecting about her in that moment, I felt my heart crack open.

'Do you love him?'

'I wish it were that simple,' she said so softly that I had to lean forward to hear her.

I had been hoping, somewhat selfishly, that she would tell me that she had secretly been in love with him, that they couldn't imagine being apart, that the video was just the result of teenage idiocy. The idea that she had done those things with Vineet simply so she could hurt Sabah sickened me.

Yet I couldn't help but feel sorry for her.

'Have you spoken to him since . . . you know?'

'No, and I don't plan to.'

'He's saying you knew about the video.'

'Of course he's saying that.'

'Did you?' I asked, desperate to know but also aware that our newly reinstated friendship was still fragile.

'How can you ask me that?' She turned so sharply it made me jump. There were tears in her eyes.

'Sorry, I just – He'll probably be there.'

'I know.'

'Are you sure you want to do this?' I asked her, no longer concerned about what Sabah wanted. I knew the kinds of things people were saying about Noor. They would rip her apart, and knowing Sabah, she certainly hadn't called her there to make up.

'I need to see Sabah. I can't stop my parents from sending me away, but I can't leave without speaking to her. We've been best friends since we were five. I have to make things right.'

We waited till the commotion had died down, till Noor's father had left and the house was eerily quiet.

'Are you sure this will work?' I whispered even though we were the only ones in the house. 'Maybe we should go out the back.'

With all the media attention, the house was even more heavily guarded than usual, but it was a massive house, and we'd snuck in and out through the servants' entrance enough times for me to know that was the easiest thing to do.

But Noor wasn't having it.

'I'm not hiding anymore,' she said, grabbing my hand. For a moment it felt as though this was just another adventure I was setting off on as we went downstairs and marched out of the front gates.

SABAH

I grip the wheel, dust flying beneath the tyres as I as swerve onto the private road leading to the Qureshi estate. Trees whir by, their wrangled branches nothing but a blur of darkness.

Though there are only two residents, the Qureshi estate has always been a busy place. Aside from the full-time cavalry of staff – maids, drivers, cooks and cleaners – the Qureshis have always enjoyed an almost endless stream of guests and visitors. Anyone could have accessed the Qureshis' wifi connection to send the tip, but the Trojan gave us one other piece of information. The email account was accessed from a MacBook Pro and as open-minded as I like to think I am, I have trouble believing that any of the staff would shell out a few months' wages on a computer, which leaves only two options – a guest or one of the Qureshis. My gut tells me it had to be one of the Qureshis, but logic tells me I'm wrong. If either Fatima Aunty or Faraz wanted to tell me something, all they had to do was pick up the phone. There was no need to go to the trouble of sending in an anonymous tip.

But I suppose there's no harm in checking it out.

I honk when I get to the big iron gates, impatient to be let in.

'I'm here to see Fatima Aunty,' I say, rolling down the window to speak to the *chowkidaar*.

'Madam *nahi hain*,' he replies, his Hindi delivered with a strong Nepalese accent.

'Faraz?'

'*Nahi hain*,' he repeats before hurrying back into his hut.

For a moment I consider ditching my car and sneaking in through the servants' entrance, as I'd done hundreds of times with Noor. But the house is shrouded in darkness and I am not a teenager anymore.

I ring Faraz instead.

'Sabah, how can I help?' Faraz sounds harried. I can hear noises in the background and I realize I've interrupted him at work. I get straight to the point.

'I thought I'd visit Fatima Aunty. I'm outside the house but the guard won't let me through.'

His voice softens at the mention of his mother. 'I wish you'd called first. She's visiting her brother.'

'When is she due back?'

'Next week.'

I'll be back in London by then.

'Could you send me her phone number?'

Faraz hesitates for the briefest of moments before speaking. 'Sure, I'll text it to you now. Anything I can help with?'

'Just a few more questions. Nothing that can't wait. But while I've got you on the—'

'Hang on one sec,' Faraz says. I hear the sound of footsteps and then a door closing before Faraz's voice comes back on the line, minus the background clutter. 'I've been meaning to talk to you about that,' he says, his deep voice concerned. 'Ammi's been a bit . . . distraught since your last visit.'

'I'm so sorry. I didn't mean to upset her.' I run my hand along the curve of the steering wheel. When I last saw her, Fatima Aunty had seemed convinced that Vineet was to blame. Was it possible that it was more than just her instinct that told her that Noor hadn't committed suicide? It made sense that she would've found Noor's diaries after her death and Faraz had already told me she was obsessed with online courses. She could easily have learned how to set up the complex VPN framework that Dan had described online. I could tell Faraz what I suspected, but if Fatima Aunty had gone to the trouble of using proxy servers to send me the diary, she obviously felt the need to keep it from Faraz. What I can't understand is why, when it seems like all Faraz is trying to do is protect her.

'I know you didn't. And it was always a toss-up. I'd hoped that talking about Noor would help bring her some form of closure but it's had the opposite effect.'

Unless it is *because* he's trying to protect her. Faraz has been doing everything in his power to help Fatima Aunty move on. He wouldn't want her getting drawn back to Noor, obsessing over her diaries, trying to prove that her death was more than a tragic suicide. It occurs to me that that is exactly what I'm doing and I turn my focus back to Faraz.

'But I've been thinking and I don't think it's good for her to keep revisiting the past, Sabah. She's already back on her anti-depressants and I . . . you remember what it was like after the funeral, don't you? What it did to her. I can't risk that again.'

I feel myself deflate. Fatima Aunty is a key contributor. Her interview in the sizzle reel had been crucial in roping in Amazon.

'I can make sure that—'

'Look, I don't want to put you in an awkward situation. You've already got the footage from the interview a few weeks ago and I'm still more than happy for you to film me. But I need to look after Ammi. She's all I have left.'

I drum my fingers against the steering wheel. It feels as though I'm stuck in a real-life slow-motion sequence. The infamous Delhi fog has descended and I am inching along on the highway, the usual orchestra of honks and beeps muffled as it travels through the thick clouds of mist.

I nearly jump when my phone rings, the shrill ringtone a sharp contrast to my current environment. I consider pulling over, but I can barely see the road, let alone try to find a hard shoulder. I put my phone on speaker and answer.

'Sabah?' Alia's voice echoes through the car. 'Where are you?'

'On the highway, heading home. What's up?'

'I've got the files.'

*

'Okay, so what have we got here?' Alia sets two cups of tea on the coffee table before settling down on the sofa next to me. Dressed in a sweatshirt and leggings, with her hair swept back into a messy bun, she looks more like the young girl I'd once known than the suave politician she is now.

I point one by one to the four stacks that I've split the contents of the police file into.

'The first information report and phone transcripts, a copy of the suicide note, transcripts of the police interviews the week after, copies of the press release issued by the police.'

'Start with the FIR and transcripts?' Alia asks, picking up the first bundle and splitting it into two.

We spend the next two hours working through all the paperwork, poring over every report, reading and rereading every transcript, but we find nothing. It is shocking how sparse the file is, lacking in even the most basic pieces of information. The incident report consists of little more than a typed-up sequence of events and a copy of the death certificate. There are no crime scene photographs or documents detailing evidence gathered, but then, I suppose, with the fact of Noor's suicide being uncontested, the police wouldn't have treated it like a crime scene.

I tear up when I come to the note. I pass it to Alia and she nods, refusing to meet my eye.

We don't need a forensics team to analyze it. The handwriting is Noor's, but the words aren't. There is a formality there, the use of a certain legalese that could never have come from her. It is obvious that she had been coerced into writing it. Or threatened.

'Did you know that Javed Uncle's bodyguard reported the gun stolen four days before Noor died?' Alia says, looking up from the sheet of paper in her hand.

I shake my head. I didn't know that but it doesn't surprise me. Noor's death wasn't an accident or a crime of passion. Her diary entry, dated a week before the party, had confirmed as much.

Someone had been threatening Noor.

My stomach drops as something occurs to me. I leaf through the papers splayed out on the coffee table till I find the one I'm looking for.

'What do you know about Brij Pratap Joshi?'

'He used to be the police commissioner. Retired three, maybe four years ago. Why?'

I hand her the copy of the FIR.

Alia scans the incident report then looks at me, puzzled. 'What am I looking for?'

I lean over and point out the name of the attending officer.

'Emergency calls are automatically diverted to the nearest patrol car,' I say. 'So why was the head of Delhi's police force first on the scene?'

ALIA

Fifteen years ago

The leavers' ball wasn't hosted or even endorsed by the school. All the school organized to send off the graduating class was an incredibly dry farewell full of speeches, awards and a dance floor in the middle of the football field that no one could be bothered to hit up. Everyone knew that the *real* farewell happened at the leavers' ball hosted by the year eleven students, a party that was much more apt for the kind of debauchery that Wescott was famous for. Our class had decided to send off the year twelve students with a ball at Yash's farmhouse in Sainik Farms.

The party was already in full swing by the time Noor and I arrived. The drive was packed with cars and I could hear laughter floating out of the house and into the front lawn. We pushed our way inside, the crowd parting as Noor and I walked through the hallway and into the front room where a dance floor had been set up, complete with overhead disco lights, smoke machines and strobes.

I wasn't naive enough to think that Noor would get a warm welcome, but nothing could have prepared me for the way they treated her, clusters of girls whispering and hissing and groups of boys shouting out lewd comments and whistling.

'Line up, boys, the slut has arrived,' someone yelled over the music.

I saw Noor's jaw tighten but she just kept walking until we were standing in front of Saloni and Addi.

'Where's Sabah?' Noor asked them.

'I didn't know the boys had hired escorts for the party,' Saloni said, turning to Addi, pretending she hadn't seen Noor.

'Come on, Saloni, there's no need to be nasty,' I said.

'Of course you would defend her.'

I looked at Addi for support, but she slid her eyes sideways, refusing to meet mine.

'Sabah doesn't want to talk to you or see you so just go back to whatever shithole you came from, okay?' Saloni leaned in close to Noor, their faces almost touching. 'Some of us are trying to have fun here.'

With that, Saloni turned to pick up her drink from the bar, something hideously pink and girly.

'How—' Noor started as she reached out to grab Saloni's shoulder, but Saloni shrugged her off with such force that Noor stumbled backwards.

'Don't touch me,' Saloni hissed. 'Slut,' she added under her breath.

Even Addi looked horrified. No matter how twisted the rumours got, we all knew that technically, Noor's only mistake had been trusting Vineet. The rest, getting involved with her friend's ex-boyfriend, getting drunk, having sex

– if they even got that far – they were all things that most people in this room had done.

Noor's eyes darkened. She took a step forward, gaze fixed firmly on Saloni.

'I suppose you only like being touched by bus drivers and conductors,' Noor said, raising her voice an octave so everyone around us could hear. 'What was his name . . . Ajay? I've always wondered how it works, do you pay them or—'

'How dare you!' Saloni lurched forward but Noor stepped aside.

'Where is Sabah?' she repeated after Saloni had straightened herself.

This time Addi stepped in. 'She's not here yet but she called me earlier, she's on her way,' she blurted out.

Is there anything better than the threat of a secret being exposed to make people talk?

'Tell her to come and find me.'

Noor reached around Addi to grab a bottle of vodka from the bar and stalked off into the garden, ignoring the stares she was getting from girls daintily sipping on fruit juice.

Fruit juice that they had spiked with whatever spirit they could get their hands on earlier.

We sat down on the concrete slabs in the corner and took turns swigging from the bottle.

It wasn't long before Sabah found us, trailed, of course, by Saloni.

'I thought you would've got the message by now. I'm done with you,' Sabah said, looking down on us.

'Oh, you're done, are you? After making sure I have no one left to go to?' Noor sneered, before her expression softened. She stood up. 'I know you're upset, Sabah, but please let me explain.'

'Explain what? How you humiliated me by kissing my boyfriend then pretended to be my friend while you continued screwing him?'

'I know what you did, and if I can forgive and forget, then so can you. Please, Sabah, I just want us to go back to being friends.'

'I could never be friends with someone like you,' Sabah spat out. 'Slut.'

'You know what, I've just about had it with you. I made a mistake but you committed a crime. The only reason I haven't told anyone is because I thought you were my friend.'

A crime? I looked at Saloni but I could tell from the startled expression on her face that she had no idea what Noor was talking about either.

'You're making no sense.' Sabah paused to frown at the bottle Noor was holding. 'Vodka straight from the bottle? Classy.'

'Come on, Sabah, you can drop the act now. Don't you think you've done enough damage already?'

'I don't know what you're talking about, and if this is your way of apologizing, you need to do better.'

'Sabah, I am trying really hard here. Don't push me. Vineet sent that video to only one person. You.'

I heard myself gasp as Noor's words sunk in. The realization rose like nausea. The guilt followed soon after.

There was only one reason Vineet would send Sabah the video.

Sabah's face was impassive. 'Stop lying.'

'When you sent that video out you ruined my life. Half the fucking country's seen it. Surely you can see what you did is so much worse than anything I've done to you,' Noor continued.

'You sound deluded. Why would I do that?'

'To punish me? You have always liked the idea of poetic justice.' Noor looked away. There were tears streaming down her face. Saloni and I shifted on our feet, neither of us comfortable with watching yet unable to tear ourselves away. 'Or maybe you didn't realize who the boy was when you sent it. Either way, you got what you wanted,' Noor continued. 'They're sending me away. I can't get into any school here, and even if I did, I think my parents would rather see me dead than—'

'So would I. I will never forgive you for what you did. And after your little porno, good luck finding anyone to talk to. You're finished here.'

Sabah flipped around and walked away, Saloni on her heels.

'Noor.' I took a step towards Noor, arms open, but she pushed me away. Loud sobs were wracking through her entire body.

'Just leave me alone.'

ALIA

Fifteen years ago

I found her a few hours later, spinning on the dance floor by herself, a nearly empty bottle of vodka in her hand and the tell-tale remnants of white powder on her fingertips.

I cast around the room, remembering too late the party favours that were being passed around earlier. I couldn't believe I had been foolish enough to think that anyone would look out for Noor at this party.

'What did you take?' I asked Noor.

'What do you care?'

'Come on, Noor, you know I care. Let's—'

'All you care about is worming your way into this world. Well, you've seen what we do to each other. What do you think about it now?' She swung her arm around, knocking against a couple as she twirled.

Almost immediately a small circle cleared around us. I felt the heat of at least fifty sets of eyes burn into my back.

I put an arm around Noor's shoulder, and tried to pull her away from the dance floor.

'Actually, no, that's not it,' she said, shoving me. 'What

you really care about is worming your way into *my* world. Poor little Alia wants a new mummy and daddy.'

The room darkened.

She leaned in close, her face inches from mine. 'Well, look somewhere else because you can't have mine.'

I willed myself to say something but no words came out.

'Oh, right,' Noor said, clocking that she had a captive audience after weeks of being the pariah. 'You all don't know. Alia's parents hate her. That's why they shipped her off,' she spat out.

I heard someone gasp.

I stood there unable to move, unable to speak. I wanted nothing more than for the ground to open up and swallow me whole, every lie, every ambition, every thought gone. I wanted to vanish, pretend I had never existed.

'Surprise, surprise,' Noor continued. 'They aren't ambassadors on some high-risk posting in Turkey. They aren't even diplomats. They're *aides*. They can't even afford to pay the school fees. And the award for Liar of the Century—'

I spun around. I didn't know how, but my feet were moving. I was pushing through the crowd, running, running, running, desperate to get away, desperate to forget.

I must have spent hours alone in the cold, staring up at the cloudless sky. It was almost midnight when people started spilling out into the garden for the fireworks. The girls had slipped off their heels and were standing on their tippy-toes, wrapped tightly in their boyfriends' coats, pretending they didn't know how cute they looked. And the boys were acting gallant, as if we didn't all know they had only one thing on their minds. It was a charade we were all experts in, right down to the fluttering eyelashes and the not so subtle hair toss. I watched from a distance as people knocked back shots and toasted their futures, kids who had said nasty things to each other and about each other clinking their glasses together and promising to remain best friends. Forever.

I pulled my coat tight around me and stood a few feet from the rest of them, close enough to find some comfort in the gathering but far enough to know that no matter how hard I tried, how many friends I made, how hard I worked, I could never be a part of their world. They might have let me visit, but they would never let me stay.

I felt a flash go off and held my hand up to shield my face. I did not want any reminders of this night.

Sabah, Addi and Saloni were standing a short distance away from me. I tried not to look at them as they pressed together, laughing and giggling, their closeness just another reminder of how alone I was.

Their heads tilted up in unison as a rocket whizzed up and showered the sky with blue and green teardrops.

It was my own fault, I thought as the sky erupted into a million colours. I hadn't been careful. I had let my guard down. I'd thought that Noor liked me for who I was, when the truth was that she had pitied me. I tried so hard not to cry, but I was drunk and tired and so completely alone that the tears slipped out. I turned my face up to the sky so that no one would see. I had suffered enough humiliation for one night.

Something made me turn around, the sound of my name or perhaps just instinct, but there she was.

Noor. Unsteady on her feet, swaying.

Vineet was hovering by her side, trying to steer her towards the house, but she kept pushing him away, clearly not drunk enough to forget what he had done. A few feet from them, Ankit stood clutching a bottle of water, perhaps waiting for an opportunity to swoop in and save her.

Let him.

'Alia,' she called out, 'I don't feel well.'

I thought about the promise I had made to her earlier that day when I told her I would stay by her side, and instantly pushed it away. She was on her own now. After the way she had humiliated me, I didn't owe her anything.

'Alia. Please. I want to go home.'

She sounded broken, desperate. I knew she needed help.

I knew she needed *my* help.

I turned around. I pretended I didn't hear her. I decided she deserved a little pain after what she had put me through.

And as the fireworks shrieked into the sky, hissing and whistling before they exploded, shattering the still winter night into a million colourful pieces, I imagined her dead. It made my love glow brighter. Picturing her gone made me realize just how much I would lose, how much worse things would get, but more than anything else, it made me realize that no matter how badly Noor treated me, I would go back to her. Because ultimately it came down to this: I needed her.

I brushed the tears away. I told myself I would let her suffer tonight. And then when she called me tomorrow, which I knew she would, I would accept her teary apology. I would forgive her.

She would see that she had been wrong to humiliate me like that.

She would see that she needed me just as much as I needed her.

I let a smile flicker across my face as a rocket sizzled into the sky and small orange lights began to sparkle, as though the entire sky was filled with fireflies, fluttering, dancing, glimmering for a few seconds before fading away one by one, leaving us in darkness.

Yes, I thought. I would let her suffer alone tonight. That would teach her a lesson.

An hour later, I went home and crawled into bed, already planning in my head the conversation I would have with Noor the next morning. The apologies, the tears, the promises.

I never had that conversation.

My grandparents woke me up at the crack of dawn. Nani held my hand while Nana uttered the words that would splinter my world forever. Noor was dead, he told me. She had bled to death on her kitchen floor.

ALIA

Fifteen years ago

The funeral took place the next day.

I was there, standing next to Javed Uncle, when Faraz burst in with his mother.

I stood with them as they lowered her into the ground.

I wept with them as we cleared out her room and packed away her clothes.

I laughed with them as after months of mourning, the grief lifted.

I was there for all of it and slowly, deliberately, I became a part of their family.

I never told anyone what I had done and even as the guilt gnawed away at me, I became her proxy in death.

Meanwhile the case that the police had brushed off as teenage debauchery became a talking point. Noor's death sparked something off in a nation that had until then made their peace with a system that failed its people again and again. The country wanted answers. The same people who had called Noor a slut took to the streets demanding justice. The candlelight vigils and silent protests continued for months and yet the police did little.

They arrested the college student who had uploaded the video on the website, then released him. They arrested the man who owned the auction site, then released him. They called in more than twenty Wescott students for questioning. But Noor and Vineet were both minors, and the act itself had been consensual so legally there was nothing to be done. I became known as the misguided, but innocent, sidekick and Sabah the mastermind behind Wescott's decadent parties. Noor's allegation that Sabah had been the one who sent the video out became something of an open secret, an unconfirmed rumour that was widely discussed in the Wescott crowd but only in hushed whispers.

I kept waiting for someone to question why Vineet would send that video to Sabah in the first place but no one ever did. The guilt was crippling. In my blind desperation to be accepted, to have friends, I'd ruined the very person I most wanted to be accepted by.

And yet, every time I saw him afterwards, I looked away, refusing to acknowledge our shared guilt, turning away from the moment when I'd set into motion a chain of events so twisted, I'd be left grappling with the repercussions years later.

After Sabah's attempt to sabotage my birthday, I'd seen Vineet at the Viva concert. The bomb that I had dropped about Sabah and Mohit had had little effect on Sabah and still seething from what she had done to me, I pulled him to one side and told him that Sabah wasn't the virgin queen she pretended to be. I hadn't quite realized the power of that revelation until I saw his face. For a moment, I was scared that he might hit me, but then I realized that his fury was directed at Mohit. I can't explain how I felt in that moment. No matter what she did, Sabah was untouchable. I knew she would find a way to spin this. She would cry and offer Vineet an over-the-top apology or tell him that Mohit had taken advantage of her being drunk or vulnerable. However she did it, I knew she would find a way to manipulate the situation and draw Vineet back to her. I couldn't stand the idea that after everything she had done to me, she would still get what she wanted.

I looked at Noor and Sabah, arms linked, hips bumping as they screamed lyrics in sync with the band. I was sick of being the outsider. No matter how close Noor and I became, Sabah kept getting in the way. The only way to secure my position as Noor's best friend was to wrench Noor and Sabah apart once and for all. I was so consumed by jealousy, I didn't stop to think twice. Vineet was glaring at Mohit, ready to pound him for touching the girl he had been pursuing for months. I stopped him. I lied. I told him that instead of focusing on the girl who cared so little about him, he should focus on the one who loved him.

Who, he'd asked, the anger on his face melting away as confusion, then arrogance took its place. I didn't hesitate. I pointed straight at Noor.

SABAH

I twist the key in the lock and push the front door open into darkness, setting my car keys and bag on the console table before wandering into the kitchen. I pour myself a glass of wine in the white glow from the fridge and go into the living room.

Something's niggling at me. A little piece of the puzzle that doesn't quite fit.

By all accounts, Noor left the party with Vineet at about one a.m. Vineet dropped her off, she went inside, a few hours later her father found her with a note to say she had killed herself.

I close my eyes and press my fingers into my temple. It's right there.

Assuming the note wasn't forged, she was coerced into writing it. Which means it couldn't have been the staff or a stranger. Someone she knew made her write that –

My eyes snap open.

I scroll through my phone and ring Addi.

I cut through the pleasantries and get right to the point. 'Where did Vineet drop her off that night?' The words tumble out as my mouth tries to get in sync with my brain. Alia had told me that when they left for the party that evening, the house had been empty. Javed Uncle had already left for the constituency and Fatima Aunty and Faraz were out of town.

'At her house. We've already been over—'

'Yes, but where?' I cut her off. 'Did he go inside?'

'No, of course not. It was late, she got off outside. Sabah, what is going—'

I hang up. We used to get dropped off outside the house whenever we were sneaking in. We would slip through the gates and go in through the servants' entrance. But if Noor was the only one at home, she didn't need to sneak in; Vineet would've driven through the gates up to the porch.

I sink into the sofa.

Someone had been at home that night.

The Qureshis had always maintained that the house had been empty that night. It was the one undisputed fact in a case that was riddled with gossip and speculation. I run through the little that I know for sure. Faraz and Fatima Aunty had been out of town but Alia had told me that Javed Uncle had been at home when she got there that evening. He had called a press conference and she'd said the whole place had been teeming with TV crew and reporters. But when riots broke out in his constituency, he was forced to adjourn the press conference and rush to the scene.

When my parents and I visited the day after the funeral,

Javed Uncle had told us that leaving the house that evening would always be the biggest regret of his life.

I think back to one of the many afternoons Noor, Alia and I had spent at my house. Alia and I were working on a Physics project but Noor had been bent over her sketch-book as usual. When I realized she was using me as a model, I insisted on seeing the sketch. I close my eyes as the memory comes back to me, as clear as if it were yesterday.

'This is incredible,' I'd said, amazed at the detail, the way she'd caught the curve of my nose, the tilt of my eyebrows. The sketch was so precise it could have been a photograph.

Alia leaned in to sneak a look. 'You should apply to art school.'

Noor hesitated for a second before laughing it off.

I can still see the pained look that appeared on Alia's face as she tried to figure out what she had said wrong.

I tried to warn Alia silently, willing her to let it go, but she pressed on, unaware that Noor's laughter hid layers of hurt and anger.

'Why not? You're so talented, any programme would have you.'

Noor flipped the page and started covering it with furious, black strokes, the charcoal crumbling between her fingers. 'Abbu won't let me.'

Javed Uncle was always described as progressive but his liberalism extended only to his politics. With his children, he was strict, harsh even, disciplining them at the slightest hint of misbehaviour. When the scandal broke, people assumed that Noor behaved the way she did because she was looking for attention, but I've always believed the opposite. The drugs, the drinking, the boys, it was her way of escaping it.

I still remember the look on Javed Uncle's face when he discovered the drugs that Noor had smuggled into the house. He had dragged her out of her room and into the guest room further along the corridor, his grip on her arm tight, the fury in his voice uninhibited, unconcerned by my presence. He had locked her in, refusing to let her out even to say goodbye as I packed my things and left. She'd told me later that he'd kept her there all weekend and that she had felt like she was going crazy, trapped in a room with nothing to do and no one to talk to. I'd always thought that his actions, however shocking, were necessary, that he was doing it out of love for his daughter, but it occurs to me now that there were undercurrents of shame there too. The more pious Muslim communities in the country expected Javed Uncle, as their leader, to embody good Muslim values and while he could, and did, force Noor into wearing a *hijab*, there was little else about Noor that he could control.

The gossip and rumours that started after the video went viral would have been embarrassing for any parent, but for someone in Javed Uncle's position, someone constantly under the gaze of the media, it had the power to destroy everything. For the first time, I find myself thinking about the impact that scandal must have had on him not just as her father, but as a politician. Something that sordid, that public . . . Political ambitions have been squashed for less than that.

The scandal should have meant the end of his career, the end of the legacy he had spent his whole life building. But before things could get to that point, the tide changed. As news of Noor's suicide swept through the nation, public opinion shifted. It didn't take a political genius to understand that Javed Uncle's win in the next election was driven, predominantly, by sympathy.

My brain struggles to put this together.

Javed Uncle loved Noor, I tell myself. He disciplined her because he loved her. He wanted the best for her. He had been distraught when she died.

But letting a scandal that big go unchecked would have meant the end of his career.

It meant he had reason enough to kill his own daughter.

ALIA

Noor hovers but I cannot afford to let myself get sucked into the past so I fill my brain with work instead. I focus on the latest version of the campaign funding spreadsheet and press on with the calls that I have to make. It's not grit, rather impatience that drives me on, pushing me to cut through the bullshit and face the worst.

Omar knocks on the door and I wave him in, gesturing to him to sit down while I grovel on the phone, kissing up to my biggest donor like a schoolgirl.

'Well?' Omar asks after I finish the call.

I shake my head. The donor's hedging his bets till the nominations come out, just like every other donor I've spoken to over the last week.

Omar nods before swiftly moving on. He hands me a slim folder. 'The call with the party president is in an hour. I've got the statistics you asked for here.'

'And?' I say, tetchily.

'It's not looking good.'

The call to go over the party's strategy for the general election has been scheduled for over a week now but

I know that's not what he will want to talk about today.

After Faraz's comments about the crisis centre, the party president had already warned me to reel him in. Whatever your differences, he'd said, our parties are still an alliance and if your allies don't trust you, why should the country? By country, what he really meant, of course, was the party and the cabinet. What it all meant was that unless I could turn things around, not only could I forget about winning the election, I could forget about getting the party's support for the nomination.

I can feel the recklessness searing through me.

I can't take that call, not until I've done some damage control first. I pick up my phone and my wallet. I need to know what I'm up against. Right now.

'Tell him I've had to go to the constituency on urgent business. Reschedule the call for next week.'

'But—'

'Just do it, please. And those interviews you were setting up about the sexual assault committees – move them all up. Mine should be the only face the country sees for the next two weeks.'

'Alia, always a pleasure,' Faraz says, getting up to greet me. He motions to the sofa across from him. 'Sit, please. Tea?'

'I'm not here for pleasantries, Faraz. I thought we were on the same team.'

'We are,' he says, unfazed.

'At least have the decency to be honest. I know what you're trying to do.'

He just looks at me with that polite, infuriating smile.

'Do you really think discrediting me, dissolving the alliance, will do anything to help you? There's no way in hell that you can win the election without us. We can still find a way to keep the alliance together, find you a more prominent position. Maybe in one of the parliamentary committees or a seat on the Rajya Sabha like your father?'

He lets me finish, then leans back in his chair, nodding thoughtfully, and I almost sigh with relief.

The promise of power. It works every single time.

Faraz stands up and takes a step towards me, his eyes level with mine.

'Who said anything about dissolving the alliance? My father built this party from scratch. He created the alliance so that he could help the Muslim community. I don't want a trophy position, I want the ministry.'

It takes me less than a few seconds to come up with a response, but I know from the glint in Faraz's eyes that I've given my hand away.

'Funny you say that, and yet in all these years, your father never let you run for even a municipal election. Because he knew you would lose.'

The smile disappears and with it any semblance of civility as a flash of malice passes over Faraz's face.

'Let's just see, shall we? Abbu always underestimated me. I'd advise you not to make the same mistake.'

★

I leave the Muslim Congress headquarters seething. I had assumed Faraz was going to dissolve the alliance and run against me in the general election and with their threats and speeches, Faraz and Saeed had inched me along, adding fuel to my belief. I had been worried, of course, but the situation was still salvageable. I could find new funding and though Faraz running against me would split the votes, I still had a decade's worth of work to rely on as proof and the backing of a large political party. The negative buzz they were generating would make it a harder fight, but it was still a fight I knew I could win.

The idea that he might be going after my position within the party was too audacious to even consider.

And yet now that I think about it, by keeping the alliance together, he gathers support within the party.

By publicly discrediting my work, he gathers support within the constituency.

By running for the seat that has been earmarked for me, with the support of the party that I have dedicated a decade of my life to, he isn't just making it harder for me to win, he is taking me out of the competition altogether.

The highlight of his political career will come from ending mine.

It's underhanded, disloyal and completely despicable but it's also masterful and exactly what I would have done.

It's what Javed Uncle would have advised me to do.

Dread trickles through me like a chill.

Faraz is right. I have always underestimated him.

SABAH

Exhaustion burns through my eyes. I've been up all night trying to sift and sieve the facts from the fabrications, working my way through the archive footage from every major network's coverage of Javed Uncle's press conference and the communal riots that had interrupted it, trying to pin down his whereabouts on the day. I hit pause on the video and get up, arching my back and stretching to release the tension. My head feels heavy, my stomach knotted after the multiple cups of black coffee I've gulped down.

I unlock my phone and press redial. I don't stop to think about how much I've come to rely on Alia over the past few days. Everyone needs a sounding board.

Her voice is breathless. 'I'm so sorry I missed your calls. I've had a hell of a day. Are you okay?'

I glance at the TV in front of me, a picture of Javed Uncle frozen on the screen. I have one day left before I have to go back and nothing except a theory that I still can't bring myself to believe.

'Can you come over?'

'I'm on my way.' There is no hesitation, no question, and that is how I know how panicked I must sound.

Twenty minutes later, Alia's at my door.

I pull her into the house, hurriedly filling her in on my call with Addi, words spilling out of my mouth as I voice my worries about the timeline.

Alia's face pales when I get to the part about Javed Uncle.

'No,' she says. 'You're wrong.'

'Alia—'

'There has to be another explanation. He *loved* her.'

I don't say anything. I'd been fond of Javed Uncle, but Alia worshipped him. He was her mentor, the man who had plucked her out of obscurity and changed her life overnight.

Alia rubs her hand over her eyes, pinching her lids, and I can see that she is trying to order her thoughts, letting the memories claw back.

It is only when she sits down that I notice the file she has in her hand.

'What's this?'

Alia looks at me, her face completely blank.

'Alia,' I nudge. 'What's in the file?'

She hands it to me without a word and I flick through it, unsure of what to make of it. It's a police report about a hit and run. It's only as I start reading through the dates and the details of the cars that it all comes back to me. The young couple, the baby, the two underage boys, the lie I'd told about Faraz being with us in Goa. The lie Javed Uncle had asked me to tell.

'Look at the name of the attending officer,' Alia says.

My eyes skim to the bottom of the page. We all know the maxim it's not the crime; it's the cover-up, but it's only now that it hits me how true it is.

Attending officer: Brij Pratap Joshi. Commissioner, Delhi Police.

The same man who had visited the Qureshi estate the night Noor died.

I go back to the archive, trawling through yet another network's footage while Alia busies herself with phone calls, trying to track down the retired policeman who seemed to be Javed Uncle's go-to cover-up guy. The motive fits, but even though I've spent the past hour convincing Alia of this, somehow I can't bring myself to believe that Javed Uncle would have put his career before Noor. Every time he disciplined her, it was because he was trying to protect her, quite often from herself. He loved Noor and Faraz with an intensity that had often befuddled me. He was passionate about his career, he was devoted to serving his constituents, but his children were his life.

I'm missing something.

I hit pause.

The blood rushes to my head as my brain links what I'm seeing with what it means.

'Where did you say Faraz was that night?' I ask Alia when she hangs up.

'Out of town. With his mum at her parents' house, I think. Why?'

I hit play.

'Look,' I say, pointing to the TV as the clip starts playing. We watch Javed Uncle run down the stairs, surrounded by his entourage of bodyguards, assistants and party workers. He climbs into the first car in the convoy and in less than fifteen seconds they drive off.

'What are we looking for?'

I rewind the tape and press play again.

'Look at the second car.'

I watch once again as Javed Uncle climbs into the car, the engine already running and the car moving before he's even closed the door. I hit pause just as Javed Uncle's car exits the frame and the one behind it comes into focus. I zoom in on the image and turn to look at Alia.

I watch her expression flit from confusion to shock to anger before it settles. Her shoulders slump.

Javed Uncle hadn't been the only one lying.

He's looking out of the window, a cap pulled over his head, his face turned away from the camera, but even from that angle, the square jaw and sharp nose are unmistakable. It's him, sitting in the passenger seat of the car.

Faraz.

Faraz had told us he'd been out of town that day. He'd said he had left the night before.

I was there when he arrived, moments before the funeral.

I'd seen him run into the house with his mother, tears streaming down his cheeks.

'It doesn't make sense,' I say out loud. 'What possible reason could he have to kill her?'

'Do you remember how Faraz reacted when the video came out?' Alia says.

I nod. I do remember. I remember standing in the crowd watching the consequences of Noor's fling with my boyfriend play out in front of the whole school.

But that was different. However misguided, Faraz was trying to protect her.

I think back to the day after the funeral. I had seen Faraz grieve. He had wept inconsolably. They all had.

I've always believed that part of his grief came from guilt over the fact that he hadn't been there that night. But the video shows that not only was he in Delhi that day, he was at the house.

'This video is from hours before. It doesn't prove anything,' I venture, clinging to hope. I'd been willing to accept that Javed Uncle could have killed his own daughter, but I cannot bring myself to think that the boy I'd grown up thinking of as my friend, as my *brother*, could have killed someone.

But why would Faraz lie if he wasn't hiding something?

In that one moment it crystallizes.

He wouldn't. And neither would Javed Uncle.

Family came first for Javed Uncle, always and without question.

I think about the lack of an investigation, the hurried funeral, the silence the Qureshis had maintained throughout the whole ordeal.

If Faraz had something to do with Noor's death, Javed Uncle would have had no option but to help him cover it up or risk losing his son as well. If an investigation had been carried out, the family would have been questioned. Their alibis would have been verified. The truth would have come out.

I think too about the diary entry. I had assumed that Fatima Aunty had sent it to me anonymously so she could avoid adding to Faraz's worries.

But what if I had been looking at it all wrong.

Faraz had refused to let me interview his mother without him being present, telling me he wanted to make sure she felt supported.

Control flipped sideways can look a lot like concern.

I press my fingertips into my eyes, trying to focus on the thought that's taking shape. What if the reason Fatima Aunty had kept it from him was not because she was protecting him, but because she was afraid of him?

ALIA

'We need to go to the police,' Sabah says, dark eyes fixed on mine.

'The police will go straight back to Faraz,' I say, the DU rape case still fresh in my memory. 'Look at the files, Sabah. The head of the force orchestrated the cover-up.'

I had tried to use my position to force the police to do their job but even a junior minister like Saeed had enough influence to get the police to dance to his tune. Faraz had inherited the relationships Javed Uncle had spent years building. The police wouldn't touch him. He had access to that special kind of power that can only come with years of privilege.

'We have to do *something*,' Sabah says. Her face has gone very pale and there is a desperation in her eyes that scares me.

The silence that follows seems to bounce off the walls.

I almost sigh with relief when my phone rings.

'Omar,' I speak into the phone. 'Did you find him?'

I'd tasked Omar with locating the retired police commissioner who was proving notoriously difficult to track down through the usual channels.

'Yes, but—'

Sabah hands me a post-it and a pen.

'Have you got an address?'

My heart stills as Omar speaks, his words delivered in a staccato manner that is so unlike his usual tone. Terror snakes down my spine. I feel the flicker of a memory. Once again, I underestimated Faraz.

I hang up without a word.

'Well, where is he?'

My skin feels hot and I have a sudden urge to burst into tears. Nothing I do will ever be enough. I will never be able to get Noor the justice she deserves. Not when I'm up against men like Faraz who wield their power with a flick of their hand, devastating entire families without so much as leaving a fingerprint.

Sabah's already standing, shrugging on her coat, cramming her feet into her boots. She's getting ready to go and see a man who doesn't exist.

Not anymore at least.

I reach out and grab her wrist.

'We can't see him.'

She pulls away. 'Why the hell not?'

I go very still. Dread churns in my stomach.

'He's dead,' I say. 'He was murdered last week.'

Sabah's expression is a mix of fear, shock and foreboding. I imagine mine is much the same. 'What do we do?' she whispers.

'I don't know.'

I cradle my head in my hands, letting the enormity of

it sink in as the sense of unease I've carried for so long morphs into something far more terrifying.

The retired head of police, the man who helped cover up Faraz's complicity in two cases, found dead in a ditch.

It is the timing that alarms me the most. Faraz is at the cusp of having everything he's ever wanted, party presidency, a seat in the parliament, if all goes well, a portfolio on the cabinet.

I look up as Sabah answers the question I haven't asked. 'He was the only remaining witness.'

It is shocking how far Faraz's power stretches, how ruthless his ambition is.

Sabah straightens up and pushes her shoulders back. 'There has to be something else,' she says with trademark determination. Her gaze is direct, unflinching. 'If there's one advantage we have, it's that Faraz has no idea we are on to him. We need to keep it like that till we have a plan. No one can commit murder without leaving a trace.'

Two a.m. Tiredness beats against my eyelids as I push the front door open and climb up the stairs, lack of sleep making my footsteps heavier, my head foggier.

Sabah is due to fly back to London in a few hours. We had talked about rescheduling her flight, then decided against it. It would be stupid to risk alarming Faraz when we had nothing concrete to go on. I was meant to be flying to London for a women's empowerment summit in a few weeks anyway, so it made more sense to regroup then.

I creak open the door to the bedroom and slip into the bathroom to undress, careful not to wake Arjun.

It's only when I come out, face scrubbed clean, pyjamas on, that I realize he isn't there.

The bed has not been slept in. The glass of water on the side table is untouched.

I search my brain, trying to remember if Arjun was meant to be at an event last night, but despite the haze that is clouding my thoughts, I am sure that he hadn't mentioned anything and he isn't due to travel to Tokyo until next week.

I grab the cordless handset and press down on the speed dial, aware of the quickening in my chest.

Please answer. Please answer.

'Hello?' Arjun's voice is deep and gravelly, the way it sounds when he reaches for me in the middle of the night. I can hear music in the background. Not loud club music, not even the light jazz that you might find in some of Delhi's finer establishments. It sounds like *sufi* music, something that Arjun usually hates and –

'Alia? Is everything okay?'

It takes me a few moments to find my voice. 'Where are you?'

'At work. I left you a voicemail.'

'Did you?' I can hear the accusation in my voice. I don't care.

'Yes,' he says. 'Look, I'm in the middle of something. Are you okay?'

He seems to take the strange sound that comes out of my mouth as confirmation that I am indeed okay.

'Good. I'll see you in the morning.'

He's gone before I can protest.

But not before I hear the identifying lyrics of the song. It's surprising really, how long it took me to recognize it, considering it had been an almost constant soundtrack to my years at Cambridge.

'Afreen Afreen.'

Nusrat Fateh Ali Khan's ode to the irresistible beauty of the unattainable woman.

Niv's favourite song.

ALIA

I flip onto my side, wide awake in the milky darkness of four a.m.

As a little girl, when I couldn't sleep, I would slip out of bed and tiptoe along the hall to my parents' bedroom. I never went in – even as a five-year-old I understood that I wouldn't be welcome – I just stood there outside their bedroom, listening to the muffled sound of my parents snoring. I still remember the sensation of that cheap, fake wood against my cheek as I pressed myself into the door. Just knowing that my parents were behind that door was soothing and I would drowsily slink back to my room and into my bed after a few minutes.

I hold myself completely still, listening. Arjun is still not back and the house is silent. And yet my hearing is amplified, my brain is on high alert. I am acutely aware of every heartbeat, every breath, but it is my thoughts that are roaring the loudest. They are the ones that are impossible to silence.

The dull thud of the front door closing.

The click of the switch as the lights flick on.

The creak of the stairs, decades-old wood groaning under the weight of footsteps.

I sit up with a jolt, reaching for the bedside lamp just as the bedroom door swings open.

'Fuck! You scared me,' Arjun says.

His shirt is rumpled. The tie I'd watched him pick out yesterday dangles from the pocket of his heavily creased jacket. My breath catches. I force my gaze to his face, to the dark shadows underneath his eyes and the tousled hair.

My voice, when I get it to work, comes out raspy.

'You were with Niv.'

It is not a question but he nods anyway. He slips off his jacket and sits down at the foot of the bed.

I am aware of the tears streaming down my face. My husband isn't.

His head is bowed. His hands, bent like claws, rest on either side of him on the bed. I can tell by the way he holds himself that underneath the wrinkled shirt the muscles in his back are stretched taut. He is bracing for impact.

His voice cracks and breaks as he speaks. 'The past few months . . . things have been difficult. I've been trying so hard . . . I thought I could steer us back on track but – oh God, I don't know how to say this. Alia, I—'

'You've been having an affair,' I finish for him. There is no point dragging this on.

It's the thing that I've been dreading since the day we got together and somehow also the thing that surprises me the most.

'What?' He flips around, his body twisting as he looks at me.

Even in the dim light of the bedside lamp, I can see that his eyes are wet. I look away. It's too much.

I thought we were good. I thought we were *solid*.

'I am not having an affair.'

'You *just* admitted you were with Niv.'

He walks around to my side of the bed and sits down in front of me.

'Yes,' he says, holding my gaze. 'And Nisha and Amit and about five others from finance.'

'What?'

'I didn't want to tell you. I thought I could salvage things.' He sighs. There is weariness in his eyes that I hadn't noticed before. 'Barclays gave the contract to Go Green.'

His biggest competitor.

'Last week,' he adds, before I can ask him when.

'The deal with John was a mistake. Niv kept trying to warn me but I was overconfident and reckless. I overstretched. We were trying to find a way to keep the company intact but . . . I have to be in the office at nine for the first round of layoffs and then straight to Mumbai to face the investors.'

'I'm sorry, I had no idea. I thought –'

'That I was having an affair. How could you even think that?'

I don't say anything. I don't need to.

His jaw tightens. 'That was different.'

Only it wasn't. It was exactly the same. Except the woman.

I thought we were past that, I really did.

Arjun runs a hand through his hair, his expression unreadable. 'I can't believe you accused Niv.'

'She *told* you?' The words slip out before I have a chance to consider them.

'No.'

He watches my face as realization dawns. I'd accused her in front of half of Delhi's WAGs. I should be grateful that my little performance hadn't made it into the dailies. 'I'm sorry,' I say, reaching for him.

I think about the people on that terrace. I'd barely even glanced at them as I walked out but the faces come back to me now. Arjun's friends, distant cousins, society women his mother lunched with and men his father met for golf. Arjun is far too mannered to spell it out but I know what he's thinking. This is not how people behave in his circle.

'It's okay,' he says, finally, pulling me into a hug. 'It doesn't matter.'

I rest my forehead against his shoulder, willing my heart to slow down.

Arjun isn't having an affair.

I should be relieved.

So why does it feel like my marriage is crumbling before my eyes?

It takes less than twenty-four hours after my meeting with Faraz for the call from the party president to come through. It's about campaign strategy and budgets, but the campaign we're discussing is not mine. He tells me the party wants me to continue visiting the constituency. They want me to attend every campaign rally and fundraiser but my sole purpose in every public appearance, every press conference, every parliamentary meeting is to talk up Faraz. They want me to throw my full weight behind his campaign. The message is clear. The party needs my help to win the election, but they don't need me. I suppose it's saying something that they aren't throwing me out of the fold. But in many ways, what they're asking for is worse. They're asking me to do the one thing I've fought against my whole life. They're asking me to become invisible.

SABAH

I pull my scarf tight around my neck as I step out of London Bridge station and walk through Hay's Galleria to the South Bank. The first thing that strikes me is how quiet London is, how people march past each other, headphones on, eyes wary, a disengaged, soundless army of grey and black hurtling towards an unknown enemy.

Funny what a fortnight in Delhi will do for your senses.

I spend the morning locked in the conference room with Andrew, Rachel and the Amazon commissioner. As is usually the case with these things, the general meeting is little more than a muscle flex, the network reminding us that while they want us to have creative control, we've got to deliver on the promise of the pitch. We talk about access, run through skeletal character arcs, go through the key narrative beats and overall tone and style. The misconception with documentaries is that there's no writing involved, and although there is an element – a huge element – of capturing moments as they happen, there's a difference between documentary film-making and news reporting. I feel like a fortune-teller as I run through all the possible arcs the story could take and the commissioner highlights the ones he thinks would be the most compelling. The suspicious death angle, of course, is top of the list and as we move on to the legalities, I shoot Andrew a look, wondering how much he had blagged to get us this deal.

We bring in Jenny once the commissioner leaves and the focus of the meeting shifts from creative to housekeeping. My insistence that the series premier on the anniversary of Noor's death means we'll be running a tight diary, and Jenny's smooth twenty-something forehead creases as she jots down the dates for the rough cut, picture lock and final delivery.

It's only when the meeting is over and the conference room empties out that I let myself acknowledge the thought that has been circling my brain all morning. An idea that if played right, will give Amazon the scoop that it wants, and get Noor the justice that she deserves.

The next few days pass in a blur. With the office closing in two days for the TV industry's traditionally long Christmas break and a delivery date of 1 March, we're all on our toes and Andrew, Jenny and I spend the rest of the week playing musical chairs as one meeting bleeds into the next. Producers, researchers, editors and camera crew step in and out of the huddle room, the cloudless sky going from blue to purple to black as we go over everything from planning and logistics to budgets and equipment. By the time Friday evening rolls around, I'm ready to collapse, my body losing the race against the heady mixture of jet lag and total, utter exhaustion.

I grab my bag and walk out quickly. I have no intention of getting guilt-tripped into going to the office Christmas do. It's one thing to pop out for a quick drink, but Andrew tends to go all out with elaborate themed events. Last year, he had dragged us all to a burlesque bar. This year he seems to have outdone himself by booking us into a boozy escape room adventure. My plan is to escape before the adventure begins.

I make it as far as the lift.

I rest my forehead against what is possibly the only concrete wall in this glass cage, its tangible solidity comforting.

'You're coming, right?'

I blame the exhaustion for what I do next.

I pull my lips into a smile and turn to face Dan. 'Wouldn't miss it.'

Dan and I trail behind the others, the conversation flowing easily as we walk down side streets and badly lit alleyways.

I turn to Dan as the group crowds around the entrance to a nondescript townhouse near Borough station. Jenny's shepherding everyone in one by one, handing out wristbands and tote bags emblazoned with the Arch Films logo.

'Here we go,' I say, falling in line.

Dan scoffs. 'Why do you hate her so much?'

'I don't hate her. She's just annoying.'

He rocks back on his feet and nods, eyes twinkling. 'Sure.'

'What?'

'It's just funny, that's all. She's a lot like you.'

His remark gives me pause. With her detailed lists and schedules and that laser-sharp focus, she *is* a lot like me. A younger, happier, infinitely more Instagrammable version of me. My own bitterness takes me by surprise.

'Right, shall we?' Dan says as the queue shuffles forward. I hang back, hesitating.

He steers me to one side, letting the group of edit assistants pass. 'Or we could skip this and go for a drink instead?'

I look at Dan, surprised at the strange sense of longing that's appeared out of nowhere. He's not handsome in an obvious way, certainly not the kind of man I'd pick out on Tinder, but with his biscuit-brown skin and softly chiselled chin there is something undeniably attractive about him. As he peers at me, thick eyebrows knotted together, I realize it's the kindness in his eyes.

I look at the entrance, where Jenny is waiting, two tote bags dangling from her arm, and then back at Dan, at those kind, sincere eyes that I want to sink into. I weigh up both the options in front of me. I think about Noor.

And Vineet.

And Faraz.

I step back. I take the third option.

'I'm sorry,' I say, with a regret so deep it feels as though my bones are made of putty. 'I have to go.'

I wake to the sound of pelting rain.

I go into the app on my phone and cancel the yoga class that I'd ambitiously signed up for the day before. I make a cup of coffee and settle down on the sofa with the thick bundle of mail that had been waiting for me at the office, secretly pleased for an excuse to avoid the downward dog crew.

I leaf through the stack of envelopes and flyers. Cards, Christmas party invites, discount vouchers and letters telling me I'm eligible for another credit card I can't quite afford. Not yet, anyway. I toss them aside one by one until an engraved envelope catches my eye.

I rip it open and pull out the thick card. It's an invitation to a private view at an art gallery in west London. I'm about to throw it away when the name of the show catches my eye. *This is Everything.*

This is everything.

My stomach drops.

I remember hearing those words, thrown away so carelessly as if they meant nothing.

I flip the card over and look at the image on the other side.

It's a picture of a painting depicting two girls on a boat.

One girl is standing at the bow of the punt, pole in hand, head thrown back in laughter. The other girl is sitting down, eyes wide, head tilted up towards her friend in admiration.

I close my eyes and I am back there, the twigs scratching my legs, the smell of the mossy banks making me nauseous, the sound of laughter grating my ears. It all comes back to me in an instant, as sharp as if I was still there, hiding in the bushes.

This is everything.

I'd bristled as those words skipped and bounced across the water.

I don't need to read the caption below the picture to know the painting depicts a summer evening in Oxford.

I was there, spying on Noor and Alia through the tangled branches.

And there's only one person who knows that.

The boy that Noor had loved toying with, giving him just enough attention to leave him wanting. The boy who had followed Noor around for years. Who had written her love letters and poems that sent us into fits of giggles.

Ankit.

SABAH

The gallery is on the corner of Westbourne Grove and Monmouth Road. It's a huge space, already packed by the time I pass through the glass sliding doors, every wall filled with paintings. A large sign on the front wall announces the name of the show: *This is Everything*. Large canvases depicting subversive landscapes hang on the walls. The detail is incredible, woodland creatures peeping through hooded forests, vast seascapes with hints of menace underneath. I find myself mesmerized as I move from one canvas to the next.

I come to a stop in front of the painting that brought me here. It's massive, nearly three times the size of the others, and even more magnificent in real life. I lean in to look at the texture, the layered underbrush, the soft ripples on the water, each detail drawn out for maximum effect. My eyes linger over the girls' faces. The girl holding the punt is dark-skinned, with deep green eyes that mirror the surroundings. Her hair is a bright red, wavy and voluminous but nothing like Noor's. The other girl, the one sitting down, is blonde and light-skinned. They look nothing like

Noor or Alia, but the expressions on their faces are all the proof I need. Even though it is just a painting, that peculiar teenage air of trepidation and invincibility is unmistakable.

My eyes travel to the edge of the frame, the overgrown branches, the mossy underbrush and that's when I notice it, the shadow lurking within the thicket. The pale man, concealed behind the branches, standing there watching, waiting. A shiver runs through me despite the warmth of the space. Ankit.

'This one is my favourite,' I hear someone say and I nearly jump. It's a man wearing a bow tie and shiny brogues. I give him a quick smile.

'Are you familiar with the artist's work?' I ask.

'Yes, as a matter of fact.' He holds out his hand. 'I'm James. I'm the gallerist. This is the third show we've had here and it looks like it's going to be another sell-out.'

'Impressive.' I flick through the catalogue in my hand. There is no artist biography or even a name, which is not entirely unexpected. My search online had provided no answers either. All I'd found was a link to the gallery's website with page after page of beautiful art and zero information. 'I was trying to find the artist's name but there doesn't seem to be one mentioned. Does he live in the UK?'

'I believe so, though I've never met the artist myself.'

I nod, keeping my eyes fixed on the painting in front of me. I'm not entirely sure what it is that I'm expecting to find, but I know that this is the missing link I've been looking for. It's like when you find a spare screw after you've finished painstakingly assembling a piece of IKEA furniture. I have the missing piece. I know what it looks like. I can feel it in my hand. I just don't know where to put it.

'That's a shame. I'm redoing my house in Delhi and I would have loved to commission a few pieces,' I say, putting on my best trophy wife impression. I lean in to whisper conspiratorially. 'My husband prefers art that hasn't been displayed anywhere else.'

'Of course.' He nods. I can see the cogs in his brain turning. One of my Tinder hook-ups had been with an aspiring art curator. I don't remember much from that drunken evening but I do remember him saying that the high-end art market in the UK is pretty much driven by rich Asian buyers. A commission in a private residence in India . . . It's the stuff of any gallerist's dreams.

'Thank you for your time anyway,' I say, smiling sweetly. 'Good luck with the show.'

I turn around, making as if to leave. I keep my face set in a nonchalant smile but my heart is pounding though my chest.

I need this to work.

I need to find Ankit to figure out just how he fits into all this.

'I could see if the agent is able to get in touch with the artist?' he says finally, the lure of a big sale too hard to resist.

I stand still for a moment, letting him fret in the silence.

I turn around slowly, my lips drawn into a grateful smile.

'That would be great,' I say.

I hesitate before I give him my email address. But if I'm

right, and Ankit is the one who sent me the invite, he already knows who I am.

'I'm only here for a few days, though, and I don't commission anything unless I've met the artist.'

'Of course,' he says, bowing his head. 'I'll make sure the agent gets back to you within the next couple of days.'

I spend the next day hitting refresh on my email and wandering through London, eager to lose myself amidst the tourists and shoppers, hoping that by rubbing shoulders with them I might be able to pinch some of their happiness for myself.

After a few hours in the exceptionally crowded British Museum, I wander into a restaurant in Bloomsbury. I thread through the outdoor tables, empty in the winter chill, and step inside. It's a cosy space, indicative of the kind of clientele you would expect in the area. Even though it's only three p.m., there are candles on every table, a vertical garden takes up the entire back wall and cosy blankets and sheepskin rugs are draped over every chair. It's an Instagrammer's dream, a woodland paradise mere steps away from the jungle that is Oxford Circus. Save for a group of ladies in their late seventies having tea, and two women with prams chatting about their NCT group, it is empty.

The waiter comes over in an instant and hands me a menu.

'Red wine, please. Large,' I say, not bothering with the wine list. 'And some olives.'

He nods brusquely, reminding me why I love London.

There is no awkward chit-chat nor any judgement about the mid-afternoon wine. People just get on with things, leaving you to yourself.

It's also why I hate London. You could go weeks without having a real conversation.

He returns a moment later and places a massive glass of wine in front of me along with a ridiculously small bowl of olives.

I take a long swallow, enjoying the familiar sensation of wine slipping down my throat as my mind takes me back to the trip to Oxford fifteen years ago.

Even though we weren't technically talking, I'd noticed a change in Noor on that trip. She had seemed on edge, disappearing for hours on end, sometimes with Alia but usually alone. I'd bet anything that Alia had never asked her where she was going, or why. She had always been far too enthralled by Noor to question anything.

I'd seen Noor slip out of the college nearly every night but on that final night, as Noor and Alia climbed out of the window, I followed them. I told myself that I was doing it because I was worried about Noor – she had just spent a month in rehab and I didn't want her relapsing – but if I'm honest, I followed them because I was jealous. I crept along after them, keeping my distance. It wasn't long until I ran into Ankit. He fumbled over his words, told me he was supposed to meet Noor on Magdalen Bridge, acting like it was all pre-arranged. It was obvious that he was lying but I was hardly in a position to tell him off. Instead, I followed them all the way to the river and watched quietly while Noor stole a punt and nearly toppled it over. I didn't pay much attention to Ankit, who was standing next to me the entire time, unobtrusive as ever. But then he'd always had a talent for becoming invisible. Noor and I hadn't even noticed that he used to follow her around until the poems started, and suddenly we began to see him everywhere, lurking, hiding in the shadows, hungry for even one moment of Noor's time. At one point, he even joined Noor's art class to try and get close to her and now that I think about it, I'm pretty certain that he'd spent half his time in Oxford bent over his sketchbook.

I run through the possibilities in my head. Though I teased Noor about having a stalker, I had never really thought of Ankit's fascination with Noor as more than a somewhat disproportionate crush. Of course, she had led him on – Noor had a peculiar power over boys and she liked to use it to toy with them – but he was a meek, skinny boy with too many pimples and no friends. Did he really think he stood any chance with the most popular girl in school? But then, perhaps a sweet smile or a kind word meant far more to him than either of us could have imagined. Perhaps it was enough to feed an obsession. He wouldn't have been the first boy to be hypnotized by Noor, but then what?

I glance at my watch, trying to work out the time in India before ringing Alia. She answers on the first ring.

I fill her in on everything, my cheeks burning as I tell her about how Ankit and I had followed them in Oxford. She has the grace to let it slide, not calling me out on my hypocrisy.

'I haven't seen him in years,' Alia says after I tell her that I've already tried looking for him online.

'He left school around the same time that you did,' Alia continues. 'He must have transferred to a different school but I don't – I don't actually know where he went. I haven't seen him at any of the reunions.'

I'm not surprised. That boy had no friends. And other than Noor, no one ever really bothered with him. But that doesn't explain the fact that I've trawled through every social media website, checked phonebooks and electoral registers, even called the school's admissions office and still drawn a blank. It's as though he just disappeared, dropped off the face of the earth at almost exactly the same time that Noor was murdered.

'I can try and –' Alia stops speaking. The gasp is unmistakable.

'What?'

'He was there. Don't you remember? At the leavers' ball. He tried to speak to Noor a few times.'

I don't remember seeing him, but then I was a bit preoccupied that night. 'Do you know what they spoke about?'

'No, sorry, I don't remember. But –' She pauses, groans, then continues. 'But I'm pretty sure he left right after Noor.'

'He must have followed her,' I say, stating the obvious before running through scenarios with Alia.

I hang up a few minutes later, promising to let her know as soon as I hear from the gallery.

There's a single thought running through my head as I swirl my wine.

If Ankit did follow Noor that night, he would have been there when she died. The thing that I need to work out is whether he was an accomplice or a witness.

Unless, of course, Faraz is innocent. I finish my wine, then order another, sipping it slowly as I turn the thought over in my mind. All that the video proves is that Faraz had lied about being out of town. Could that just be the result of overcompensation on Javed Uncle's part? An attempt to shield his son from any baseless accusations? It would make sense considering Faraz's history and the kind of gossip they'd already been subjected to. The threat of losing Faraz might have been enough for Javed Uncle to cover up his own daughter's murder. I have almost convinced myself of Faraz's innocence when I remember the dead police commissioner.

And then there is the card. I find it hard to believe that the invitation to the private view was a coincidence. But if Ankit really is guilty or hiding something, why would he reach out to me? No, it makes far more sense that he's hiding *from* something. Or someone. No one disappears this completely out of anything but fear. Before I know it, a few hours have passed and the waiter starts hovering, pointedly reminding me that they are starting dinner service.

It's not until I'm back home that my phone pings. It's the email I've been waiting for all day.

Dear Ms Khan,
  I hope you are well.
  I have been in touch with James from Wolf Arts and I

am pleased to include below the artist's contact details as requested by you. You will be welcome at the studio anytime next week.

The artist has requested that you respect their wish for anonymity and treat this information in complete confidentiality. Please do let me know if you need anything else and I hope you will enjoy your trip to Scotland.

Burnside Studios,

Fanagmore,

Scourie,

IV27 4RT

Kind regards,

Katie Briscoe

I read through the email again. Scotland?

ALIA

It's still dark when I step outside.

I climb into the hotel car and let myself sink into the soft leather seats before plugging in my earphones, a futile attempt to drown out the thoughts that have been circling my brain all night. I had rescheduled my flights when Sabah called, choosing to fly in a few days before the summit in Westminster, but now that I'm here, I cannot escape the feeling that I've made a mistake. We're going in blind to a situation that neither of us have any way of controlling, but then, I suppose I have no control over anything anyway.

The life I've spent years building is unravelling around me.

I cast a quick glance at my phone as we drive out of the hotel grounds and past the sprawling designer shops and cafes. Arjun and I have barely spoken in weeks, our conversations growing more and more stilted as the cracks and crevices where I stowed away all my lies and secrets warp and widen. When I told him I was going to London a few days earlier than originally planned, he didn't ask me why or when I'd be back. He just nodded. I'm hoping there is a message or a voicemail from him, checking to see if I arrived safely. There isn't.

I try to remember the first time I met Arjun, the *real* first time. I was working as a waitress at The Ivy when Arjun walked in with his girlfriend, the astonishingly beautiful and proportionately vain Tanya. The hostess had seated them by the window and I watched them for a few minutes before walking over with the menus. I knew who he was, of course, but we'd never spoken. We spent a few minutes chatting while Tanya debated between the green salad and the caesar salad and by the time I walked away with their orders – steak for him and caesar salad without the dressing for her – I knew I liked him. He was different from all the other trust fund kids I'd come across in Cambridge. He had that easy confidence that can only come from knowing your place in the world but he was far too well mannered to flaunt his money or status.

I was still thinking about him when we ran into each other a few days later in the library checkout queue. I smiled, expecting a hello, but the brief conversation that had made such an impression on me seemed to have meant little to him. I could practically see the invisible shield that came with years and years of privilege go up between us. I walked away, library book still in hand, my face burning.

I had always known it but that's when it really hit me. People like him didn't notice people like me.

I quit the job at The Ivy and started teaching English at the local women's institute. The pay was lower, leaving me with little to spare, but I was willing to trade in drinks at the student bar for a last name like Arjun's.

I knew he was friendly with Niv and I made sure that the next time I saw him, I had a boy on my arm. Not a boyfriend – that would be too crass – but an admirer whom I was trying to fend off, an announcement that I was unobtainable. Something to be coveted. I met Arjun as if for the first time at Niv's birthday party. It didn't take long before we became friends, hanging out as part of a group to begin with, but gradually, as we grew closer, our meetings became more and more intimate. We always found excuses to justify it – none of our friends like obscure French cinema (neither did we), they don't really get Nietzsche (I still can't stand the man), no one else wants to spend an afternoon at a cryptozoology exhibition (we didn't make it past the entrance hall) – but the truth is, both of us knew exactly what we were doing.

And when six months later Tanya walked in on Arjun and me having sex in their rather spotless white kitchen, I knew exactly what I was doing.

Tanya had an appointment at the hair salon that afternoon.

But there was a mix-up. *Someone* called the salon and told them she wanted to reschedule her cut and colour for the next week.

I got dressed in thirty seconds flat and ran out while Tanya wept in the corner.

Arjun told me the next day that they'd broken up.

Six weeks later, we started dating.

Six years later, we were married.

I twist away from the memory as my phone lights up with a text from Sabah: she's waiting on the platform.

I sit up straight as we pull up along the concourse. The weight of what we're about to do anchors me. I might not know what we're walking into but if there's even the slightest chance that I can bring Faraz to justice, I have to try.

I step out of the car with renewed determination just as the sun peeks through the clouds and the sky explodes in shades of pink and orange, bathing King's Cross station in shades of innocence.

SABAH

Though it's less than a hundred miles from Inverness, Scourie feels like the end of the world.

After the seven-hour train ride to Inverness, the drive takes another three and a half hours, most of which Alia and I spend in complete silence.

We haven't seen another car in miles, not since we got off the motorway an hour ago. We've been driving along the coast, with the ocean on one side and the forest on the other. Every so often the road curves, bringing us dangerously close to the edge, and I tighten my grip on the steering wheel, painfully aware that one wrong move could send us teetering over.

No one knows where we are. Once the thought occurs to me, it's all I can think about. Other than the boarded-up pub we passed an hour ago, I haven't seen any sign of life for miles. We'll have to go all the way back to Inverness for a meal or a room. The remoteness hits home and I wonder if this trip is a mistake. We could drive off the cliff and not be found for weeks. Alia's parents think she's visiting friends in London and her husband . . . judging by the way Alia clams up every time I ask about him, I'm pretty sure she hasn't told him much about why she's in the UK, let alone where we're going. We could disappear and no one would even think to look in this part of the country. They might be able to follow my credit card trail up to the car hire agency in Inverness but beyond that, they could spend weeks searching and not find a trace. With it being New Year's Eve, we'd had to pick up the car keys from a collection box outside the station. There had been no banter with an over-friendly Scot, no talk of Hogmanay plans or chat about the freezing Scottish weather. The last people to see us were the students who had got into the carriage at Aviemore.

I think, irrationally, of Dan. I wonder what he would make of this trip, if he would think it was crazy trying to track down a creep I haven't seen in fifteen years in the middle of nowhere on New Year's Eve.

When I first read that email with Ankit's address, I couldn't help but smirk. It felt like I'd somehow tricked the gallerist and the agent into revealing Ankit's location. But now, as we move further and further from civilization . . . I daren't think why Ankit's brought us all the way here. If he wanted to reach out, why not just pick up the phone or ask to see me in London or even Edinburgh?

It's illogical and reckless, and yet, something compels me to keep driving.

I refuse to look at Alia. I can't risk seeing my fears reflected, not now, not when we are so close to finding out how Ankit fits into all this. I switch on the radio, desperate to change the topic in my head, but all I get is static. GPS stopped working about twenty minutes ago and our mobile signals dropped off about ten miles after Inverness.

I catch sight of some lights in the distance and my heart leaps at the sign of life, but before we are close enough to see what they are, Alia looks up from the A to Z she has open in her lap.

'Take the next left,' she says.

The road is little more than a dirt track and I slow down as we wind through it.

I shudder to a stop.

'Are you sure this is it?' I ask Alia.

There is nothing but wilderness around us.

'Yes,' she says, her irritation evident.

I continue up the path, unease prickling my skin.

All I can see now is an expanse of water and a ramshackle cottage. It doesn't look like an artist's studio. It doesn't look like anything. We circle the lake, which doesn't even appear on the map. It is only when we come to the end of the track that I catch sight of the small sign saying 'Burnside Studios'.

The sight of another car in the drive bolsters me and I pull up next to it, trying to peek into the car to look for clues. It's an SUV, fairly new, but completely anonymous. No stickers, no jackets strewn on the back seat, or coffee cups in the front. No clues.

I look at the cottage backlit by a sky that's slowly turning black as the last light leaves and then at Alia, who is already climbing out of the car.

I take a deep breath and follow her to the front door.

I step forward when the door swings open and as the features fall into focus, every last bit of constraint disappears. I crumble to the floor, the weight of fifteen years' worth of guilt and regret too much for my body to handle.

I had seen her unspool at the party.

I had wept at her funeral.

I had lit a candle every year for the last fifteen years.

I had nearly lost myself in the guilt of what I had done.

I had dared to hope, but the hope felt so sharp, so desperate, that my mind had refused to accept the possibility.

And yet, here she is. Alive.

Noor.

SABAH

Inside, the cottage is cosy. A log fire is roaring in the living room. A mug of tea sits on the coffee table. A record player in the corner is playing jazz. A book lies open, spine up on the armchair.

The scene is so ordinary it takes my breath away.

Noor goes straight to the drinks cabinet and carries three glasses and a bottle of Scotch over to the kitchen table.

'When in Rome,' she begins but her words are met with silence.

She sighs. That deep, this-world-is-coming-to-an-end sigh that I never thought I'd hear again.

The sound that leaves my throat is entirely unfamiliar. A gasp. A cry. A thousand emotions rolled into one tiny little sound.

Noor pours the Scotch out, the deep gold liquid glinting as she slides a glass each towards Alia and me. I swallow it back, hoping a drink will steady my nerves, but the smoky liquid feels rough against my throat as I try to make sense of the scene before my eyes.

My hand trembles ever so slightly as I set the glass down.

'You're alive,' I say, uselessly.

'Yes,' Noor says, the hint of a smile on her face.

'Did you run away?' I ask.

I look at Alia. She hasn't said a word since we stepped out of the car. I follow her gaze around the kitchen. Her drink lies untouched on the counter. The fridge is covered with photos, evidence of a life well lived. Souvenirs litter every surface, displayed proudly amidst the chaos of a kitchen that is used often.

I take in the chiselled features, the wild hair, the face that I used to know so well. My heart flips in my chest as it tries to decide what to feel.

'What did we bury?' I whisper.

'Let me start at the beginning.'

'I moved to Scotland a few years—' Noor begins, but I cut her off.

'I *mourned* you. I've been punishing myself for fifteen years.'

'I know,' Noor says. 'I'm sorry.'

The apology is delivered far too effortlessly to mean much. I flinch. Alia doesn't. Indignation curtains her face.

'You're *sorry*?' Alia demands. 'What the actual fuck, Noor?'

Noor takes a sharp breath as Alia continues, her fury rippling out as words tumble out of her mouth unre-strained.

'You faked your own suicide! What the hell happened? How did you convince yourself this was okay?'

Noor's face crumples. Her voice, when she speaks, is

soft. 'I didn't. I didn't convince myself it was okay.' She bows her head. 'Abbu did.'

'Remember the protests in Kanpur that summer?' Noor asks, her eyes darting from Alia to me.

I nod, vaguely recalling the arrests at the university and the communal violence that had ensued.

'We came back early from Shimla because of the riots. Sabah, you probably don't know this because—'

It's my turn to bite back. 'Because we were fighting about how you decided one fine day that you wanted to be Head Girl?'

Noor looks at me, waiting perhaps to see if there's more. I sigh. 'Go on.'

'After we came back, Faraz wanted to go to Kanpur. He was planning on running for the student elections the next year and he wanted to show his support towards the youth and students. He managed to convince Abbu to let him tag along.'

Alia and I look at each other, unsure what the riots have to do with any of this.

'While he was there, Faraz became friendly with a few of the party workers, mostly from the youth division but also some of my dad's older *karyakartas*. We didn't notice anything at first, but over the next few months, he became tetchy. He started commenting on things he'd never cared about, telling Ammi off for not wearing a *hijab* at home, skipping college to hang out at the party headquarters. He'd never liked the idea of me having boyfriends, but he went off the rails with Sameer; he started spouting off obscure passages from the Quran. It was odd, he wasn't religious at all – I don't think he ever even went to a mosque and I saw him come in drunk more than a few times – but he became quite extreme. There were a couple of incidents at his college as well,' she says and I nod, remembering. 'Faraz had started hanging out with radicals and when his friends called him out on it, he got into a fight with them and the whole thing escalated. Some of Abbu's supporters went over there the next day and they beat up a bunch of boys at the college. That was the first sign that something was going horribly wrong.'

I remember that. I remember hearing some of the boys talk about it at school, veering between idolizing Faraz and ridiculing him.

'Abbu sent him away, and for a while things got better. When he came back, Faraz would still get really riled up about little things, but Abbu had forbidden him from going to the constituency or meeting the *karyakartas*. And being cut off from them seemed to help.'

Noor looks away, out of the window.

'But then the video went out and it was like overnight everything changed. Things were already so bad at school, but as soon as it was on the news . . . everyone was judging me, questioning my morals. No one ever published my name. The clip was never shown on TV. People knew it was me because they had searched for the video, downloaded it and watched it. Half the fucking country got off on it and then they called me a slut.'

I feel an even greater stab of guilt than before as Noor pauses, her voice hoarse. The country had crucified her. *We* had crucified her.

'What you both saw, at school, that wasn't even half of it. There was so much pressure on Abbu to resign. Usually Abbu was really strict about not allowing party workers to come home. He only ever met them at the party office or in the constituency but even though he was still the party president, it was like he had no control over them anymore. They started coming to the house at all hours, calling me immoral, a bad Muslim, demanding Abbu do something about it. It was just this constant stream of pressure. We all tried to ignore it at first, but then the death threats started coming in. And then one day, a party worker snuck into my room. I came out of the bathroom and he was just standing there, waiting. I was lucky that Abbu was in the house and he heard me screaming, but I was terrified. I wasn't even safe in my own house.'

I close my eyes, finally understanding what that diary entry was about.

'That's why he wanted to send you away?' Alia asks.

Noor stares into her glass, as if begging the amber liquid to magic away the past. 'He said it wasn't safe for me in India, and he was right. But what we didn't know was that the real threat wasn't coming from some stranger; it was coming from within our family.

'Faraz had been ringing and texting me non-stop that night. Abbu was still in the constituency but Faraz had come back home and realized I wasn't there. I didn't want him to see me with Vineet, so after Vineet dropped me off I snuck into the kitchen through the servants' entrance.'

I nod. That house was guarded like a fortress, but no one ever bothered with the servants' quarter. There was never any need and once Noor and I figured it out, that became our main route in and out of the house.

'I was so wasted, I must have woken Salma up.'

'Salma?' Alia asks, confused.

'The maid,' I say. 'The girl who Noor gave her old clothes and books to.'

'She followed me inside,' Noor continues. 'I wanted to go to bed but she insisted on making me a snack. Faraz must have heard me come in, because the next thing I knew, he was there in the kitchen, shouting at me, telling me how I was an embarrassment to the family, how I had brought so much shame to the Qureshi name they'd all be better off if I was dead. I'd seen him high before, but not like that night. He was completely wasted. I kept trying to speak to him but anything I said only made him angrier. At one point, he lunged at me. He had his hands around my throat.' Noor takes in a shaky breath, her hand going automatically to her neck, as if to reassure herself that she's safe.

'Salma,' she says, her voice breaking. 'Salma tried to intervene. She tried to pull him off but she was just a slip of a girl . . . I was terrified he was going to kill me, right there in our kitchen.' Noor shuts her eyes and presses her fingertips to her forehead. 'The next thing I knew, she hit him on the head with a rolling pin.

'She had been making *parathas* for me,' Noor adds, as if that detail is somehow significant, before shaking her head. 'I don't think she actually hurt him, but he just snapped. I thought he was angry before but . . . she was a servant and she'd hit him.'

Faraz had always been arrogant and I can imagine the indignation, the anger he would have felt.

'I didn't even know he had a gun until it was in my face,' Noor says, finishing her whisky in one long swallow. 'Salma struck him again a second before the gun went off. He was pointing it at me, but then she hit him . . . he was already unsteady on his feet. He swerved and . . . it went off . . . He shot her, right in the head.'

Even though I'd known it was coming, the gasp that escapes my mouth is genuine.

'You see it in films, but it's not the same. There was so much blood. It went everywhere,' Noor says, setting her tumbler down.

'Did he try to—'

'He passed out. He didn't even realize he shot the wrong girl.'

'Did you call the police?' Alia asks.

Noor pours out some more Scotch and then carefully replaces the stopper in the bottle. Her eyes are glistening when she looks up.

'I called Abbu.'

SABAH

'I didn't find out until months later,' Noor continues, 'but while Abbu had been busy trying to manage the mess I'd made, Faraz had started mixing with the party workers again. They were always around the house and I suppose they'd been filling his ears, grooming him almost. Later, Faraz told Abbu that they'd convinced him he had to kill me for the sake of the community, the family, Islam. They gave him the gun. Told him they could do it themselves but, as my brother, it wasn't just his responsibility, it was his honour to repair the family name that I had sullied.'

Her eyes well up with tears, and she blinks them away.

'I don't expect you to understand but I think for Abbu, it was the only way he could protect both his children. We had a dead body there that we had to deal with, Faraz was passed out on the floor clutching a gun, there were people threatening to kill me. It was just too much. Even if we found a way to cover up Salma's death . . .' Noor runs a hand over her face. 'It didn't seem like my going away would stop them. These people . . . they were after blood.

Abbu said the only way I'd be safe was if everyone believed I was dead.

'He called the police commissioner. They'd been at university together, Abbu had helped him get his post. And . . . and I got the sense that there was history there, maybe Abbu had something on him.' Noor shrugs. 'Either way, Abbu was sure he would help, and he did.'

Alia makes as if to speak but I stop her with a quick shake of my head. Now is not the time to tell Noor.

'It must have taken no more than fifteen minutes for him to arrive . . . but those fifteen minutes . . . Once the commissioner got there, he told us exactly what to do. Salma was the same age as me, and lots of people thought we looked similar anyway.'

I try to picture the young girl who had often ferried snacks up to Noor's room. The first time Alia visited Noor's house, she had asked me about the girl. I still remember the surprise on Alia's face when I'd told her that she was a maid, not a cousin.

'He had me dress her in my clothes. I also – I also put one of my *hijabs* on her. With the scarf covering her hair and half her face . . . He was being cautious but there was really no need . . .' Noor trails off.

I get it. Even without the backing of the head of the state's police force, no one had any reason to doubt Javed Uncle. Why would any father lie about his own daughter's death? And to ask him to return to the morgue for a formal identification when he was the one to report the death would just be callous. It was easier, kinder to close the matter then and there and let Javed Uncle get on with the trickier business of arranging a funeral for his sixteen-year-old daughter.

'He cleaned up the gun and put it next to her. Abbu and I had already carried Faraz upstairs and—'

'The note –'

Noor nods, as if to say she's getting to it. 'The commissioner dictated it to me. He wanted to make sure it was phrased just right, in case there was ever an investigation. He was the one who insisted that Abbu have the funeral the very next morning. The body had to be moved to a morgue overnight, and even though it was unlikely that anyone would question his authority, he didn't want to take a chance.'

'What about the post-mortem?'

'They never did one.'

I draw a breath. Surely Javed Uncle's power couldn't stretch that far?

'Legally, the police are only required to request an autopsy if they suspect foul play or if the cause of death is unclear,' Alia says, slowly.

'That's why the note was so important,' Noor says.

'And Faraz . . . he never realized that he'd shot Salma instead of you?' Alia asks.

Noor shakes her head.

Something occurs to me, a little piece of the puzzle that doesn't quite fit. 'But he must have wondered about the suicide note, right?' I say.

Noor nods, as if she had been waiting for one of us to

question this. 'Maybe, but the only person who actually saw the note before it was handed to the police was Abbu. And, honestly, at the time I think Faraz was just grateful that he wasn't going to prison. He probably assumed that Abbu forged the note to protect him.'

It's incredible. Javed Uncle had orchestrated the perfect cover-up, getting rid of a dead body, saving his daughter's life and protecting his son's freedom in one move. There was only one loose end. 'No one asked about Salma?'

'I don't think so, no. She was an orphan. Abbu took her in after she ran away from her village. People probably assumed she had run off with a boy or something, but even if they were worried about her, no servant would dare to bring it up with my father, right? Not when he was grieving the death of his own daughter.'

The sound of a key in the door startles us and we hush as footsteps echo through the cottage.

'Hello,' I hear a woman call out moments before she walks in, dog trailing behind her.

I look at Alia. She looks just as confused as I feel as I take in the blonde woman standing in front of me, dressed in a puffer jacket and skinny jeans. Why hadn't Noor mentioned that she had a guest?

I watch as the dog leaps forward and runs to Noor.

The woman drops a set of keys on the counter and then leans in to give Noor a kiss.

'Babe, these are my friends from back home, Alia and Sabah,' Noor says to the woman, before turning to us, a nervous smile plastered on her face. 'And this is my wife, Kate.'

ALIA

I pass the bowl of salad to Sabah. We are sitting in a cottage in Scotland having dinner with Noor and her wife. The whole thing feels so ridiculous that I want to burst out laughing.

'I'm sorry this is all a bit slapdash,' Kate says, setting down a platter of cold cuts on the table. 'If Nida had remembered to tell me you were coming, I would've made sure we had a proper meal organized.'

Nida? Sabah and I exchange a glance. Of course she changed her name.

'Please don't worry about it,' Sabah says, smiling as she helps herself to some cheese. 'It was pretty last minute. Alia and I realized we were both going to be in Edinburgh at the same time and we just had to come and see *Nida*.' She throws a sharp glance at Noor. 'It's been, what – fifteen years?'

Noor nods.

'So you must have known each other when Nida was in Nepal?'

'That's right,' I say, picking up my wine glass. 'Though

I'm not quite sure where you went from there. Remind me, Nida.'

'Dubrovnik, then Tallin, Bucharest –'

'Where she met me,' Kate says, smiling. Her left hand rests on the back of Noor's neck. I blink when I realize I'm staring. The cottage might seem cosy, but it's clear that Noor's been living like a fugitive.

Noor gives her a quick smile and then continues. 'And then Scotland. Kate's family is here so it made sense for us to move.'

'Which reminds me,' Kate says, 'we were going to go to the loch for a small Hogmanay celebration. Nothing fancy but it should be fun. There are only about seventy people in the village, and everyone will be there.' She turns to Noor, a slight frown creasing her forehead. 'Except Bo. She's having trouble with her hip again. I told her we'd pop in next week.'

Noor nods. 'Of course.'

'Anyway,' Kate says, turning back to us, her easy smile back in place. 'It's all very low-key, some fireworks and drinks by the loch to bring in the New Year. Would you like to come?'

'We'd love to,' Sabah says.

The ride to the village takes us along a different route, deeper into the valley. The village itself is a cluster of houses around a lake, the water glimmering black and silver in the moonlight. We help Kate and Noor carry the flasks of mulled wine and whisky down to the shore. About fifty-odd people are gathered around a campfire and there is the faint strain of Gaelic music in the air. We linger on the fringes while Noor greets everyone. It's odd, seeing her here, with a blonde wife and the hint of a Scottish accent, chatting, laughing, bending down to pet a dog, bouncing someone's baby. All the drama, the constant need for attention, the restlessness that she used to carry with her, all of that is gone. She seems to have transformed into someone calmer, more grounded. I watch as she laughs at something a white-haired man is saying before reaching out to Kate and pulling her close, her action thoughtless. That's when it hits me. She's found it. She's found where she belongs.

'How much of it is true?' I ask Noor as we walk around the lake.

'All of it. After the body had been moved, the commissioner drove Faraz out to my grandparents' and I hid in one of the unused servants' quarters. The next day, Faraz came back home with my mum. Ten days after the funeral, Abbu and his commissioner friend drove across the border into Nepal. Between the two of them, they knew no one would stop to check the car at the usual checkpoints. And then a few miles before the border, I got into the boot of the car.'

'It was easier once we were in Kathmandu. Abbu had already arranged a new passport. I flew to Dubai the next day and then on to Dubrovnik for a few days and then, finally, Tallin. I enrolled in a boarding school there. Abbu had always been very clear that I couldn't stay in one place for too long, especially not a European capital, even if it was Tallin. He said it was too risky. So after I graduated, I went to the arts university in Bucharest. I met Kate and when she said she wanted to move back home, I came with her. I could be an artist from anywhere, but after I'd finally found someone who understood me, I didn't want to be alone again. I had always known I'd have to spend my life in hiding, but it became easier with Kate by my side. And a Scottish village with a population of seventy seemed like the perfect place to disappear.'

'But you never told Kate?' I ask.

Noor shakes her head. 'I can't risk it,' she says simply. 'There's too much at stake.

'I never knew what I wanted in school,' Noor continues. 'The boys . . . I acted experienced, blasé almost, but the truth is, I never really had the impulse and for the longest time, I couldn't figure it out. I didn't understand why I didn't have the same urges as the other girls, why I always wanted to stop halfway . . . I knew something was wrong but I couldn't figure out what. Until we went to Oxford . . . You remember the student guide?'

'Simon?' Sabah asks.

'No, Michelle.'

I have a sudden memory of the other student guide, the slightly plump, cheerful brunette. She had always been friendly and she was particularly kind to Noor, coming to fetch her every night when her parents called.

'I used to hang out with her quite a lot. To begin with we'd just meet up to smoke or talk about art, but at some point I realized I was attracted to more than her sense of freedom. But it was hard to process, you know? I struggled enough just being myself, but to be a lesbian, especially back then . . .'

I nod. When I first moved to India, I thought the concept of honour killings was limited to far-off villages and that the stigma of homosexuality was only acute in the rural pockets of the country, driven entirely by poverty and a lack of education. But all it took was a few weeks of watching the news to realize how common such crimes were even in the most metropolitan cities, how much the educated, modern middle and upper classes cared about social standing and reputation. I still can't think of a single openly gay person I'd known as a teenager – it just wasn't an option, not in the least because until a few months ago, it wasn't just taboo, it was illegal.

Noor turns to Sabah. 'You knew, didn't you?'

Sabah nods. 'I had a feeling.'

'That's why you gave me that dare. It was a test.'

Sabah looks away. Her voice cracks. 'And that's why you picked Vineet?'

'I was angry with you. I knew you suspected that I liked girls so the dare . . . it felt like an attack. I wanted to get back at you . . . but shooting that video was a stupid thing to do. I never intended for it to get out.'

My heart stills. I'd always thought that the rumours about Noor knowing she was being filmed were just rumours. Once again, I feel like the trespasser as Noor and Sabah talk about things I had only ever guessed at.

'No,' Sabah says, tears running down her cheeks. 'That

was all me. Sleeping with Mohit was the worst thing I'd done and when I found out that you'd told Alia about that . . . I'd trusted you with my darkest secret. And then when Vineet sent me the video . . . I thought someone had sent it to him and he was just passing it on. I didn't even realize the boy in the video was Vineet until the next day. I was so angry, and so humiliated, I just wanted you to feel the same. I didn't realize what it would lead to. I am so, so sorry, Noor.'

'So am I.'

I watch quietly as they hug. I try to come up with the words to tell them what I had done, how I'd manipulated Vineet, how my obsession with ending Noor and Sabah's friendship once and for all had kicked off the chain of events that led us here, to this day, but the words dry up in my mouth. I have regretted my actions for years and yet I am not brave enough to own up to them. I turn my attention to Sabah as she speaks.

'You could have stayed. You could have fought,' Sabah says. 'There had to be another way –' Sabah breaks off, her voice catching.

'There wasn't,' Noor says softly, looking at the group assembled across the lake as we walk back to join them. 'And I may have left because Abbu wanted me to, but I stayed away because that's what *I* wanted. I was so ashamed of what I'd done. And after that night, it felt like there was nothing left for me to come back to. Half the country had seen that video, my own brother wanted to kill me, my parents and all my friends hated me . . . Running away was the easiest option. And once I found Kate, it didn't feel like I was running anymore.'

We tip our heads back as the first rocket sizzles up, lighting the midnight sky with sparks of red and green.

I link my arms through Noor's and Sabah's as I realize that once again I am back there, watching the fireworks. But this time instead of tearing us apart, the fire in the sky is bringing us together.

ALIA

The drive back feels sober, each of us lost in our own thoughts. Kate attempts conversation a few times but in the end she gives up and we return to the cottage in silence. She heads upstairs without a word, leaving the three of us in the living room.

'Nightcap?' Noor asks.

It has been agreed, without anyone bringing it up, that Sabah and I are spending the night here and I am reminded of all our impromptu sleepovers at Noor's house, curled up on the sofa or squashed together in her bed.

'Why did you reach out to me?' Sabah says when we are settled in, a fire crackling in front of us. 'The card – it was you, right?'

Noor lifts her feet up onto the sofa, resting them against my hip. She looks at Sabah, sitting across from us in the armchair. 'Do you know how I heard about Abbu's death?'

I can guess but I don't say anything. I remember how I felt when I found out that my grandfather had died. I couldn't believe that I was finding out on the phone from my mother, instead of being there by his side. The idea that I had been tucked in my bed watching a film while he took his last breath was appalling and even though the doctors had warned us it was coming, the intensity of the loss took my breath away. I was furious, but more than anything I felt cheated, like I'd been robbed of the chance to say goodbye. All that when I'd seen him just the night before.

'On the BBC,' Noor says, her voice bitter. 'My own father . . . and I found out through the fucking BBC. I couldn't believe it. I hadn't seen him in years . . . and I know it doesn't make any sense but I'd always thought that I'd see them again at some point. Him and Ammi. And in one moment, that whole possibility, as unlikely as it may have been, was gone.

'I spent weeks reading every article about Abbu, watching every YouTube clip from the funeral, again and again and again. I'd been able to stay away for fifteen years because I spoke to Abbu every week. Even though I wasn't there, I still felt connected because I knew what was happening in their lives. I felt involved. Suddenly there was just this void. My father was gone and I knew how much pain Ammi would be in, but I couldn't do anything about it.' Her voice cracks. 'I am not an orphan but I felt like one . . . I don't know if I would still have had the courage to do anything. But then I saw that article about your documentary,' she says, looking at Sabah. 'And that video of Ammi . . .' Noor swallows.

I remember seeing the teaser that had accompanied the article. Seated in her dilapidated garden, Fatima Aunty had looked distraught as she spoke about Noor. It had torn through me, her pain so visceral, so immediate even after fifteen years. I can't bear to think what it would have done to Noor to see her mother in such obvious agony.

'I'd always assumed she'd moved on . . . but seeing her in so much pain . . . and knowing that you were still looking for answers after all these years.' Noor pauses, takes a breath, then starts again. 'I couldn't let it go. I had to reach out.' Her eyes dart across to Sabah. 'And frankly, after reading that article, I was worried about you.'

'Why?'

'That bit about foul play? I didn't know how much you'd already figured out, but I knew that if Faraz so much as suspected you knew about his involvement . . .' She breaks off, presses her fingertips into her forehead. 'You don't know what he can be like. He would've killed you. I couldn't risk coming to London and I didn't want to endanger you by ringing or emailing in case Faraz was keeping tabs on you, but I knew that if I could just get you to the gallery, you'd figure it out.

'A few months ago, Abbu told me he was planning to retire and hand over the party leadership. Faraz had always assumed the position would be his to inherit. He'd been pushing Abbu to support his nomination for the next election and Abbu had been putting it off. When Abbu told him that he had no intention of recommending Faraz for party president or even as a candidate in the next elections, Faraz lost it. Their relationship was already splintered but

I think that's when Faraz realized that although Abbu had protected him, he had never forgiven him.'

I think about all the times Javed Uncle had pushed Faraz towards strategy, or accounting, or campaign management instead of supporting him to run as a candidate himself. I'd always thought it was because Javed Uncle needed someone he could trust behind the scenes. Now I realize it was the opposite. He never trusted Faraz.

'He finally has everything he's ever wanted,' Noor says, looking from Sabah to me. 'While Abbu was there, he managed to control Faraz but now . . . he's not going to let anything get in his way.' Noor says. 'The last time I spoke to Abbu, he sounded worried. Really worried. He'd been talking about moving away, cutting Faraz off –'

I close my eyes as I take this in. I have seen Faraz's ruthlessness first hand, but how far might it stretch? Surely he would draw the line at hurting his own father. I feel myself going off on a tangent and I remind myself that Javed Uncle had died of a heart attack. I try to ignore the little voice in my head that tells me that I don't know that for sure. It would be easy for Faraz to influence the coroner, and just like with Noor, the funeral had happened so quickly . . . But the idea is too horrific to voice. I reach for an easier question instead. 'Your mother never knew?'

Noor shakes her head. 'That's the only – the biggest regret I have,' she says. 'Abbu told me that Ammi begged him to let her see me before the funeral so she could say goodbye but he couldn't let her. He made sure Salma's body was embalmed and wrapped before Ammi and Faraz arrived. He told her that seeing me like that, with a gunshot wound piercing my face, was the hardest thing he'd ever had to do and she wouldn't be able to handle it.'

There is a pause while Sabah and I take this in. Javed Uncle had thought of everything. Of course, Fatima Aunty wouldn't want to see her daughter like that. No parent would.

'No one deserves that kind of pain,' Noor continues, 'but Abbu and I knew from the beginning that she could never know the truth. Letting Faraz be her perfect son was the best way to keep her safe. Faraz would never jeopardize that.'

'Unless she does something that might endanger his position,' Sabah says.

Sabah and I glance at each other, coming to a silent understanding. It's time to lay all the cards on the table. Noor's face crumples as Sabah tells her about the diary entry, about how Faraz made sure Fatima Aunty never spoke to her unaccompanied. Her eyes widen as we tell her about the police commissioner, found dead in a ditch.

Noor shakes her head as realization dawns. Fear wraps itself around my throat.

If Faraz is as dangerous as we think he is, Fatima Aunty isn't safe.

None of us are.

It's nearly dawn by the time we get up from the sofa.

I look at our faces reflected in the huge mirror above the fireplace and I think back to the girls we once were. We had lied to each other, we had plotted against each other and we had hurt each other, but ultimately, when it came down to it, it was always us against the world.

Three girls and a whole lot of spunk.

Noor catches my eye in the mirror and I turn to face her. 'What do you want to do?'

Her answer is instant.

'I want to go home.'

SABAH

The walls of the studio are filled with Noor's paintings, at least fifty canvases showing the world we grew up in, the world that once upon a time Noor and I ruled. I move from canvas to canvas, stopping every few minutes to admire a particular landscape or examine a detail that I'd missed earlier.

I end up next to Alia, both of us drawn towards the painting of the Qureshi estate. The house is dark and empty. The fountain on the drive is covered in moss. The forest that surrounds the house is overgrown; sinewy branches, plants and vines twisting together, threatening to engulf the estate. And in the corner is the same figure that I'd spotted in the painting I'd seen at the gallery. Lurking in the forest, hidden almost entirely from view, but watching. Waiting.

I'd assumed that the figure was Ankit. A stalker. An outsider trying to get in. I realize now that I had it all wrong. The figure is Noor. An insider trying to get out.

I think through the plan one more time.

If we go to the police with everything, Faraz might find

a way to escape the consequences. He could flee the country, make sure the case takes years to reach the courts or, worse still, he could find a way to silence us before he's even arrested. We have all seen it done enough times to know just how easy it would be for him.

There is only one way to guarantee that he gets what he deserves. We cannot trust the police or the judiciary, but we can trust the public.

I am still scheduled to interview Faraz for the documentary next week and I wanted to catch him out during filming, find a way to trip him up, and have him confess on air. It seemed like the easiest, and safest option. He wouldn't dare try anything while the camera was running, especially if it was a live broadcast, I argued.

It had taken Noor mere seconds to dismiss my idea. 'And what, you think he'll just confess? On camera?' she'd demanded.

'He thinks you're dead, Noor. If you confront him during the shoot, then yes, he might incriminate himself. What is he going to do, deny that you're his sister? We can find a way to surprise him.'

'Stop kidding yourself. You know that he will find a way to twist the story. The only way he's going to admit to anything is if it's just me.'

'Are you insane? He already tried to kill you once.'

'And he thinks I'm dead,' Noor said slowly, using my own words to convince me. 'He won't see it coming.'

'How exactly are you going to get in? That house is guarded like a fortress.'

'Not anymore, it isn't,' Alia said, apologetically. 'The bodyguards were all for Javed Uncle. Faraz isn't even an MP yet . . . he's not important enough for the state to provide security.'

I glared at her.

'He's always paid for private security, though,' Alia hastened to add. 'One armed guard, I think.'

'Which means I have to confront him at home and it has to be in the middle of the night. That's the only time I'll get him alone.'

'What is wrong with you? Both of you!' I yelled. 'We know what he's capable of. It's far too dangerous. The only way I'm agreeing to any sort of a confrontation is if we do it together, with proper backup.'

We had batted back and forth, Alia stepping in every few minutes to referee, but I'd known from the beginning that this was a battle I was going to lose. Noor is nothing if not stubborn but it's more than that. Alia is invested, and for years, I've wanted nothing more than to unearth the truth, but this is Noor's fight. She's lived in fear for fifteen years and I can't blame her for wanting to face her brother alone. I can see that for her this is as much about confronting her demons as it is about bringing Faraz to justice.

But that doesn't mean I think it's a good idea.

And it definitely doesn't mean I'm going to let her go in unprepared.

I turn around at the sound of footsteps behind me. Noor wanted to speak to Kate before we did anything. Alia had seemed surprised that Noor had kept such a big part of her life hidden from her wife for years, but to me it makes complete sense. The events of that year had left me so scarred that I'd all but isolated myself, not even trusting anyone enough to go on a second date. I can't begin to imagine what it must have been like for Noor. She had been lied to, betrayed, let down by pretty much everyone she had ever trusted.

'Hey,' Kate says.

'All set?' I ask, looking from her to Noor, hoping that this time Noor's got the ending she deserves.

I smile as Noor takes Kate's hand, their fingers intertwined. 'All set.'

SABAH

'Are you nervous?' Alia's voice pierces through the silence.

I look at Noor in the rear-view mirror. I can't keep the exasperation from bleeding into my voice. She *knows* how dangerous this is – she had refused to let Kate accompany us to India on that account – and yet she is adamant about doing this alone. 'There's still time to back out,' I say. 'You don't have to do this alone.'

Noor shakes her head, but the movement is too quick for it to be convincing. I ignore the knot of anxiety twisting in my chest and focus instead on the road. We are driving in near darkness, the headlights switched off, just the milky glow from the moon illuminating the narrow road. 'Noor?'

I flick a quick look at Noor, the twinge of hope taking me by surprise. But she shakes her head again. Her voice is quiet, but there is an edge to it. 'I need to do this,' she says, before turning to look out of the window. 'On my own.'

We park in a clearing behind the house, the small black hire car hidden amidst the overgrown bushes and gnarled trees. I twist in my seat to look at Noor. I talk her through the kit I'd managed to borrow from Arch Films.

'Remember we can only see what you see so try and keep some distance between you and Faraz,' I say, buttoning up Noor's jacket and checking that the camera is secure, before tapping into her phone to set up the hotspot.

'What if he's behind her or there isn't enough light?' Alia asks.

I'd asked Gillian, the producer on the covert filming team, the exact same question. 'The night vision on this camera is pretty good, so I wouldn't worry about lighting too much,' I say. 'And even if Faraz isn't in the frame, it'll still pick up the audio.'

'And you'll be able to see everything from here?' Noor's eyes scan my face. Her voice carries a hint of apprehension. Her fingers twist around themselves.

'Hey, look,' I say, pointing to the laptop on the dashboard. I fiddle with Noor's phone and see an image of my face appear on the screen. 'The cameras are linked to the app on your phone, which transmits directly to my laptop. We'll be right outside watching.'

And promises be damned, if anything starts to go wrong, I will come in, I think, silently reassuring myself.

'Great,' Noor says. Her voice is shaky but the panic I'd sensed a moment ago is gone. She nods at Alia and me, then picks up the scarf resting on the back seat and swirls it around her face, draping it so that all I can see are her eyes.

She doesn't hesitate as she climbs out of the car and slips back into the house that had almost swallowed her whole.

It's odd seeing what Noor's seeing, the camera feed showing us her route in. It's a route that I'm so familiar with I can almost feel the grass prickle my ankles and the splinters in the wooden fence press into my back.

My breath catches as she slips into the kitchen.

The camera stills. I picture Noor taking off her *hijab* and tucking it into her pocket.

I steal a quick glance at Alia. Her eyes are fixed on the screen.

We watch the view change as Noor walks into the living room.

She lifts a vase off the coffee table then drops it onto the floor, the sound of glass crashing onto marble deafening.

She follows with another, a ceramic bowl that she drops at the foot of the stairs and then another vase, dropped from halfway up the curved staircase.

It takes less than five seconds for the lights to switch on. Faraz appears at the top of the stairs, phone in hand.

Noor continues walking up the stairs.

'I wouldn't do that if I were you,' she says, her voice steady.

I watch the phone slip out of Faraz's grip and bounce down the stairs. He remains frozen in his spot as Noor climbs the remaining steps to the first-floor landing.

When his face finally comes into focus, it is ashen.

He has quite literally just seen a ghost.

Even with Noor standing right in front of him, Faraz doesn't speak.

Noor's hand reaches out to touch his chest and he jumps back. The expression on his face goes through a hundred different iterations from disbelief to shock to panic as he realizes that the scene before his eyes is real.

The woman before his eyes is real.

'You're dead,' he says, taking a step back, the panic obvious as his voice gains volume. 'You can't be . . . You're *dead*.'

Noor's hand curls around his arm, her grip on him tight. 'No, I'm not.' She pauses. I can't be sure, but I think I detect the hint of a smile in her voice when she speaks again. 'You aren't disappointed, are you?'

We watch quietly while Noor talks, explaining to her brother the machinations of the lie that kept her alive and him outside prison for fifteen years. Faraz doesn't interrupt or ask any questions, just nods along as Noor speaks. His features crumble as understanding dawns.

'I'm sorry,' he says when Noor stops talking. 'I'm so, so sorry. I wish I had known, I wish Abbu had trusted me enough to –' His voice fractures. 'Not a day has gone by when I haven't thought about you. I was supposed to protect you and I . . .' He trails off.

Alia leans forward. 'What is he doing?' she whispers.

I hold my hand up as he starts speaking again, his deep voice filling the car.

'Those people, they brainwashed me, Noor. I spent that entire year walking around in a daze. I had no idea what I was doing. My sister. My own sister.'

Alia and I look at each other. A few beats pass in which neither of us say anything, so shocked are we at Faraz's presence of mind. I allow myself a breath before speaking. 'He's building a defence.'

*

Around us, the velvet blackness is lifting as dawn breaks, forcing all the hiding places of the night to disappear one by one.

I slide my eyes back to the screen. The shock and paranoia from earlier are gone. Faraz's face is contorted, his features twisted in a show of anguish. His hand shakes as he runs it through his hair. 'If there's anything I can do, to make it better, to take it back,' he continues.

His hands reach out and I picture him gripping Noor by the shoulders. I try to imagine what it would feel like, his grip gentle but bolstering. The grip of a brother who made a mistake and has regretted it ever since.

Or the grip of an experienced politician trying to talk his way out of a crisis.

The silence is deafening.

'He's trying to manipulate her,' Alia mutters and I nod, hoping that Noor doesn't get swept up in this grand apology.

The frame tightens as Faraz steps closer and there is the sense of zooming in as he pulls her into a hug. The screen blacks out, the camera pressed between them.

'I'm sorry, I am so, so sorry,' he murmurs over and over again and for a moment I am reminded of the boy I used to know.

What if he is telling the truth? What if he really was brainwashed?

The murmuring continues for a few moments before they part and the camera zooms out again. We get another glimpse of Faraz.

'Do you need some money?' Faraz says. 'Abbu must have

been looking after you all these years. How much do you need?'

He almost had me.

The pounding behind my ribcage intensifies. I feel my hands ball up into fists.

I can only hope Noor can see through him.

'Come on, Noor, get the fuck out of there,' Alia whispers under her breath. 'We have him.'

More silence. Noor breaks it this time.

'I don't need your money.' The bitterness in her voice is unmistakable, but there is something else there too. Something that scares me. 'Did you kill him?'

Next to me Alia gasps. My entire body goes cold, an icy chill spreading through me as I realize what Noor is doing and why she was adamant about going in alone. If Faraz really did kill his father, the only person who can get him to admit it is Noor.

On screen, Faraz's face freezes. 'What?'

'Abbu. Did you kill him?'

The pause lasts less than a second, but that second, that slight hesitation, is all I need. He's lying. I watch as he rearranges his face into a picture of indignation.

'How dare you ask me that? Abbu had a heart attack.'

Noor's voice doesn't waver. 'His heart was perfect,' she says. 'It was about the party presidency, wasn't it?'

Faraz stills. His face darkens.

'He told me. He told me that you were desperate to take over but he couldn't trust you. Why would he? After what you did.'

I can see the anger ripple across his face. She's pushing him too hard.

'Shut up,' he says, his words cut from steel.

'He told me he was worried about what you might do.' Relentless. 'You threatened him, didn't you?' Noor presses on. 'What did you do to—'

'I said shut up,' he yells. 'He got what was –'

I only have to hear the fury in his voice and I am out of the car, scrambling through the bushes, rushing into the house, a single thought running through my mind. *Not again.*

Please.

Not again.

SABAH

I burst through the back door and into the kitchen.

I run into the living room, my heart hammering against my chest. I can't believe I let Noor talk me into this. I know what Faraz is capable of. I should have stopped her. I should have—

'How dare you?' Faraz's voice echoes through the room. 'You have no idea of the sacrifices I've had to make.'

I stop in my tracks. Alia is seconds behind me.

Faraz has Noor pinned to the wall at the top of the stairs, his hands gripping her arms, his face inches away from hers. Even from this distance, I can see that she is terrified, the confidence from earlier long gone. I step forward instinctively, but Alia's hand on my shoulder holds me back.

'Wait,' she whispers, coming to stand next to me. She holds up her phone. It takes me a second to work out what she's saying. Her bodyguards. Of course.

'Do you think it was easy for me?' Faraz yells. 'I earned that post. After all those years of doing exactly what he wanted me to do, playing by his rules . . . But he still couldn't see that I had changed. That I was sorry. All he ever cared about—'

Faraz cuts himself off.

We all hear it, the sound of a door opening, the sound of footsteps over the marble floor.

It feels as though even the walls are holding their breath.

A knot of worry swells in my throat. No one is supposed to be here; if a guard sees us . . .

My heart drops at the sound of the voice booming in from the entrance hall.

'Faraz? Are you awake, *jaan*?'

Faraz's head jerks backwards but he doesn't let go of Noor.

She's supposed to be away. It was the one thing we had all agreed on. We had to make sure Fatima Aunty was away on the night that Noor snuck in and I had double, triple checked, ringing her late last night at her brother's house to make sure she was still there.

Alia grips my wrist, her fingernails clawing into my flesh as we watch Fatima Aunty walk in. She stops abruptly at the foot of the staircase. Her hand flies to her head.

A single word escapes her lips. 'Noorie.'

She takes a step forward, clutching the banister for support.

'Noorie,' she repeats, her voice thick with disbelief and longing and something else. Hope. She stutters. 'You – you're alive.'

Faraz turns, his grip on Noor loosening, and as he twists to look at his mother, Noor shoves him. She slips out of his grasp. I've almost exhaled, relief fluttering through me, but before she can get away Faraz lunges forward and grabs her. He drags her away from the stairs and forces her back towards the wall, his hands twisting around her neck, choking her.

The sound that Noor makes is chilling. Her voice is strangled and it takes me a second to realize she's saying something.

'Ammi.' Her words come out garbled. 'Faraz . . . Abbu . . . he –'

I know without a doubt that he will kill her. Faraz will do anything to keep his mother from finding out what he did. I yank myself free of Alia's grip and run across the room.

I'm halfway up the stairs when Fatima Aunty screams. The raw, guttural sound of her wail is enough to distract Faraz and in that split second of confusion Noor presses herself back into the wall, her features warped with effort and concentration. One look at her and I know exactly what she's going to do. She's going to use the wall as leverage to push Faraz away. I look at the banister behind Faraz and the marble floor underneath.

I want to shout, warn Noor, but I can't get my voice to work. I watch, paralyzed, as Noor pushes Faraz. I see the look of shock on his face as he realizes what is happening. It's over so quickly he doesn't even get the time to scream. All I hear is the horrible, sickening sound of skull against marble.

Followed by excruciating, chilling silence. Until Fatima Aunty's scream pierces the air.

Noor bolts past me in a flash, prompting me out of my shock.

I run down the stairs.

Alia is crouched on the floor next to Fatima Aunty. Less than a second later, Noor is there, arms wrapped around her mother, holding her up.

'Is he dead?' I whisper but my words are lost under the sound of Fatima Aunty's wails.

'Is he dead?' I shout and Noor whips around, registering my presence. There is blood on her hands, on her sleeves. Her neck is bruised, bluish streaks highlighting the space where Faraz's fingers had been.

I take a step to the side and look past her. My knees buckle. Faraz is lying on the floor, neck twisted, limbs bent in awkward angles, blood pooling under his head.

The relief is to be expected; it is the lack of remorse that catches me off guard.

I close my eyes. In some ways, I had known this was the only way it could've ended, that any hope for justice was unrealistic.

I am vaguely aware of Alia shouting into her phone, calling an ambulance.

The two bodyguards that Alia brought along as a safety measure hover uselessly.

My eyes drift back to Fatima Aunty. She is clinging to Faraz, cradling his head, begging, pleading with him to wake up. Her only son.

I turn away, unable to watch.

What she's asking for is impossible.

She got her daughter back, but she won't be quite as lucky with her son.

He is dead, gone forever.

ALIA

Fifteen years later

I stand in the shadows and watch the last few members of the audience settle in. The lights have been dimmed but the mid-morning sun filtering through the windows is enough to illuminate the auditorium. It's packed, nearly every seat occupied by ministers and party workers.

I take a deep breath and hold it in for as long as I can. It's a meditation technique I've come to rely on in the last few years, a gentler way to calm my brain than fidgeting, though the anxiety that used to unnerve me as a young politician has long since dissolved.

It's been fifteen years since Faraz died. Fifteen years since I let go of the guilt that had been holding me hostage since I was a teenager.

I think back to everything I've done since then to get here, to this day, my mind replaying every risk, every sacrifice, every little step that took me in the right direction, even when it didn't feel like it.

After the paramedics took Faraz away and the police left for the night, I pulled Noor and Sabah into the kitchen. We had a choice to make – Faraz was dead. He couldn't be tried for his crimes posthumously, but we could release the recording to the world. Let people know the truth behind the facade. Or we could forget about justice and focus on rehabilitating our lives.

The decision was simple, really.

The video of Noor confronting Faraz got more than two million hits in twenty-four hours. I still remember the pride that rippled through me. I held on to it for a long time. That video, the public outpouring of support, that deep sense of justice – it became about more than just Noor and Salma. I turned to it every time a rapist walked free, every time a victim was slut-shamed, every time a woman was silenced.

I held on to it when the party president called me and asked me if I'd consider running for the general election.

I held on to it when I won by the highest majority the party had ever seen.

I held on to it when I was sworn in as the WCD Minister two terms in a row.

I even held on to it when under the weight of all the lies and the secrets, my marriage finally crumbled.

Noor, Sabah and I tried to keep in touch but as the years wore on, the lunches turned to phone calls, then to emails, finally trickling down to the odd birthday message.

Sabah's documentary about Noor broke records, winning every award under the sun and establishing her as one of the best documentary film-makers in the UK. Since then she has made a dozen more documentaries, focusing on everything from war crimes to human trafficking, fraught subjects always presented with a sensitivity and compassion that seems so unlike the girl I went to school with. The last I heard, she had married an archive producer and moved to LA.

Noor went back to Scotland as soon as the investigation was over, taking her mother with her. I saw a picture of her beaming, standing next to Kate and their two little boys at the opening of her first solo show at the Saatchi Gallery a few years ago. I've toyed with the idea of buying one of her pieces for years, but I never get around to it. Her paintings remind me of a version of myself that I'd rather forget. They remind me of the outsider, always lurking in the shadows, waiting to be let in. That's not who I am any more.

My mind flashes back to an evening nearly thirty years ago. It was a few weeks after the funeral – Salma's funeral – and the Qureshis had organized a memorial at their house. It was a small affair, limited to the immediate family and a handful of friends, which is why I was surprised when a uniformed officer, the man I would later come to know as the police commissioner, walked in. I followed him down the corridor. I hung back while he spoke to Javed Uncle, their whispers getting more and more urgent as they talked about Noor and Faraz and the crime that they had covered up. I understood that day what power meant. What it could do. How it could alter perceptions and change truths.

It was astounding.

Years later, I used the power that I had to balance the scales of justice. Javed Uncle treated me like a daughter and for years, I kept quiet out of respect for him. But what happened to Noor was an injustice that had gone on too long and after Javed Uncle died, I knew it was up to me to do something. Faraz seemed determined to claw his way to the top and he was so entitled, so power-hungry, he couldn't see that he was destroying lives in the process.

He was destroying the career I had worked so hard to build.

I couldn't let him get away with it. He had to be stopped. But I knew Faraz and I understood that the only way he would own up to his crimes was if he was brought face to face with Noor.

And the best way to reach Noor had always been Sabah.

I sent that diary entry to Sabah. After she told me about the Trojan Horse trap, I drove up to the Qureshi mansion and logged in to the burner email I'd set up, knowing that Sabah would assume it was Fatima Aunty who had sent it. It was simple, but necessary. Sabah had always liked playing saviour to Noor and I was certain that even the slightest hint that Noor was murdered would be enough to get Sabah going. I was right. Less than two weeks after I sent her the 'tip', Sabah was in India, digging, asking questions, trying to uncover the truth under the pretence of making a documentary. Sabah had always had a dogged determination, especially when it came to Noor, so all I had to do was nudge her along and wait in the sidelines until she managed to draw Noor out.

I pull myself out of my thoughts as the compère finishes introducing me. I hand my phone to Omar.

Javed Uncle used to say that the most dangerous people are the ones who believe that they're doing right, doing *good*. He said that there was nothing more toxic than the combination of steely resolve and self-righteousness. I never understood that. The world needs people who are willing to do whatever it takes to balance the scales.

I take a breath, adjust my *sari* and then move out of the wings.

The applause as I step onto the stage is deafening. People are shouting, chanting my name, yelling out the campaign slogans we spent months perfecting. I smile as two words rise above the din and settle into my ears, my heart, my soul.

Prime Minister.

ACKNOWLEDGEMENTS

First, thanks must go to my outstanding editors, Vicki Mellor – whose intelligent, incisive and tactful feedback has made me a better writer and *Can You See Me Now?* a better book – and Gillian Green, who guided this book to publication with extraordinary enthusiasm and a multitude of ingenious ideas.

Huge thanks also to everyone else at Pan Macmillan: Matthew Cole, Kate Tolley, Mel Four, Rosie Wilson, Ruth Killick and all the other people working behind the scenes. Your passion, attentiveness and all-round brilliance never fail to amaze me.

My agent, Annette Green, always has my back and I'm constantly grateful for her support in getting to grips with everything that comes with being a published author. Calling myself a published author still gives me goose bumps – something that I'll always (happily) blame you for, Annette.

Thank you, Simon Yeoman-Taylor, for sharing with me so candidly everything that goes into making a documentary. Needless to say any mistakes are my own, but there would have been a lot more without your help.

The hardest part of writing a novel is starting it, and I've got my brilliantly supportive Faber Academy writing group to thank for reading the first few chapters and cheering me on at that crucial early stage.

Anjola Adedayo, thank you for stepping in to help with the part of the writing process that I hate the most: outlining.

Huge thanks, as always, to Anvi Mridul and George de Freitas, both of whom took time out of their very busy lives to read stacks of pages and helped me figure out which ones not to light on fire.

Rishabh Sakhlecha and Ashmi Mridul, thank you for listening to me go on and on about murders and plot twists, offering world-class feedback and calling me out, in the way that only family can, on my more ridiculous ideas.

Having grown up in a political family, I was lucky to have access to a number of people who helped with research and offered invaluable advice on the political set-up in the book. However, this is a work of fiction and I must acknowledge that while I've tried to stay true to the essence of modern Indian politics and used several real-life cases as inspiration – as eagle-eyed readers will have no doubt noticed – the criminal cases, constituencies (and their demographics) and political parties depicted in the novel are fictional.

There is nothing that feeds my soul quite like a Nirula's hot chocolate fudge sundae, nothing that brings me greater joy than Sunday brunch overlooking Delhi Golf Club's greens and nothing that makes me smile as quickly as stepping off a plane and walking across the depressingly brown carpets of Delhi's IGI Airport. This book is a love letter, albeit a slightly dark one, to the city that I grew up in that, no matter where I live, will always, always be home. *Dilli meri jaan* ♥

I cannot possibly talk about Delhi without mentioning the people who make it home: my family. Thank you for always believing in me and for always being up for a Nirula's HCF.

Next, the girls I grew up with, Avny, Prerna and Shivani, who are nothing like the characters in this book and who remain, nearly thirty years after we first met, my middle-of-the-night friends (I'm looking at you, Shivani) and the keepers of my secrets.

And finally, huge thanks to all the readers, booksellers, authors, bloggers, reviewers and bookstagrammers who have been so supportive of my writing – I appreciate every one of you.